# REVOLU

# NUMBER ONE

# REVOLUTION NUMBER ONE

## ZIN MURPHY

ISBN: 1540750477
ISBN–13: 978-1540750471

Cover design and typesetting: Trevor Cook, cover photograph: ©Trevor Cook

*For Juventino and Maria Alice*

# CONTENTS

# ACKNOWLEDGMENTS

I would like to thank the following for help, encouragement and inspiration down the years: Antônio Sousa Fernandes, Barbara Skolimowska, Carey Elcome, Carole Garton, Chester Graham, Vicky Hartnack, Colin McMillan, John Elliott, José Manuel Moreira, Julieta Tuson, Mao Qing, Margarida Costa, Maria do Céu Sousa Fernandes, Peter Wise, Rui Rocha, Sylvia Lumley and Tunbridge Wells Writers.

To refresh my memory, I also drew on the online archive of the Centro de Documentação 25 de Abril, University of Coimbra, and 'A minha passagem por Caxias. Como a CIA ensinou os portugueses a torturar' by Christopher Reed.

# 1  Birthday Boy

The egg lent Joséphine's thin throat an adam's apple as it slid down.

'Ten!'

Joséphine diluted the taste with a gulp of her whisky and coke.

Warm autumn air carried the sound of music from the colonies across the city neighbourhood. Inside the party flat, on the top floor of a low-rise apartment block, Simão looked at the remaining hard-boiled eggs, all of them neatly shelled. His face had started to lose its Mediterranean colouring after the fourth egg. Now his skin turned even paler. He reached for the smallest egg, then drew his hand back.

'I can't.'

'You give up?'

'Yes. I give up.'

Simão looked crestfallen, though his eyes gave away a flicker of relief.

The guests set up a chorus of 'Jo-sé-phine! Jo-sé-phine!!' Joséphine raised her skinny arms in triumph.

Ed Scripps observed his young landlady from the back of the room. This was a new side to her. He was glad to see her so enthusiastic about something other than money. His party was warming up.

'Eleven!' he shouted.

Ed wondered whether this party game was a local tradition or a French import. Either way, his landlady had clearly had plenty of practice.

Joséphine grabbed another egg from one of the plates and stuffed it into her mouth. She chewed a couple of times, then swallowed.

'Jo-sé-phine! Jo-sé-phine!!'

'Twelve!' called Ed.

Joséphine paused. Pride fought unease on her face.

'All right,' she said, 'but take off that ugly African music and put on one of my beautiful Brazilian records.'

Ed interrupted the voice of Rui Mingas, his own choice, and replaced it with the record he found at the top of the stack of Joséphine's collection.

Accompanied now by the sound of Maria Bethânia, Joséphine eased her twelfth egg into her mouth and started to chew. Then stopped. Chewed again. She placed one hand on her throat and began to massage it. With her other hand, she snatched her tumbler, raised it to her lips, and took a draught. And another. She belched. The egg was down.

'Jo-sé-phine! Jo-sé-phine!! Jo-sé-phine!!!'

Clutching her belly, Joséphine rushed out of the lounge.

'Don't go!'

'One more!'

A couple of people patted her as she went past, but no-one risked trying to stop her.

The cries of 'Jo-sé-phine!' died down. Conversation resumed, rose and swirled to the background of Brazilian rhythm.

Ed's guests, Portuguese and foreign, talked mainly about music, cars, football, politics and clothes. And supermarkets, of course, when they spoke to their host. The heated political discussion was a surprise to Ed. He did not expect people to speak so openly, living, as they did, under a fascist regime.

'Things have got to change,' said Hélder, one of his business contacts here in Lisbon. 'The days of standing 'proudly alone' are over. We've got to open up to the outside world and get trading. Like it or not, that means becoming more democratic.'

'It means ending the wars in the colonies,' put in Mário, a friend of one of Ed's acquaintances back home. 'Give them their independence. Let them run their own damned show.'

'Bring our boys home! And keep them here!' This was Lourdes, a woman in her mid-30s whom Ed had met at the rowing club. 'Can you imagine it, spending four years in the jungle, with the natives shooting at you?'

Ed shook his head. She was exaggerating, surely?

'Can you picture,' she went on, 'what those boys will be like when they get back? Traumatised and dangerous.'

The only dissenting voice was that of Jorge. Ed had met Jorge in a bar frequented by teachers at the Sussex School, a language institute where Ed was taking Portuguese lessons. One of the teachers must have brought Jorge along this evening. Jorge prised Ed away from the group by asking him for a bottle of beer.

'Help yourself,' said Ed. 'The beer's in the fridge in the kitchen.'

'Can you show me where that is, please?'

Ed excused himself and propelled Jorge down the corridor to the kitchen. He opened the fridge, pulled out a bottle of Sagres, handed it to Jorge and went to the drawers to rummage for an opener.

'Must be in the lounge,' he said.

'That's OK.'

Ed turned to see Jorge drinking from the bottle.

Jorge wiped his luxuriant moustache with the back of his free hand. 'Having one yourself?' he asked Ed.

'Not just yet. I like to get some plain water inside me first. Gotta stay sober in front of my guests.'

'Look, Ed, the things those people were saying, they've got it all wrong. You don't want to listen to them. For one thing, we don't have any colonies. Mozambique, Angola, Guinea, they are not colonies. They are all part of Portugal, just as much as Lisbon is. Giving them away would be like cutting our arms off!'

Jorge caught Ed's quizzical expression.

'Ed, tell me, how long have you been in Portugal now?'

'Two months to the day.'

'Right. That's nothing, is it? Of course you don't understand the way things are here, what is going on. But with time you'll get to know us and to respect what we're doing. We are only doing what we have to do.'

'Ooooh!! What are you two boys doing in here alone?'

The voice was followed into the kitchen by the voluptuous body of Anne, one of the English teachers from the Sussex School. She evidently knew Jorge quite well, because she pushed her hands into the thick hair over his collar and brought his face forward and up to meet her lips, shoving him back against the fridge at the same time. They did not part. Indeed, Jorge's arms closed around Anne's back and pulled her tighter to him.

Ed removed the bottle of beer from Jorge's hand, which then disappeared under the back of Anne's blouse. Ed placed the bottle on the kitchen table and went back to the lounge, where an argument about music was brewing.

Lourdes wanted to go back to the classical music with which Ed had started the evening. Some of the others were adamant about sticking with Brazilian, or at least South American, music. One or two were arguing loudly for rock. None of them, it appeared, shared Ed's taste for African music, or wanted to hear Portuguese sounds.

Ed did not recognise the woman at the centre of the argument. He found her attractive, despite her boyish haircut. She was short, olive-skinned and curvaceous. Her eyes were dark and flashed fire to accompany the strong words shaped by her full lips. He reckoned she was about twenty years old. She was waving the disc she wanted played. Ed recognised his copy of *Genesis Live*. Mário and others had planted themselves between her and the record player, which was playing a number by Chico Buarque that had no words. Every so often, they would supply a chorus with relish. It sounded medical to Ed: 'Tantum R' – not much fun. Rock would be better. Especially Genesis.

Ed approached the young woman.

'I see you like Genesis. I got that just before I left England. It's so new, most people here won't know it.'

She looked at him steamily.

'Can you just *play* it?'

'Sure. As long as you dance to it. With me.'

'If that's what it takes.'

Ed removed the record from her hand and strode over to the player. He turned off Chico Buarque and replaced it with *Genesis Live*. It was his party, after all.

Genesis were not the easiest of groups to dance to, but on the dance floor, or even in a crowded room at a party, Ed could dance to anything, his slight limp invisible. His partner danced without speaking, lost in the music. When the track finally ended, she hugged Ed, looked up into his eyes, thanked him and drew him into a corner, where she manoeuvred him onto a chair and perched herself on his knee.

'I'm on your level now,' she said, looking him evenly in the eyes, 'whoever you are.'

'Ed Scripps. It's my party.'

'Oh, the supermarket fellow. Who likes classical music.'

'Yes, that's me – among other things.'

The floor below them began to reverberate with more than the vibrations caused by Genesis. Someone was banging from below.

'Neighbours!' said the source of the warmth spreading along Ed's thighs.

'I expect they want us to turn the music down a bit,' said Ed. She slid off his knee, pushed her way to the record player and raised the volume even higher. When she got back to Ed, she had two glasses in her hands. She gave the one containing water to Ed and took a sip from the other.

'That'll teach them,' she said. '*Genesis Live* is the most important record of this year. A live album by the best live band in the world. It's got to be heard!'

Ed listened to the music for a couple of minutes, then asked 'Who did you come with?'

'I'm a good Catholic girl. Or so my parents think. I come by myself.' She giggled. 'But Calvin brought me here. I'm his student at the Sussex

School. He teaches me German. And I have a name: Maria da Conceição. Most people call me Ção.'

It sounded awful to Ed.

'I know what you're thinking. Just nasalise the vowel, then it'll sound a lot better.'

'Mary of the Conception,' Ed translated.

'It's a good Catholic name, wouldn't you say?'

'Kind of sexy, if you think about it.'

'I can tell you are doing just that. Yes you are, don't deny it. Why don't you try me sometime, mister blue-eyed handsome man.'

'How about tonight?'

'Not tonight. Unless you can empty this room in the next twenty minutes. I've got to head home while the Metro is still running. Mummy and Daddy don't want their little Conception turning into a pumpkin.'

She slid slowly along Ed's thigh, letting her short skirt ride up so that he could see her black knickers, then slid slowly back again, exhaling a breathy 'Aaah!' into his ear, before standing on her own feet, giving Ed a long sultry gaze, turning, and plunging into the party.

Ed stayed put. He was next to an open window. Warm, damp air blew in, dissipating some of the tobacco smoke, underneath which Ed could smell not only his own perspiration, brought out by the dancing, but also a sweeter aroma left on his clothes. He identified it as cinnamon.

When the second side of *Genesis Live* had finished, someone put on Milton Nascimento. Ed got up and went to look for Ção, who was no longer in the main room. As the evening progressed, the party had spread to the corridor and the kitchen, but she was not there. Nor was Calvin in evidence. The toilet door was open, the light off. Either she was being a good Catholic girl in one of the bedrooms or she had left. Ed was about to investigate the former possibility when his new friend Rui, a well-connected student of economics, buttonholed him. Rui was tall; almost as tall as Ed, and had the habit of looking people directly in the eye. This evening, though, his gaze was faltering.

'What's going on, Ed? You stop talking your guests? Here, have some of this.' For once, his enunciation was less than immaculate.

Rui proffered a jug of light red liquid and looked around for Ed's glass.

'No, thanks, not just yet. What is that? Seems powerful.'

'Nah. Just the opposite. Is *água pé*. The newest, newest wine. Foot water, it means. After the grapes have been trodden, we tread the grapeskins. Produce this. 's lovely. Weak, weak, weak. You can drink litres of it without falling in. Over.'

'Sounds disgusting.'

'Nah. 's lovely. Try some.'

'Not just yet. Have you seen –'

'Nah. She's not so lovely, under that skin.'

Ed's fingers tingled at the thoughts that last word evoked.

'Forget the womans. Tell me about supermarket business. What's new on the shelves?'

'Since you ask, lots of Brazilian products, because they're mostly Brazilian chains. But that's not my department. I'm here to introduce loyalty cards. Haven't I told you?'

'Loyalty schmoyalty!' Rui was a fan of Woody Allen and Philip Roth. 'In this country, we are loyalty only to our football team and our Church. And even that … You heard what these people say about our government. And these are the middle glass! You know you gotcha rival?'

'Calvin?'

'Not for Ção, for loyalty. Mark Rotherfield. One other English.'

'He wants to introduce loyalty cards to Portuguese supermarkets?'

'Noooo! Trading stamps. Much better idea. Things people can collect, hoard. You should –'

Rui's nascent suggestion was aborted by loud, insistent banging on the front door of the flat. Ed wondered why whoever was knocking couldn't see the bell, but he went to answer all the same. He opened to four men in uniform, behind whom were two who looked like the stereotypical spies from Mad magazine in their hats and raincoats. The uniform nearest him started speaking in rapid Portuguese. It was too fast for Ed to understand. Lourdes appeared at his shoulder and interpreted.

'He says your neighbours have complained about the noise. And about the suspicious people arriving at this flat. So they're going to check identities.'

'I'm –'

'They know who you are. They're more interested in your Portuguese guests.'

Lourdes drew her ID card from her handbag and showed it to the policeman. He nodded perfunctorily at it and pushed past them, followed by a companion and the two plainclothes men. The two other uniformed men stayed at the door.

'Judite and Pides,' Lourdes whispered to Ed.

'Huh?'

'The ordinary police and the so-called secret police. Everyone knows who they are. They're powerful enough not to need secrecy. Nasty.'

The men in uniform had turned the music off and were glancing cursorily at the ID cards produced by the Portuguese women. One of the Pides was examining those of the men with great care. The other was asking the names of all the foreigners present and writing down their answers.

Without warning, Ed was knocked against the wall as a man rushed past. The man shouldered one of the uniformed police guarding the door out of his way, too, but the second policeman there grabbed his arms from behind and secured them in a full nelson, shouting for his companions to come and help. One of them rushed over and expertly handcuffed the man. One of the Pides sauntered to the doorway and exclaimed, 'Look who we have here.'

It was Jorge.

With neither words nor ceremony, the men in uniform marched Jorge down the stairs and out of sight. The two plainclothes men stayed on the threshold of the flat. The harder-looking of the pair told Lourdes they had better not turn the music back on. One of the neighbours who had phoned the police to complain was a retired judge from the colonies. He'd said he had a gun and knew how to use it. Lourdes relayed the information to Ed, who could see that she was badly shaken.

The man turned his sour gaze onto Ed.

'Happy twenty-third birthday, Mr. Scripps,' he said in English.

His companion chuckled, though his eyes stayed cold.

'Good luck with the loyalty cards,' Cold-eyes added.

*How did they know that? I've never seen these guys before in my life.*

The plainclothes men turned and left. The party was over. The guests spoke little as they gathered their coats and hurried away into the night as though a curfew had been imposed.

On her way out, unaccompanied, Lourdes asked Ed if it was really his birthday.

'Well, it was until midnight,' he answered.

'Why on earth didn't you tell us?'

'I didn't want anyone bringing presents. Not my style. My party, I provide. Though all your contributions were very welcome.'

Dazed and perturbed, Ed went through the hand-shaking and cheek-kissing routines that he was getting used to, and then he was alone.

Lost in thought, Ed shuffled down the corridor to the bathroom. Inside, there was a stink of vomit, though the toilet bowl, like the sink, was empty. He relieved himself, flushed the toilet, washed his hands and splashed cold water on to his face. As he turned to leave, he heard a groan. Wondering who the police had missed, Ed drew back the shower curtain.

Curled up in the bath, fully clothed, clutching her belly, was Joséphine. She was so thin that Ed was able to lift her out of the bath and carry her to the room she set aside for herself for her occasional visits and trysts.

Ed laid her in the middle of the broad bed and put a blanket over her. Then he fetched a large jug of water and set it on her bedside stand. Over the bed, a giant poster of Joséphine looked down benignly on its occupant. She was muttering something. Ed bent to listen.

'Who turn off my beautiful Brazilian?'

Ed left Joséphine's bedroom and closed the door behind him. He went into the kitchen, located an untouched bottle of *água pé*, and took it into the lounge. He resumed his seat by the window, which he now closed. Ed sat drinking from the bottle as he pondered the evening's events and his nose sifted the room's layered scents for a hint of cinnamon.

## 2 PLAY ON!

The boy held a gun; but he was still a boy.

*Bloody hell, he's younger than me.*

The young soldier stiffened his posture and narrowed his eyes as Ed passed in front of the sentry box.

*Poor bastard. Four years' military service! Could that be right? If Lourdes was telling the truth, he'll be thanking his lucky stars he's on sentry duty in the middle of Lisbon, rather than in a tropical hell-hole where everyone hates him.*

The gate swung inwards to let a military vehicle pass out. Behind it, Ed glimpsed tropical vegetation and the façade of an ornate old building. He carried on and turned into the side street that housed the Sussex School in a modern block with a fine view of the city's Army Headquarters but no distinguishing features of its own. Ed thanked his lucky stars that he was young enough not to have been called up for even one year of 'national service'. He had been able to finish his studies at Stevenage Tech in peace.

Ed followed a trio of pretty teenage girls into the building. On the stairs, they glanced back at him and giggled, resting their hands on each other's arms and whispering words he caught but failed to understand. They stopped in front of a notice board at the top of the stairs. It was adorned with portrait photos of people who did not look local, with the exception of one whom Ed recognised as Carlos, his teacher of Portuguese for Foreigners. He assumed the people portrayed must be members of the School's teaching staff. One of the girls backed into Ed as he passed. He felt her firm bottom against his thigh. Ed raised his hands, palms outward. 'I'm so sorry,' he said, smiling. He brushed past and into the reception area, looking for Ção. The sound of giggling followed him.

The reception area held dozens of students milling around between classes. Ção was not among them. He saw Anne, her head bobbing above the students surrounding her, and hailed her. She excused herself and came over to him.

'Recovered from the party, Mr B?'

'B?'

'Mr Businessman! Good business, man!'

'Fully recovered, thanks. You?'

Anne nodded.

'Jorge?'

Anne's face clouded.

'I haven't seen him and I haven't heard from him, either. Have you?'

'No news.'

'I'm quite worried, actually.'

Ed caught an aroma he remembered from his party. Hands covered his eyes.

'Guess who!'

He turned around. The hands fell away, leaving him gazing into the seductive eyes of Maria da Conceição.

'Olá, querido!' she whispered, then kissed him full on the mouth.

A bell rang. Everyone started moving towards classroom doors. Ção skipped past him and caught the arm of a dark, stocky young man wearing thick spectacles. Ed recognised their mutual greeting as German. The door closed behind them. Even though the man looked more Latin than Teutonic, Ed assumed that he had just caught his first sight of the redoubtable Calvin. And his first, sweet, lingering taste of Calvin's delectable apparent admirer.

Ed turned to face the long reception desk, behind which three young secretaries sat. Laura and Assunção were engrossed in their work, but Célia smiled and winked at him.

'They'll be out in fifty minutes.'

As though he did not know. Ed sighed, and sat on one of the functional chairs lining the walls.

Laura put down her phone.

'The boss would like to have a word with you. He's in his office. Just down that corridor, on the left.'

'With me?'

'Yeah. Get to know the students. Reminisce about Blighty. You know.' She sounded as though she'd just stepped off the plane from London herself.

Ed found it strange to be considered a student again, but he was taking Portuguese lessons there, a couple of times a week if he could make it.

He got up.

'Hello, Mr. Scripps. May I call you Ed?'

The speaker was a man of medium height with blond hair curlier than Ed's. There was a canny glint in his green eyes. He looked old to Ed – well over thirty. His handshake was firm; his smile was relaxed.

'Sure.'

'I'm Keith. Would you come down to my office?'

Ed followed the Director of the Sussex School down the corridor. Keith ushered him into a medium-sized office, gestured to a chair and sat himself behind a broad workaday desk.

'How are you getting on with Carlos? Learning?'

'Carlos is fine. Has a good classroom manner. I'm a bit slow, but I think I'm getting the hang of the lingo.'

'You'll learn a lot more outside the classroom than in it, Ed, if you put your mind to it. But you really should try to attend Carlos's lessons regularly, especially in these early stages.'

'Yeah, I know, Keith, but it's not so easy.'

'Busy man, eh?'

'That's right. Luckily for me.'

'Businessman, Carlos tells me.'

'Right. Sort of. I'm not independent yet. Still working for Retail Support Services. But no-one from England keeps tabs on me. I'm practically my own boss.'

'Nice feeling, isn't it?'

'Not half!'

'Can you tell me about your business?'

'Sure. I'm a man with a mission. I'm here in Portugal to bring loyalty cards to stores and supermarkets.'

'Loyalty cards? That's a new one on me.'

'It's simple really. The idea is that you, the customer, take out a special card with your name and the supermarket's name on it. The card entitles you to special discounts at that supermarket. This gives you an incentive to become a loyal customer of the supermarket, though, of course, there is no compulsion.'

'Like the trading stamps we already have in Britain?'

'No. I think it's much better. Trading stamps only give you things you might not want, whereas my scheme gives you a discount on stuff you do want, otherwise you wouldn't be buying it. If it takes off – and I'm sure it will – I plan to expand it, so that your loyalty card to a certain supermarket will give you discounts at, say, 'partner' clothes shops. That kind of thing.'

'Are you sure Portugal is ready for all this?'

'I reckon Portugal is the ideal place. It is just right for business. Full of untapped potential and so, so stable.'

'Yet, you know, Ed, everyone in the cafes moans about the government, the war, and so on.'

'And what do they do about it? Nothing. They're too damned scared.'

'With good reason, too.'

'Come on, Keith, a regime that has lasted forty-eight years isn't going to crumble any time soon. And what would you do if it did?'

'Oh, I'm well placed. Education. Everyone needs education. And if Portugal comes in from the cold, it's going to need English even more than it does now. A need which the regime has kindly neglected to fill.'

Ed was relishing this chance to talk up his business with a compatriot who understood these things.

'There's other things I can do for this place, too, as well as loyalty cards. Like plastic. You hardly ever see it, and when you do it's expensive and low-quality. They still hand-make everything. Of course, there's stuff I'm going to send the other way. Some of the hand-made and hand-grown things. The fruit and veg here doesn't always look too good, but the taste is fantastic! You know that better than I do. Most farmers can't afford pesticides. And they let the chickens run around their smallholdings before they kill them! There's going to be a market for that kind of thing in the West again, Keith, just you wait and see.'

'Yes, well, Portugal is actually part of the West.'

'On the map. And I'm going to help turn the map into reality. I can just see this country in twenty years' time: rolling in oil wealth from the colonies, building a second bridge across the Tagus, a Caetano bridge even longer and more impressive than the Salazar Bridge, holding a World Fair, the World Cup, you name it.'

'Best not get carried away, Ed.'

'You're right, Keith. I'll concentrate on my own little mission. Tell you what. What is it now? November. Give me six months. May the First, 1974. If they don't have loyalty cards by then, I'm a Dutchman. And if they do, you can buy me lunch at that posh place in the main square. Deal?'

'If that's a lunch-buying Dutchman, it's a deal. I'll be happy if it works out for you. If it doesn't, Ed, have you got a Plan B?'

'Go somewhere else. Home even. Wherever the company sends me.'

'You know, teaching English isn't a bad option. Gets you around the world.'

'So I see. But I'm not a man of letters, Keith. And I don't have the training.'

'A lot of people don't. Though you're right that they need it.'

The phone rang, but Keith ignored it.

'I put people – whatever their background,' he continued, 'through a month's intensive training, and they're ready to start teaching. You've got drive and enthusiasm, and that's contagious. I can see a future for you in this business. You do that course and you can have a job here next autumn, maybe sooner.'

'Thanks, Keith. I guess I've just got a new Plan B. Next autumn? By then I'll be thinking about buying a stake in your business.'

Both men laughed and studied each other.

'Well, thanks for dropping in, Ed. I was sorry to hear your party got raided.'

'Me, too. Do you know that man they took away? Jorge? Hangs around with several of your teachers.'

'Not personally. But don't worry about him. He'll show up.'

'The guys in the raiding party seemed to know a lot about me.'

'They do. They will. That's something you need to remember.'

Ed left the Director's office and went up to the School's small coffee lounge on the floor above. He hadn't finished his insipid milky coffee when the bell rang. He abandoned his drink and took the stairs two at a time to get back down to the reception area. There was the inevitable crush as students and teachers left, arrived or changed classes. Thanks to his height, Ed could see over the sea of heads. When Ção emerged, she was with Calvin, again leaning on his arm, engaged in animated conversation. Ed waved at her. She looked at him, through him. She walked straight past him and down the stairs with Calvin. Ed felt as though he had been punched in the solar plexus.

Never one to waste time, nor to dwell on slights, he swallowed the bile his mouth and spent the next ten minutes asking the teachers he knew if they had news of Jorge. None of them had heard a thing.

Once the next set of lessons was under way, Ed changed his focus to the secretaries, and to charming them into divulging the phone number of one of the School's students.

*

Ed was pleased, and relieved, when Ção answered the phone herself.

16

'Oh, Ed, I'm so glad you called. I've been thinking about you. Constantly.'

'I saw you at the School yesterday. I wanted to talk to you.'

'Oh, Ed, there was no time for that. I mean, I can't just talk to you, like you're some teacher or student.'

'Well, I am a student of Portuguese, you know.'

'I can teach you Portuguese. Then you'll never forget.'

'You're on! When can I see you?'

'I don't know. I just seem to be so busy these days.'

'Look, you know Milton Nascimento himself is in town next weekend? I've got tickets.'

'Hmm, yes, I had heard. Which day?'

'Saturday of next week.'

'Oh no! I'm so sorry. You see I'm busy on Saturday. I've got a big family dinner. I'm sure you know the kind of thing. He's playing on Friday, too, right?'

'Yes, I think so.'

'Change the tickets and I'll come with you.'

'OK, I will!'

'Now give me your number.'

Ed did. Ção read it back to him.

'I'll confirm.'

She made a strange, liquid sound and rang off.

*Damn! I forgot to ask about Jorge.*

\*

On a balmy autumn evening, Ed waited for Ção among the many people outside the São Luiz theatre. The crowd buzzed with expectation and good cheer. Ed expected Ção to arrive by taxi, but caught sight of her getting out of an unmarked car, a large black Opel. She blew a kiss at the couple in the front, and the car drove off. Ed waved at her and caught her attention. She rushed over to him, and gave him a quick kiss on the lips; then a second, lingering one.

'I'm here!'

'Wow! I noticed.'

Ed was wearing his usual sharp jacket with a white shirt, thin striped tie, narrow dark trousers and black leather shoes. It was chic in Stevenage, but the people here seemed to dress more formally when they went out for an evening. Çāo had feminised her hair style, and the heavy kohl around her eyes made her look Persian to Ed. He liked that look, and the cinnamon aroma that wafted over him when she came close. In the vestibule, she took off her smart ankle-length overcoat to reveal a high-cut dark red velvet dress that just covered her knees. Ed caught his breath.

He had forgotten how little he liked the music of Milton Nascimento. Joséphine had subjected him to long bouts of it when she was at the flat, and to Ed it was just background, not something he would choose to sit and listen to. He spent the first half of the concert looking at Çāo and fantasising.

He took her to the bar during the intermission.

'I guess you've heard about the police raid on my birthday party. After you'd left.'

'Oh, sure. I heard all about it. It must have been exciting.'

She seemed distracted, more interested in surveying the other concert-goers than in talking to Ed.

'It happens all the time. It's really nothing to worry about.'

'They seemed to know a lot about me.'

'Why shouldn't they? It's their job, you know.'

'And Jorge? They took him away. Nobody has seen him or heard from him since.'

'It happens. Don't worry about it.'

'Do you know him?'

'Oh, yes. Everyone knows Jorge.'

'When did you last hear from him?'

'At the party. I remember every minute of the party. He wouldn't talk to me, and I met you.' She was giving Ed all her attention now.

'But aren't you worried about him?'

'No. He'll turn up. It was probably all a big act. A warning. I wouldn't be at all surprised if he's laughing about it with those policemen right now.'

'It didn't look like a laughing matter.'

'Laugh it and leave it, right? Anyway, I'll ask Daddy. He often knows about such things.' The bell called the audience back to their seats.

*Summoned by bells*, thought Ed.

Their gin-and-tonics did not make the slow music appeal to Ed any more after the break.

Çāo seemed restless, too. Without looking at Ed, she placed her hand on his knee and ran it slowly up and down his thigh. He stiffened. Ed knew where this might end, and though he wanted that ending, he didn't want it in the midst of a theatre audience. He put a hand over Çāo's and held it at mid-thigh level. Breathing deeply, he thought of the Queen.

During the next song, Çāo caught Ed's eye and gave him a mischievous grin. She intertwined their fingers and moved them from his thigh to hers.

On the stage, the star of the show and his band began a long instrumental number. Three minutes into it, Çāo adjusted her dress, and Ed found his hand under it, and free. Çāo moved her bulky handbag from beside her to cover her lap. For the next half hour, Ed became acquainted with the silky texture of her inner thighs and, as her contractions and relaxings alternately halted and allowed, the contours of her shaved vulva.

As the audience clapped stolidly and shouted for an encore, Çāo drew a handkerchief from her handbag, dabbed dry eyes with it and pressed it to her lips with her right hand, removed Ed's hand with her left hand and placed the handkerchief over his fingers. Ed closed his fist over the handkerchief, wiped his fingers with it the better to capture and preserve her aroma, then placed it into his own jacket pocket.

Ed jumped the queue to retrieve Çāo's coat. As he helped her on with it, he whispered into her ear.

'Do you fancy a drink? Or a dance …?'

'No. I have better things in mind.'

That sounded promising to Ed. As they came out of the foyer into the now damp air, he asked:

'My place or yours?'

'Mine.'

She skipped towards a large black Opel parked right in front of the theatre. A middle-aged man got out from the driver's side and opened a rear door for Ção. She kissed him on the cheek and got in. The man nodded curtly at Ed, got in himself, and drove off. From the passenger side, an over-dressed grey-haired woman stared at Ed as though auditioning for the part of Medusa.

## 3  LANGUAGE LESSON

Ed went rowing with Lourdes. She was supple, strong, and more experienced than Ed at this, too. They set out upriver from the Rowing Club's base near the new monument to the medieval Portuguese 'discoverers' of places where people had already lived for centuries or more. The damp air settled like a mantle over the broad estuary, muffling the traffic-heavy din of the bustling city, letting the rowers concentrate more fully on the feedback from their rising and dipping oars and enjoy their temporary isolation from the cares of landlubbers. As the broad estuary narrowed along their path, the chemical stench from the river's southern bank assailed their nostrils. Its pungency gave them strength to row back against the tide.

'My Grandad is responsible for some of that. Just a whiff. He owns a small factory over there in Barreiro. It makes him a small fortune, actually.'

Ed filed Lourdes' comment away for future reference. He tried to take people at face value, but it was interesting to discover their background, and how it could change the meaning of what they said.

'Do you want to get changed and grab a snack?' said Ed, as they stacked away Lourdes' boat.

'Change is coming, Ed boy, to this part of the world, whether we like it or not. Do you think you are ready for it?'

'I'm ready for anything.'

'Me, too.' She smiled.

She was still drying her long, dark hair on a heavy-duty towel as they left the Rowing Club. She took his arm and shivered in the chill air. Ed

21

put an arm around Lourdes' shoulder.

'This is warm compared to England.' It was a revelation to Ed that the weather he had grown up with was not universal. He was starting to appreciate Lisbon's more clement climate.

Lourdes slipped her arm around Ed's waist and propelled him towards her car. She unlocked it; they dumped their kit-bags in the boot. Ed held the driver's door open for her, then went round and got in himself.

'What do you fancy, one of our famous custard tarts or me?'

'I'm a sucker for Portuguese tarts.'

Ed cursed himself for his hasty retort, and tried to make amends.

'So my answer is both. But not at that touristy place next to the monastery.'

The thin, neglected columns of the nearby Jerônimos monastery reminded Ed of the fragility of life. He did not like that, but he liked the thought of its being eroded by commerce even less. Ed loved commerce; but in its rightful place, not everywhere.

'To hell with tarts and monks!'

Lourdes did a U-turn and stamped on the accelerator. She headed west along the cornice towards the river's mouth and the sea. Lourdes concentrated on driving dangerously, while Ed sat back and enjoyed the way the setting sun changed the tones of the river and of the smooth, tanned skin that made up Lourdes' fine, intense face.

Lourdes double parked on the seafront of a small town beyond the city, beyond the river mouth.

'The end of the line. Cascais. The railway goes no further.'

The sun had set, but the temperature seemed to have risen, on land. The sea air of Cascais was pleasant to breathe. Ed and Lourdes sat at a café terrace outside a hotel facing onto the bay. It was full, and the noise level rose and fell with the incoming waves.

'Tarts, lobsters or beer? Or any combination of their. Thereof.'

Ed laughed. 'I'm a beer man myself. Dark, if they've got it.'

They started with beer, went on to lobster, and finished with flaky custard tarts. Lourdes asked to hear about Ed's business plans in detail, and he was happy to oblige.

'I'm not a businesswoman, but it all sounds good to me. I just wonder why no-one here has thought of it. Do you see what I mean, Ed?'

'I'm sure they have. But, you know, inertia. If it ain't broke, don't fix it, have another beer.'

'Have another beer yourself.'

'Thanks. I will.'

Lourdes drove back into town more carefully than she had on the outward leg. Her car had a built-in cassette-player, and the voice of Rui Mingas provided a counterpoint to the horns of the more exasperated drivers.

'Angolan, right?'

Lourdes nodded.

Ed noticed that Lourdes' eyes were moist.

'Mal d'Africa?'

She nodded again.

'You know, Ed, we've built a hell there in paradise.'

'The Africans I've met weren't so keen on their so-called paradises.'

'And what did they think of the hells we've built for them instead?'

'Weren't keen on them either. You're right. But with you, Lourdes, it seems personal.'

'What is your marital status, Mr. Scripps?'

'Resolutely single, for the time being. You?'

'Widow.'

She speeded up as they entered the ill-named square in which Ed's flat was located. Since there was nowhere to double-park, Lourdes hit the brakes right outside his building's street door. She kept her foot on the brake, put on the hand-brake, but left the engine running. Ed felt desire sweep over him, a comforting, familiar emotion in an alien city. Lourdes grabbed his lapels, pulled him towards her, kissed him ferociously then pushed him away from her.

'You taste of beer and lobster.'

'So do you.'

'I wasn't complaining. Normally, I'd follow you up, and follow up by fucking your brains out. But tonight I don't feel like it. And neither do you, Ed. I can tell.'

*Lady, you are so wrong.*

'It's that little fat chick, isn't it? Ill-conceived Maria. Well, if you want to impress her, you'll need a car. I can lend you one. Go on, get out.'

She kissed him again, with less hunger.

Ed pulled her to him but she pushed herself away. He opened the door and got out, almost losing his footing. He turned to insist that she come up, just for a coffee, but the door had slammed and the car was already moving off. He watched it turn out of the square and realised that the older generations really were different.

Lourdes was as good as her word. Two days later, Ed was indulging in a rudimentary breakfast of biscuits and milky coffee when the doorbell rang. He ambled down the corridor and lifted the intercom from its cradle.

'Special delivery. You have to come down and see if you like it.'

Ed slipped on a jacket, pocketed his keys and took the lift down to the ground floor. He opened the street door to a smartly dressed young man with an infectious smile.

'Good morning. I'm Paulo. Lourdes' younger brother. I have something for you.'

He held out a key ring bearing a single key.

Ed took the key and shook the hand. Paulo gestured to a white Renault 4 in need of a wash double-parked behind him.

'Special delivery. I came in it, so you have to drive me back home. Let's go.'

'Nice! Where's home?'

'Near Sintra. I'm still in the family mansion. Up in the hills. They've given me a granny flat. It makes life even easier.'

Ed drove out of town through some unusually grim suburbs whose new high-rise blocks already looked weather-beaten as well as soulless. Then they were among lush vegetation in the hills that held the former royal palaces of Sintra.

Paulo insisted on showing Ed around the historic buildings. He proved to be a knowledgeable and entertaining guide. It was mid-afternoon before he would allow Ed to drop him off at his 'family mansion', a turn-of-the-century building that was functional rather than ornate.

'Next time, you must come and dine with us. Right now, though, unfortunately, I have business to attend to. I expect you have, too.'

'Yeah, always. Mostly planning. What line of business are you in?'

'Oh, a bit of this, a bit of that. Import-export for the most part. Charcoal out, household appliances in. Plus some stuff with the colonies. While we still have them.' Concern only crept into his voice with his farewell:

'Be nice to my sister. She has suffered a lot.'

Ed headed down to the coast road, stopped at Cascais for a coffee at the café that Lourdes had introduced him to, then drove along the cornice back to Lisbon with extreme care.

The following afternoon, Ed was at the Sussex School for his Portuguese lesson. He noticed that he was not keeping pace with the other students. That would not do. He should be streets ahead if he was going to be able to persuade local business people to take up his ideas and invest in them. He resolved to go over the material by himself for the lessons he could not attend, and to study ahead for ones he could. He was not going to let language difficulties hold him back.

There was also Ção's offer. Ed knew she would not be at the School till later, for her German class, and he did not have time to wait for her. As he was leaving, Célia called him over. A dark, svelte young woman was standing in front of her.

'Someone wants to meet you. Our new French teacher, Simone, friend and colleague of your landlady, Joséphine. Simone, Ed.'

Speaking in rapid French with a strong Paris accent, Simone

apologised for missing his party. In decent French with only a slight Stevenage accent, Ed told her of Joséphine's exploits, and they exchanged anecdotes about their friend's eccentricities. The bell called Simone back to her classroom, and she bid Ed an effusive farewell. After the frustration of trying to speak a new foreign language, Ed had revelled in showing his ability to speak a more familiar one well.

'Lovely lady,' he said to Célia. 'Quite different to Joséphine.'

'Yes, you're not kidding. Everyone around here likes her. Well, almost everyone.'

'I like them both, myself. *Vive la différence.*'

Célia gave him a look that he could not decipher.

Ed collected his car and carefully drove the short distance home, thinking about the way Çāo walked.

He phoned Çāo that evening to set up a date, but she would not see him. He phoned her daily, but she always claimed to be busy. She was casual with him at the School when their paths crossed. Then, one evening, she called him.

'I've got some news for you, Ed.'

'What?'

'Are you going out? Tell me you're not.'

'Not tonight.'

'Don't. I'm coming round.'

When she arrived, Çāo looked flustered. She pushed past Ed, and strode to the kitchen. Ed followed her slowly.

'I wouldn't mind a cup of tea, if you can make some for me in your English way.'

Ed put some water on to boil in a saucepan.

'I asked Daddy to enquire about Jorge.'

'Did he? Is Jorge OK?'

'Daddy spoke to people who should know. They told him Jorge was a dangerous communist militant who specialised in recruiting new members for the Party.'

'Doesn't sound like him at all. But is he all right?'

'They told Daddy Jorge had escaped from custody. They said they don't know where he is now.'

'Well, that's a relief.'

'We can't be sure. In Chile, the new military régime makes people "disappear". Sometimes their bodies are found, and sometimes they aren't.'

'But this isn't Chile. Is it?'

'No, my love, it isn't. Our régime doesn't feel the need to hide the people it tortures, nor to kill them, usually. Except in Africa. At least, it didn't. Now, with the example of Chile, who can say?'

'I didn't know all this.'

Ção looked at Ed sceptically.

'And what did you just call me, Maria da Conceição?'

'That's where I've seen it before!'

'What are you on about?'

'The car! That dirty white French job! The one parked outside this flat. I've seen it outside the School. Don't tell me it's Joséphine's! I saw Paulo drop Lourdes off in it for your party!'

'Calm down. There's no mystery about it. Lourdes has lent me one of her family's cars. They must have quite a fleet.'

'Where is she, that miserable rich-bitch whore?'

'I'm quite alone this evening.'

'That upper-class floozy! Where is she? Or he. Is that it?'

Ed smiled. He was enjoying this.

'Are you jealous?'

'Of course I'm jealous!'

Ção once again pushed past Ed. He thought how beautiful she was when anger coloured her cheeks. She looked in the bathroom; she looked briefly in Joséphine's room. Ed turned off the cooker and followed her. She looked in every corner of the spare room, which was unrented just then; she burst into Ed's room, looked under the bed, opened the wardrobe and rummaged among his shirts. Ed caught up with her, took her by the shoulders.

27

'I didn't know you cared.'

She turned to him.

'Oh, Ed, you don't understand anything, do you?'

There was nothing for Ed to do but lower his head, drink in her aroma of cinnamon and crush her soft lips with his own. He began to manoeuvre her towards the bed, but she disengaged.

'Why do you think I've been avoiding you?'

'Maybe you've got bad taste. You don't like me.'

'Ed, I'm crazy about you. Can't you tell?'

Another long kiss. Another disengagement.

'Well, then, you're frightened of me.'

'That's more like it. Ed, I know you'll turn my world upside down if I give myself to you, the way I want to. And what can you give me in return? Only chaos and confusion.'

'Right now, I can give you a life. A life that doesn't depend on Mummy and Daddy. And with time ... with time I'll be able to give you whatever you want. This boy is going places.'

'Oh, Ed, if only I could believe you. I'm still only a girl, but my ears have already heard so many fine words ... that were no more than just that.'

'You can believe *me*.'

The pleasure in Ção's misted eyes turned Ed over and turned him on.

She pulled Ed's shirt out of his trousers and dabbed at her eyes with its hem.

'Well, now that I'm here, I might as well teach you some Portuguese. I think it's a good idea to start with parts of the body. I'll show you what helping a stranger really means.' She unbuttoned Ed's shirt and slipped her arms around his torso.

'*Mamilo*,' Ção said, and kissed his nipple.

Ed threw his head back and tried to repeat '*mamilo*' as he drew in his breath.

'*Mamilo*,' she said as she kissed the other one.

'*Mamilo.*'

'*Mamilos,*' Ed said as he placed his thumbs on her breasts.

'Hands off! I'm the teacher, today.'

Çāo eased Ed's shirt off and batted his hands away from the buttons of her blouse. She pushed him backwards until the bed-frame caught his calves and he sat on it. Çāo moved around the bed and knelt on it, behind Ed. She put her hands on his cheeks and pulled his head back.

'*Orelha,*' she said, as she kissed an ear.

'*Olha.*'

'No, I won't look. You look. And listen. *Orelha.*' She kissed the other ear.

'*Orelha.*'

She took her time, until she was convinced that Ed had learned the words for ear, forehead, eyes, nose, lips, tongue, teeth, chin and neck. He wished he was a slower learner, but he knew it would turn out to be a valuable lesson.

'No!'

Çāo removed Ed's hands from the backs of her thighs. She got off the bed and came round to face him.

'Now get naked.' Çāo showed no sign of getting naked herself.

'This isn't fair.'

'Nothing is fair in this world. Get naked. Now!'

Ed complied, then lay back on top of the bed. The cold in the room made no difference to him: his flesh was burning. Çāo came and sat on its edge. She cupped his balls in her hands.

'*Colhões.*'

'*Colly oish.*'

'*Colhões,*' she repeated, emphasising the nasal vowel.

'*Colhões.*'

'*Caralho.*' She brushed the tip of his erect penis with her lips. Ed's whole body tried to leap into the air.

'*Cawalho.*'

'*Carrrrralho,*' she said, rolling the 'r' in her throat as she took Ed's penis into her mouth for an instant.

'*Cawalho.*'

'*Carrrrralho.*' This time, she tried to get Ed to feel the vibrations at the back of her palate around his penis.

'*Caralho,*' he gasped.

'Bravo. *Carrrrralho.*'

'*Caralho,*'

'Bravo! Carrrrralho.' Ed's restraint came to an abrupt end, but the language exercise did not. Ção sucked all the semen from his penis as her lips finally moved up and off it. She looked at him triumphantly.

'*Broche,*' she spluttered.

'*Broche.*'

She swallowed.

'*Broche,*' she repeated, giggling.

'*Broche.* What's that?'

'It's what you say when ...' Ção was unable to contain her mirth. She got up and hurried to the bathroom, laughing and repeating '*broche*' with an English accent.

Ed got under the blankets and awaited her return. He did not wait long.

'That's it. Get dressed, my English gentleman, because the lesson for today is over.'

'I don't want a lesson. I want you.'

Ção came and sat on the bed.

'Just how much do you want me, Ed Scripps?'

'Very much. Very, very much!'

'You want my body?'

'I want all of you.'

'That includes my body. Ed, I'm a virgin.'

'What?!'

'Yes. Little Miss Conception doesn't want to conceive. Not before she's married. So she keeps her hymen intact until she has a ring on her finger.'

'But nobody cares about that any more!'

'In this country, they do. In my family, they do.'

'Even in Portugal you must know about contraception.'

'The surest way for me not to get pregnant is to keep my hymen intact. Until I'm married.'

'And that – '

' … is precisely what I am going to do.'

'You're joking!'

'No, I'm not. On the other hand …'

'I don't believe this!'

'On the other hand, you've just seen what I can do. By way of giving you pleasure. Not bad, eh, judging by the look on your face?'

'That was wonderful!'

'I can give you pleasure in a thousand and one ways. Using any part of the body that you like. In any way you like that leaves my little hymen intact.'

'I think I can handle that.'

'As long as you make me Mrs. Scripps. As long there is a nice diamond to tell everyone you are going to make me Mrs. Scripps.'

'I'm not sure I'm quite ready for that.'

'One small ring and a long engagement. Think about it, and think about me.' She moved to the door, wiggling her bottom. Ed threw off the blankets.

'No, don't get up. I'll let myself out.'

She was gone. Ed heard her taking the stairs; he heard her chuckling; he heard the word '*broche*' a couple more times.

Ed climbed back into bed and thought about Ção and the terms of her offer all night.

## 4 FUTURE PERFECT

Business was booming on Europe's south-western extremity. The big conglomerates were doing well in a corporate state designed to serve their interests and protect them against competition. Labour-intensive, low-tech sectors did well, as long the labourers were content with low wages or afraid to demand better conditions. Enough money trickled down to the slowly-forming middle class for it to have income to dispose of in the new supermarkets which Brazilian chains were opening to compete with the myriad small, over-priced, poorly-stocked local shops that were part of the nation's social fabric. Ed saw opportunity on every corner, saw it far more clearly than the cautious supermarket managers with whom he dealt and whose outlook he tried to broaden as he expounded his schemes and expanded his contacts.

Ed's parents welcomed him like a prodigal son when he came home to spend Christmas at his father's vicarage. Stevenage itself seemed cold and sad compared to Lisbon. The afternoon light disappeared earlier, and the familiar aroma of coffee, as well as the occasional olfactory treat of cinnamon, was absent. Nevertheless, Ed relished the home comforts that he could not provide for himself in Portugal.

He did not tell anyone how close he was to becoming engaged, and Ção, who was always present in his mind, would rarely stay long on the end of a telephone. Besides, calls were expensive and his father's stipend was low; nor would the vicar have accepted money from his son to pay for them. After Christmas, Ed managed to get a few evenings out with his pals in their habitual watering holes in town. He relished their company and the familiar English beer served at room temperature, which they downed in large quantities, though he was disconcerted that their interest in Portugal went little further than the sexual proclivities of its young people, with a view to possible summer holiday jaunts there. Ed began to feel that his own centre of gravity was fast moving south.

He was back in England in March, in London this time. Although his business prospects were shaping up nicely, Ed still had nothing concrete to show for his efforts, so he decided to put some flesh on the Plan B that Keith had outlined to him. He enrolled for a two-week course in teaching English as a foreign language. To keep his independence and increase his options, he signed up for it not at a Sussex School but at the headquarters of the Interlingua International organisation, which was located in Wimbledon. The organisation housed its trainees in student-type accommodation above its classrooms and offices. Most of his fellow-trainees were used to the lifestyle, but it was new to Ed, and he found it to his taste. Moreover, he found the training sessions to be light, enjoyable and practical.

In the evenings, those who polished off their assignments early tended to head out as a pack to sample the limited nightlife of Wimbledon or else go in small groups into the heart of the metropolis. They were more interested in Portugal than his Stevenage pals. After all, Portugal was a potential workplace for them. Ed, in his turn, was keen to see if any of them had potential as business partners.

One who did was Clarice, who had worked for over a year in Brazil and whose Portuguese, when she tried it out on him, sounded to Ed more mellifluous but even less comprehensible than the Lisbon version. She was the kind of willowy blonde who appealed to Latin men, so Ed assumed she had acquired her fluency in bed rather than in the classroom. She looked upon the training course, like her time in Brazil and learning a minor international language, as sound investments for the future. She let Ed infect her with his enthusiasm for Portugal and its prospects, while insisting that Brazil was the real jewel of the Lusophone world.

'Why don't you come to Rio with me, Ed? You could set up a language school there. I'll be your star teacher!'

'Money, honey. Got to make it before I can waste it.'

They were in a pub near the Common, with five fellow trainees. A rare football match on the television set at the side of the bar had claimed the others' attention. Neither Stevenage not Liverpool was playing, so Ed was not especially interested.

Clarice was more interested in Ed than in football, as became obvious when she slid up close to him, and put her hand over his under the table. Ed freed his hand but moved even closer to her, enjoying the human warmth she emanated. They talked more about life in Brazil and Portugal; Clarice's experience gave her more to say. When they moved on to their career plans, Ed's enthusiasm took centre stage. By the time England's football match came to its disappointing conclusion, they were spending the small fortunes they would make, and were more inebriated with future success than with drink. An hour later, at closing time, the drink was catching up. All seven of them left the pub and stumbled across the Common together. Clarice snuggled up against Ed, and this time he drew her closer to him as they joined in the unsteady rendition of the Wombling Song.

By the time they had also murdered 'Jambalaya', 'Rebel, Rebel', 'School Love' and 'Jealous Mind', they were back on the streets, outside the suburban stronghold of Interlingua International. Frankie, the trainee with the least resistance to alcohol and the strongest resistance to its effects, invited everyone to his room to finish a bottle of tequila. Ed was up for it – he had never drunk the stuff and wanted to do so. Clarice was willing to tag along, but once outside Frankie's room, three of the others cried off, citing the need for sleep, leaving only Martha to share it with them. Frankie gave Ed a pointed look, and the penny dropped.

'Yeah, well. I've got some plans to discuss with Clarice, and we really ought to discuss them alone. Right, Clarry?'

Clarice nodded.

'If there's any tequila left tomorrow, bring it down to breakfast, will you?'

'Sure thing, Edward.'

Clarice's room was along the same corridor, so they headed for that.

'This is not what it looks like,' Ed said to an imaginary audience as Clarice unlocked the door.

Ed stepped inside and waited for Clarice to remove the key and follow him in. When she did, he caught her in an urgent embrace and pushed her back against the door as his lips sought hers. The door slammed shut. He opened her mouth with his tongue as his hands unzipped her jacket and homed in on her breasts, which were protected by a thick woollen jumper. He jumped back when Clarice lightly bit his intrusive tongue.

'Whoa! What's the hurry, Ed? You'll be missing half the fun. And we've got all night.'

Ed thought of his own bed. He had intended to spend that night in it.

'Don't look so forlorn.' She kissed him teasingly, then moved past him to the writing table in the small room. Above it were two shelves with a few books and folders dumped on them. From the lower one, Clarice brought down two tumblers and a bottle containing a transparent liquid.

'This is not tequila,' she said. 'It's even better. It's called cachaça. Brazilian white rum, our national drink over there. Hang on a minute, Ed, I'm going to the kitchen for more ingredients.'

She picked up her keys and went out into the corridor. Ed felt glad she did not lock the door behind her. He drew the curtain closed, sat on the chair by the writing table and awaited her return with interest.

Clarice was soon back, clutching a saucer with slices of lemon on it, a mug full of ice cubes and a few sachets of sugar. Humming what sounded like a lullaby, she poured two generous shots from the bottle into the tumblers, stirred in a little sugar, threw in a few slices of lemon and filled the remaining space with ice.

'*Caipirinha*!' she announced, handing one of the tumblers to Ed. 'It means "country bumpkin". Or something. Here's looking at you.'

'Cheers!'

The first sensation was the cold. Then Ed's throat felt the sweetness of the sugar and the burn of the rum. His lips smarted from the lemon. He smacked them.

'I could get used to this.'

'I'll bet. Now look at me, good sir, if you don't mind.'

Clarice shook off her jacket and pulled her jumper over her head. She threw it on a chair beside the bed.

Still humming, she began to dance.

Slowly, she undid her blouse and let it fall to the floor.

'You like what you see, I hope.'

'Very much.'

Clarice turned her back to Ed, wiggled her bottom, undid a short zip at the side of her long skirt and stepped out of it. She moved backwards to where Ed was sitting and stopped just in front of him. She got to her knees, still facing away from him.

'Unhook my bra, please.'

'With pleasure.'

He did so. Slowly, Clarice crawled to the bed, rose and then lay on top of it, on her back. All she wore now was a pair of flesh-coloured tights.

'Come and take these off me, please, Ed. Slow and easy.'

Ed gulped the rest of the caipirinha, stood up, methodically took off all his own clothes, folded them and laid them on top of the writing table. Then he turned his attention to the woman squirming on the bed.

'Come on!'

Ed sat on the bed, slipped his hands under the elastic of the tights. Clarice arched her body to help him as he eased them from her waist, down her thighs and calves, over her feet and off. He left them on the bed, moved his hands to her knees and parted her legs. His lips brushed the inside of her thighs.

'Wait, Ed. Satisfy my upper lips first.'

Ed moved up until he was lying on top of Clarice. He wanted to move swiftly but his reactions were slow.

'Kiss me tender. Kiss me long.'

Ed wondered what song she had taken those lines from. Then he pressed his lips on hers and fought his instinct to enter her at the same time.

Clarice held his face in her hands and let her tongue play with his.

Ed tried to think of Clarice as an old woman, but his excitation failed to diminish; he brought an image of Ção to his mind, but this only strengthened his erection. Ed tried to empty his mind. He succeeded, and, as he did so, the rum washed over his brain like an incoming ocean wave, catching him up in its ineluctable embrace and dumping him on the shore of sleep.

Ed awoke with pain in his brain, nausea in his throat and a barely-suppressed revolt in his intestines. Even his watch was against him: it read 4:17. He forced his eyes fully open. He was lying next to somebody. Who was it? Where was he? Then he remembered, and his pain was intensified by remorse: towards Ção, towards Clarice and even towards himself. Clarice had the look of a Rossetti angel as she snored lightly. Ed managed not to wake her while he got out of the bed, put on his underpants and trousers, gathered the rest of his things and let himself out of the room. He hurried down the corridor to the bathroom, where he relieved himself, splashed his face and put on the rest of his gear before going up to the next floor and finding his own room. Once inside, he located and swallowed a couple of painkillers, set the alarm clock, collapsed onto his bed and fell asleep again before his conscience could torment him further.

Ed was one of the few trainees at breakfast the next morning. Clarice was not there and he did not go looking for her. She showed up mid-morning and shunned him. Ed understood. He did not understand why he got a request to see the course director at the end of the day.

Lisa Davies was a slim, dark, intense woman who told everyone her ambition was to write successful romance novels featuring strong female characters. In the meantime, she was doing well in the teaching profession. She appreciated Ed's honesty in admitting that teaching was not his first-choice career, either.

The shelves of her temporary office were lined with someone else's books.

'Just another couple of days to go, Ed. Then it's back to the real world for you, isn't that right? Sad, eh?'

Despite his hangover, Ed chuckled.

'Yeah, it's been good. Time off. New people. Interesting ideas. Crap coffee.'

'Going Latin already, are we? I've been there, too, as it happens.'

'Portugal?'

'Yes, among other places. A few years ago, I taught in Oporto for a time.'

'The frozen north. I've only been up there once. Flying visit. Good coffee.'

'When are you heading back to Portugal?'

'End of next week. Seeing my business bosses in Croydon, then taking some time to see the family.'

'I'm asking because we're a teacher short next week, and I haven't got cover. It's mornings only. You've done well on the course. Would you like to stand in?'

'Are you going to pay me?'

'Sure, a pound an hour, the standard rate.' She noticed Ed's raised eyebrow. 'It'll be good experience for you, a chance to put into practice what you've learned.'

'Plus board and lodging here, I take it.'

'No, actually.'

'You said you haven't got cover. Is my room booked for next week? There isn't a new training course.'

'OK. Deal!' She laughed. 'You never know, you might get a taste for

39

it. We run Business English courses, too. Don't forget to give us a good evaluation.'

'Sure. But only because you deserve it.'

The course ended a couple of days later. Ed's status was high, not only because he had been invited to teach at Interlingua International but also because he was presumed to have laid the blonde bombshell, Clarice. Evidently, she had not scotched the rumour. Most of the trainees and trainers stayed for a raucous party on the Friday evening, and a few of them, including Clarice, were still around for a late pub lunch on Saturday. Afterwards, Ed would set off for King's Cross to get the train to Stevenage, where a weekend of preparing lessons and avoiding church awaited him.

'Goodbye, *Morfeu*,' Clarice said to him outside the pub. 'Here's my card. If you're ever awake in Rio …'

'I will be. One day. Here's mine.' He turned down one corner of it, in the Portuguese style, before handing it to her. The others looked on quizzically.

'By the way, Ed, there's some kind of uprising going on in Portugal today, according to the radio. It might set your plans back a bit.'

Ed watched Clarice amble back towards Interlingua International to pack her things, then ran to catch up with the group walking briskly towards the Underground station.

None of them had heard any news about Portugal; nor had anyone he spoke to on the train; nor had his parents, who were mighty glad to see him. The BBC's early evening news was preoccupied with the Golan Heights and British party politics. With his father's permission he called Ção, who was getting ready to go out for an evening with her elder sister, Maria da Agonia, and Agonia's husband, Sebastião.

'Ed! I miss you so much! When are you coming back to me? I've been going to the gym to practise my moves for you.'

Ed asked about the uprising.

'Oh, that. That is just some soldiers playing. They have nothing better to do, poor things.'

Ed asked exactly what had happened.

'If you want details, ask your girlfriend.'

'*You* are my girlfriend, Ção!'

'I mean Miss Rent-a-car Rich-bitch Lourdes.'

'Ção, I've been thinking. I don't need a car. I'm going to give it back to her as soon as I'm in Lisbon again. All I need is you. Desperately!'

'Oh, Ed! Do you mean that?'

'I do.'

'Ed, you can be so sweet. I just melt for you.'

Nevertheless, he did phone Lourdes, because he wanted details of the uprising and Lourdes kept herself informed. She was not at home, though. Instead, Ed spoke to her brother, Paulo.

'Seems like a failed coup. A rather half-hearted one. Have you heard of a place called Caldas da Rainha?'

'I've heard of it, but I don't know much about it. Some kind of spa, isn't it?'

'That's right. A bit like your Cheltenham. Only there's an infantry regiment based there, and they decided to march on Lisbon today. Caldas is only fifty miles north of here.'

'What happened?'

'They got stopped at the gates of the city. Loyalist units arrested the lot of them.'

'How many of them were there?'

'A couple of hundred.'

'What did they want?'

'Who knows? More money? Shorter conscription? Democracy? The earth?'

'Was anyone killed?'

'Not a shot was fired, apparently. They saw they were outnumbered, outgunned, alone, so they gave up.'

'Where are they now?'

'No-one knows.'

The idea of people just disappearing reminded Ed of his party.

'Any news of Jorge?'

'No. Not a word.'

'After six months, nearly!'

'Anyway, everything is quiet here. No-one is on the streets and no-one is getting shot in the streets. You don't need to be afraid of coming back, although Lourdes doesn't seem to like you the way she used to.'

Ed was not afraid of getting shot; he was afraid of losing Ção, losing her even before he had truly made her his.

The week he spent teaching in Wimbledon was a revelation to Ed. It was a pleasant surprise to find himself in a classroom full of students who wanted to learn. And he enjoyed helping them to do so, even though teacher-pupil exchanges did not have the *frisson* that business dealings held for him. After lunch with his students on Friday, his stint completed, he went to thank Lisa for giving him the break.

'We have a branch in Lisbon, you know. And in many other cities that young people tend to like.'

'Thanks. I'll bear that in mind. It's been great learning the Direct Method with you.' Ed noticed the cheque book in front of her.

'Can you pay me cash, please? I'll be back in Portugal before the banks open again here, on Monday.'

Lisa sighed.

'It's only fifteen quid, Lisa. It's not going to leave you short.'

'Yes, all right.' She opened her handbag, pulled out a wallet, took out some banknotes, counted them and handed over the exact sum to Ed, together with a pay slip. 'Just sign for it, would you?'

They chatted for a while, then Lisa asked Ed if he'd be interested in acting as an agent for Interlingua International, recruiting Portuguese students for their summer courses in England.

'Sorry, I can't. I've got too many friends at the Sussex School there. Your rivals.'

'Friendly rivals.'

'Even so. You've got to have ethics in business, I believe. And I want my ethical standards to be high.'

'Good for you, Ed. Have you got any ethical business tips for us, then?'

'Your business ethics are fine, as far as I can tell, but I have got a couple of business *suggestions* for you.'

'Let's hear them.'

'First, all your schools here are in the south of England. You should open up in places like York, Durham, Edinburgh.'

'Too cold for our students.'

'You're joking! Your Scandinavians are used to the cold. So are the Swiss, Germans …'

'And the Latins?'

'For them, it's so cold anywhere on this island that they hardly notice the difference. If they can put up with London weather, they'll happily come to Edinburgh as well. Though in a few years, I expect they'll be going to Los Angeles instead. Which is why you should be looking ahead for new markets. Russia and China won't be Communist forever. And you should be thinking of teaching their languages to our lot, too.'

'OK, Ed. Thanks. I'll pass those ideas on to the Boss. They sound good to me, but I know what he'll say: pie in the sky.'

'Yeah? It's funny, that's what they said at Stevenage Tech when I suggested they go private. They could be right, too.'

On the train to Croydon the next day, Ed took out Lisa's business card and made a note on the back of the dates when she'd said she was likely to be visiting Interlingua International in Lisbon. He had offered her a dinner if she did show up, and he intended to make good on his promise.

Retail Support Services operated out of premises in Oakfield Road, near the Masonic Hall, though they were planning a move to more spacious offices in the glitzy business district that was emerging in the town centre. Ed's appointment was with his boss, James Towsey, a short, dapper man in his early forties who was sharp and serious about business, yet apt to articulate his appreciation of art and to philosophise about reincarnation.

'Ed! You look like the day I first clapped eyes on you. When was that?'

'1970?'

'You were still a teenager. Just out of the Tech.'

'No. I'd done a year with Tesco's in Manchester.'

'Yeah, well, say no more about Tesco's. What's the secret? You got a portrait in the attic that's wrinkling and greying already?'

'Come on, I'm only twenty-three. And I live a healthy life.'

*Apart from the occasional binge.*

'Good man. So tell me about Portugal. Especially loyalty discount cards.'

Ed explained all that he had done, the contacts that he had made, the difficulty of introducing new ideas into a deeply conservative society. He drew out and passed over to James a list of all the supermarkets and managers who had shown openness to his ideas, and ended by predicting that at least one major chain would take up his offer of Retail Support Services' technical assistance in introducing a loyalty card scheme in the autumn, once people were back from their holidays spent by the sea or visiting relatives inland. He was well aware that he had nothing concrete to show.

James nodded, then gave him his own assessment.

'Look, Ed. Apart from your reports, we've gathered reports about you.'

Ed swallowed.

'People there like you. They say you're warm, friendly, polite. You explain things carefully and clearly. They like your ideas, even if they don't leap to take them up. Not just loyalty cards, but ideas of your own. What have you been advocating? Evening opening, shopping advisers, mechanical checkouts. Hmm, not too sure about that one myself. The point is, we think you're doing a good job. Only ...'

'No concrete results as yet.'

'This is it. So how do we square the circle? Maximise our exploitation of what you have achieved in terms of preparation, but not pay you money forever without getting anything in return?'

It didn't sound like he was getting the sack.

'Yes?'

'Here's how. We give you two things: promotion and a deadline. From now on, you still report to me, but just to keep me informed. From now on, Ed, you *are* Retail Support Services, Portugal! You make your own decisions, and you make sure that by July 31 you have firm commitments that Retail Support Services, Portugal will generate an income for the mother ship starting next autumn, at the latest.'

'Or else?'

'What do you think? No more money, no job, no reference; no future!'

'Do I get a rise?'

'Don't push your luck, Ed.'

'Look, I really need my own transport out there. Public transport is good in the city, and taxis are cheap. But outside, it's a disaster.'

'Most supermarkets are in the cities, but you do have a point. How about this? As soon as you generate an income for us, we'll feed some of it back so that you can purchase a jalopy. I mean a company car.'

'Deal! Thanks for your patience, James, and thanks for the challenge. I appreciate it.'

For the remaining hours that he was in England, and on the plane back to Portugal, Ed Scripps thought long and hard about his future. He knew that he wanted very much to spend his life with Ção, and that Portugal was a great place for a young, aspiring businessman to be. However, he realised that Retail Support Services, Portugal, was unlikely ever to generate the income and consequent lifestyle that he aspired to. Ed Scripps International would be a surer bet. The outlook was rosy.

A greasy rain fell on the city as Ed's plane landed. Ção surprised him by meeting him at the airport, and he luxuriated in her aroma of cinnamon as they held each other close.

'I've missed you so much,' she whimpered.

'Never again!'

They enjoyed an amorous taxi ride into the city, despite the driver's tut-tutting. Ção wanted to go to her parents' but Ed had the driver take them to Largo do Andaluz and wait while he took his case upstairs, then drive them downtown to a self-proclaimed luxury restaurant known for its slow service. Since it was Sunday, the servants' traditional day off, the restaurant was full. Ed had to bribe a member of staff to curtail their wait.

Over coffee, Ed produced the engagement ring he had lashed out on in London, and proposed.

Ção said yes.

'There is just one small condition, my love.'

'Ed darling, I told you. Not until we are actually married.'

'I understand that. That's why I want us to get married as soon as possible. Next month, at the latest.'

'But my parents – '

'In secret.'

'Oh, Ed! How romantic! Oh, yes! Yes! Yes!'

Waving the diamond on her finger, Ção had him walk her back up the Avenida da Liberdade towards his flat, holding her other hand. The rain had ceased and the humid air felt warm. Ed felt a sudden curiosity about the name – Freedom Avenue.

'What is it, fascist irony?'

'No. It celebrates our freedom from Spain, or the Moors, or both. And the park at the top, where the boy prostitutes hang out, is named after your King.'

'We've got a Queen now, in England.'

'Edward the Seventh.'

'Way before my time.'

Ed laughed and quickened their pace.

That night, Ção gave Ed a comprehensively satisfying introduction to her extended catalogue of non-vaginal sex. Then she demanded a taxi to her parents'. When Ed got back from seeing her off, he noticed that she had left the ring next to his pillow. He sighed, and started planning.

## 5  LOVE IN THE TIME OF CARNATIONS

Ed did not return Lourdes' car immediately. He had too much to do, too many places to go in a hurry.

His first stop was the British Consulate, located on one of the city's many hills. He found a parking space close by. The Consulate had a relaxed and sleepy air, as did the man on duty, who seemed pleased to have a fellow Brit to chat with. Together with his opinions on the outlook for the coming cricket season, he gave details of the documents Ed would need in order to get married in Portugal, and produced a Certificate of Marital Capacity then and there, sharing a chuckle over the title.

That was the easy bit. Ed was glad he had brought a whole raft of documents with him from England, but it was a question of getting them to the right people in the right offices, with certified translations into Portuguese, and fast. He drove to the docks to see Hélder, the business contact who was most like a friend, and asked him if, for a fee, he would see to it all. Hélder had installed a comfortable modern office for himself in a dilapidated waterfront building. He beamed at Ed's request.

'Ed, it will be my wedding present to you, and my pleasure. You just need to leave me some grease for the palms that my requests will undoubtedly open like carnations in Spring.'

He asked for a relatively small sum for the purpose.

Hélder put the money in a drawer, then ambled to the office's noisy fridge, from which he pulled a bottle of white port and poured two small measures.

'To the health, wealth and happiness of Edward Scripps and Maria da Conceição dos Santos e Cunha!' Ed would drink to that any day.

One small measure followed another, and it was mid-afternoon before Ed left the docks, after much hugging, back-slapping and hand-shaking. Feeling pleased with the world, he stopped at the first snack-bar he found on the road back into the city centre, and got some food inside him to counter the effects of the alcohol. Then he drove very carefully home.

His late-afternoon series of business phone calls ended when Ção arrived. The phone was in what they called the party room, a name which sparked good memories for both of them. As they embraced, Ção pressed her teeth into Ed's shoulder, then pulled him through the connecting door into his bedroom. She closed the curtains on the cool April evening, then turned to Ed.

'How quickly do you think you can take my clothes off'?

'One minute.'

'Come on, then.'

It took longer than that, with frequent interruptions. They were under the covers by the time Ed freed Ção of her last remaining item, a choker, leaving her as naked as she had made him. Twenty minutes later, the covers were littering the floor. Both of them were lying back against the pillows. Ed watched Ção as she rubbed his sperm into her breasts. Ção caught sight of the engagement ring on the bedside table, reached across Ed, lifted it off the table and slipped it over her sticky ring finger. She got off the bed and waved it in the air.

'How do I look?'

'Magnificent!'

She had let her hair grow since the day they met. In Ed's eyes, that made her even more seductive.

'What else?'

'Good enough to eat!'

'Again?'

'Again and again and again!'

'What else?'

'Good enough to marry!'

'When?' She pouted.

'Monday, April the Twenty-second.'

'Are you serious?'

'I've never been more serious.'

'Oh, Ed, that is wonderful!'

She really did jump for joy.

'Wonderful! Wonderful! Wonderful!'

She skipped to the door.

'Your flatmate isn't here, is she?'

'Joséphine? No, she's away. Says she can't follow her diet when she's here. Too much temptation to steal my food.'

'There's a clean towel in the bathroom, I hope.'

Ed nodded. Ção let herself out into the corridor. Ed heard her light but energetic and vocal progress along it.

Well after dusk, they went out to eat in the neighbourhood. Ed did not want to drive Ção anywhere in the car Lourdes had lent him. Ção tackled him about the car over their dinner.

'You see, Ção, my love, I'm going to need it over the next couple of weeks. I have to get to as many small towns as I can – the ones that aren't served properly by public transport. I need to see their supermarket managers and enrol them for my loyalty card scheme. If I can convince them to join. After that, I can hand back the car and concentrate on the big cities again.'

'Why don't you just buy a car if you need one so badly?'

'Because my company is going to buy one for me - as soon as I start making some sales.'

'Oh, Ed, is that going to be soon?'

'Very soon, my love. I feel I'm on the verge of something big. So I'll be travelling a lot this next month. Until the Twenty-second.'

'Don't leave me, Ed, not all alone with my parents. And when is it you're going to tell them?'

'Tell them what?'

'About us. That we're getting married. Getting married next month, when they're going to lose their little Conception.'

Ed had assumed they would present the stony couple with a *fait accompli*.

'Don't worry. I'll deal with it.'

He did not relish his infrequent visits to Ção's family home. The only time they had invited him to eat with them, he had suffered symptoms of food poisoning afterwards. Since no-one else had been affected, Ed wondered if they had deliberately targeted him. He had not burdened Ção with his suspicions.

When they left the restaurant, Ção asked to be taken home, but then relented and accompanied Ed back to his flat. In bed, she seemed cool at first, but quickly warmed to their 'not-quite' activities. Ed asked himself about the experience that she demonstrated, but held back from asking *her*. He hoped she would be as inventive, and as little restrained, when it came to the real thing.

The next morning, Ed Scripps rose from his empty bed and set off on a mission to conquer rural Portugal. He spent nearly three weeks making contacts and pushing his luck among the supermarket managers and storekeepers in the area within striking distance of Lisbon – the Alentejo to the south, the Ribatejo and Estremadura to the north and east. A few had no time for him, but most were welcoming, if slightly baffled by his proposals, and some were keen, though they tended to want more reassurance and guarantees than Retail Support Services was able or willing to provide.

Each evening, he phoned Ção and consoled her for his absence and the hard time her parents were giving her with their cold, authoritarian ways, times that he could assure her were coming to a rapid end. He also phoned Hélder regularly to ask about progress with the bureaucracy. Thanks to Hélder's diligence and his extensive network, progress was smooth and relatively swift.

As he drove back to Lisbon, Ed reflected that those definitely on board for him to roll out a prototype of the scheme were nearing the critical number. He turned his thoughts to the make of car he would have the company buy for him. *Not another Renault*, he decided, as the one he was driving jerked him in and out of another pothole.

Back in his flat, Ed set aside his papers for a thorough going-over the following day, washed, ate, rested, and then phoned Lourdes.

'It's been great driving around in your car, Lourdes. It's helped me a lot, but now I've finished with it. My company is going to buy one for me. Can I bring yours back to you this evening?'

'No need, Ed. I'll come and collect it. Are you sure you won't still need it?'

'I'm sure, thanks. It's been a tremendous help, really, but it's actually become something of an embarrassment.'

'Oh, I see. I can imaging the kind of jealous bitchery you're having to put up with.'

'Thanks, Lourdes. For everything.'

An hour later, she turned up at his flat, clutching a blanket.

'What's that for?'

'It belongs in the car. Paulo dropped me off. He sends you his best regards and all that. No make-up girl tonight?'

'If you mean Ção, she's being suffocated by a Sunday family evening.'

'Good.'

Ed thought it best to get Lourdes away from his flat. He took her down to inspect the car. She opened the rear, pushed the back seats down and spread the blanket over them. She gave Ed her seductive look, which he found hard to remain indifferent to.

'Why don't we drive up into the hills and put this blanket to its proper use?'

Ed steeled himself.

'I find that suggestion distasteful.'

Lourdes laughed.

'Please yourself. You always do.'

'What do you mean by that?'

'Forget it. Goodbye, Ed.'

She got into the car, started it, then rolled the window down.

'And good luck.'

Lourdes drove away in her mud-splattered Renault.

\*

The wedding took place a week later.

Ed and Çāo were married in a registry office in the city centre, with only Çāo's best friend and confidante, Estrela, as witness. The atmosphere was as jolly as such a small group could make it. Çāo insisted on wearing white, though not a wedding dress. Afterwards, in the warm but humid air of the Spring morning, the photographer Ed had commissioned did his work, then the three of them piled into the hired Rolls that Ed had filled with roses and drove first to Estrela's home, where they left her with thanks and instructions not to breathe a word to anyone, then headed to the railway station for trains to the Algarve. Ed had already bought the tickets, so the first thing they did was to get on a ferry and cross the broad estuary southwards.

Çāo was ecstatic.

'Oh, Ed! We've done it! I'm free! I'm free!'

'You're not free, my love, you're tied to me. Till death us do part!'

'Nothing and no-one will ever part us, will they, Ed?'

'Nothing and no-one!' They kissed; then Çāo buried her face in a bunch of roses to blot out the acrid smell from the chemical plants on the south bank as they approached the ferry terminal.

The journey to Portugal's south coast, the region known as the Algarve, lasted all afternoon. The train sauntered through the vast cork plantations of the Alentejo, then among the citrus farms of the northern Algarve. Ed had never felt happier. Singing for joy, they changed trains at a place called Tunes and eventually disembarked at the end of the line at the small resort town of Lagos, where they got straight into a taxi for their seaside hotel at a beach named 'Dona Ana', which, even so late in April, was almost deserted.

'The perfect place for a honeymoon!' Çāo's enthusiasm was infectious, and she took it into the bedroom with her.

They got up late the next morning. Çāo was a little sore, and Ed had breakfast brought up to them.

After a bell-boy had collected the empty dishes, Çāo had Ed get out of bed and rummage in her suitcase for the camera. Then she made him go out and get the day's newspaper. When he came back with it, she asked him to pull down the covers from the bed.

'What on earth is this in aid of?'

'Tradition, Ed.'

Çāo took several snaps of the blood-stained sheets, with the day's paper propped on a clean patch. She was particularly concerned that the date should be legible.

Ed shook his head in disbelief. 'Now I've seen everything!'

'Oh come on, darling, it's just a little present for my dear ones. Proves to them I really was a good little daughter of theirs all these years.'

'Don't I know it! Was it your mother who taught you –'

'Don't make a fuss, Ed, my sweet. It's just a little thing to please Mummy and Daddy. After all, they're losing me. You never know, I might need them again some day.'

On the Wednesday night, Çāo's deep, contented snoring kept Ed awake. He got up, picked up a bottle of dark beer and his transistor radio and took them out on to the terrace with him. His watch told him it was nearly eleven. He listened to the radio for a while, relishing the joy of being wedded to Çāo and in charge of his own fine destiny. Then the radio started on Portugal's entry for the recent Eurovision song contest, and he quickly switched stations. With the sea air caressing his skin, and the beer calming his racing thoughts, he soon dozed off in his chair.

He was awakened by the sound of men crunching on gravel. Lots of them, rhythmically, as though they were marching. Ed leaped from his chair and looked down at the beach, but there was nobody below him. Then the men started singing and he realised it was the radio, which he had left on. The voices reminded him of a Welsh miners' choir, and he listened intently until their song finished, though he made out few of the words. Then he went back inside, fastened the window, got back into bed and snuggled up beside the now-silent Ção. Within minutes, he was dreaming of mine shafts, excavations and red shirts.

Elsewhere in the country, men had taken the Eurovision song as confirmation of their plans, and the Alentejo miners' song as a signal to put them into action.

The next morning, clean sea air pervaded the hotel as usual, but the atmosphere was different. The staff stood around in knots, talking animatedly among themselves and paying only perfunctory attention to their guests or their needs. Ed and Ção did not mind: they had eyes and ears only for each other, and nothing could sour the mood of their honeymoon. They spent the day on the beach, in the water, and in bed back at the hotel.

It was when they came down for dinner that it became impossible for Ed to ignore the news being broadcast on the television in the hotel dining room. The news had transfixed all the staff and most guests.

'Ção! Look at that. There are tanks in the centre of Lisbon!'

'It's probably some boring military parade. Why haven't they laid out the fresh fish today?'

'No, look! There are soldiers and civilians next to each other. Something big is going on. I want to know what it is.'

The live broadcast showed a man whom Ed recognised as the Prime Minister, and others he did not recognise, being driven out of a military building in the heart of Lisbon into a square packed tight with ordinary civilians. The crowd reluctantly parted for them. Lines of soldiers kept the people back as the convoy of armoured cars drove away.

'Oh, Ed, it looks like a military coup. We're probably going to be ruled by some even worse fascists from now on.' She looked on the verge of tears.

It seemed the hotel staff supported the coup, for they broke into an almighty cheer when the television announced that both the Prime

Minister and the President of the régime were on their way to the airport to be flown to the Atlantic island of Madeira. Then someone started singing the song that had woken Ed up during the night. Soon everyone was singing it.

'Ção, I heard this on the radio last night! Who's the singer?'

'I think it's Zeca Afonso. His songs are usually banned, because he is too left-wing.'

'Ção, my love, this is not a right-wing coup.'

'Then maybe we're all going to be free!'

'Maybe we'll find Jorge. Or, at least, find out what happened to him.'

The mood in the dining room grew increasingly jolly and exuberant. It was as if everyone present had made each other into new friends for life. Then came news that sobered people up like a cold shower: the secret police, holed up in their headquarters, had opened fire on the crowd of civilians massed outside. People had died; scores were injured. For a while, in Lisbon, it seemed as if the situation might get out of hand, but gradually it became clear that those murders had been the last brutal act of fury of a dying régime. A new leader was announced: General Spínola, who had been fired from the Army just months before for opposing the colonial wars. A National Salvation Council, with Spínola at its head, promised peace, freedom and justice.

Ed thought this was all very exciting, but what he really wanted was to get that fish grilled and Ção back into bed. It was past midnight when he fulfilled that wish. Ção was on fire.

'Ed, this is the first day of the rest of our lives! From now on everything is going to be better. Ed, promise you'll always love me like tonight.'

Ed did not need to promise anything so obvious, but he said the words, lest there should be even a speck of doubt. When they paused in their love-making, he had Ção teach him the chorus of Zeca Afonso's song.

*

The black and white television images made clear the disbelief in the men's faces as they walked quickly along the corridors, as though a heavy hand might fall upon their shoulder if they paused. They descended a flight of steps, some with difficulty, some with bravado, and emerged into light and the flashlights.

Ed searched the pallid faces on the screen for that of Jorge, but he was not among the first prisoners whom the television showed repeatedly on Saturday evening, emerging from Caxias, the political prison on and below the banks of the River Tagus, making light of the beatings they had received and the psychological torture that the PIDE had inflicted on them with techniques taken straight out of their American cousins' new training manual.

It had been a day between two new worlds for Ed and Ção. Throughout it, they had indulged alternately in sand, sea and sun at Dona Ana beach, and in honeymoon sex at their hotel.

At dinner, staff and customers were again glued to the news broadcasts. The *Armed Forces Movement* had confirmed its grip on power across the nation. Everywhere, it seemed people were in the streets to support them and to celebrate freedom. They had made carnations, plentiful that Spring, the symbol of the Revolution. No soldier could refuse a carnation placed in the barrel of his rifle by a young woman in full public view. The two hundred soldiers who had unsuccessfully marched on Lisbon from Caldas the month before, testing the régime's reaction, were released from the fortress prison of Trafaria. Then came the release of the long-term political prisoners from Caxias, and from the fort at Peniche, on the windswept Atlantic coast. The joy of those who came to greet them, and the evidence that the prisoners' spirit had not been broken, affected everyone.

The following day, Saturday, was their last in the Algarve. As the light faded, Ed and Ção took a taxi into Lagos. The driver refused a tip. They strolled around the town, and were caught up in the enthusiasm of a large rally in a small square near the sea front. A stage had been improvised. So, too, had banners, speeches and music. It became clear that people were going to take full advantage of the new-found freedom to speak their minds. The repetition of fine words stimulated the young lovers' appetites, and they soon left the square to seek an open restaurant. Ed was elated, but Çāo was pensive.

'Did you notice how few women were in that crowd? That is something we will simply have to change.'

'We?'

'We Portuguese women.'

Ed had not seen this side of Çāo before. He was happy to endorse it.

'The sooner the better. Get women into business, too.'

Later, he added: 'And waiting on tables.'

'And driving taxis. This Revolution has a lot of work ahead of it.'

On Sunday evening, they were standing in the hallway of Çāo's parents' home. The lines in her mother's face bent her mouth firmly downwards.

'What do you want, young man?'

'I've come to tell you and your husband how happy I am to be your son-in-law.'

She screamed. Her husband appeared at her shoulder.

'What the hell have you done to my wife? And my daughter?'

'Daddy, can't you be a bit nice to my husband?'

'Your what?'

'My husband. Daddy, we got married last Monday morning.'

'That's not possible! I won't allow it! You, get out of here, and leave my daughter alone! Do you hear me?'

'Come on, Çāo, let's go. You don't have to listen to this, and neither do I.'

'OK, just help me with some bags.'

'I'll set the police on you! I'll have you arrested!'

They collected the suitcases that Çāo had prepared well in advance and carried them past the now-speechless man and the wailing woman, out onto the landing and down the stairs. Ed was grim-faced but Çāo was giggling. In the taxi, though, her laughter turned to tears.

'Oh, Ed, they're my Mummy and Daddy. What if they never speak to me again?'

'Don't worry, my darling. Anyone can see that they love you. They just have to accept the facts and get used to them. They'll come round.'

Now that it was her home, Ção did not find Ed's flat as enticing as she once had. She claimed that it was too small for all her things. Ed was aware that it was no palace. He mollified her by saying he would pay to rent the spare room as well.

'In any case, we'll be out of here as soon as I start earning some decent money. We can start thinking now about where we'd like to live.'

Despite her misgivings, Ção set to work to make the flat as clean and comfortable as she could. Ed appreciated her willingness to pull her weight, and tried to adjust his domestic standards to match hers.

Wrapped up in each other as they were, the outside world was still very much with them. Ed tuned in to radio stations broadcasting in English and French. Many of them relayed fears of a counter-coup by the deposed fascists, or else a bloody struggle for power among left-wing factions.

Events on the streets belied such fears. The most prominent fascists packed their bags and left the country. Others decided to shut up and put up with the waves of freedom washing over the land, at least for the time being. Many of the lower-ranking supports of the old régime deemed it expedient simply to switch colours and embrace socialism more blindly than Karl Marx ever had. The leaders of the Socialist Party and the Communist Party returned from exile to massive popular welcomes. May 1st, International Workers' Day, was declared a national holiday.

May Day, indeed, was the Revolution's public party.

In Lisbon, the previously clandestine trade unions organised the biggest demonstration in Portugal's history. People flooded onto the streets, not only to support the idea that workers should have rights, but also to show that they identified with the soldiers who had toppled the old régime, and simply to enjoy a holiday, the Spring air, the carnival atmosphere.

Ed and Ção were swept up in the general euphoria. They met up with a group of Ção's classmates from the Sussex School, none of whom failed to notice the two adornments on her ring finger. Although the main route followed the broadest of the city's avenues, they quickly got detached from Ção's friends. Ed made sure that her arm was firmly linked with his all the time, and avoided spots where the crowd got too thick. When they approached the stadium where speeches were due, newly baptised in honour of the day, he guided them away altogether.

'There's somewhere special I want to go to celebrate this day. It's quite a walk.'

'Today, as long as I'm with you, I could walk to the ends of the earth!'

The walk was made longer, but no less enjoyable, by their having to keep to side roads to avoid going against the biggest flow of human traffic the city had ever witnessed. Eventually, they found themselves in a small square with a monkey-puzzle tree at its centre. The square was full of exuberant people. There were banners and animated conversations, but no speeches.

'Stage One, Praça da Alegria – Happiness Square.'

From there, Ed led Ção down a steep hill and on to a familiar main artery of the city centre.

'Stage Two, Avenida da Liberdade. At last it can live up to its name!'

Indeed, the Avenue was packed with celebrants drunk on freedom. They had driven off the motorists who normally monopolised its cobbled pavements, and caused consternation among the black swans which thrived along its narrow internal lakes. At the top, where it met the Park, Ção found a spot where they could rest and talk on a stone bench.

'Ed, this is lovely, but what's going to happen? Every day can't be like this. What's going to happen to the economy, and to your business? What's going to happen to us?'

'Don't worry about us. We'll be all right whatever happens. I'll look after you. We can't go wrong!' He kissed her tenderly. The tenderness in her own eyes was still clouded with worry, but Ed was bursting with joy and optimism.

'As for the country, look around you. All this energy! If the new leaders can harness this and put it to good use, they can't go wrong, either.'

'And the economy?'

'Same thing. Now that the corporate state is dead, individual entrepreneurs who are not part of the corrupt and fossilised system will have a better chance. Believe me, it's just what the country needs. Truly free enterprise plus meritocracy, with the benefits going to everyone. My life – our life – is going to get easier and better from now on!'

## 6  TEMPERATURE RISING

Ed found married life very much to his taste. It was not just waking up beside Ção or falling asleep inside her or imbibing a constant night-time aroma of sex and cinnamon. It was also the knowledge of having an anchor in a transient world, even as the world before them changed for the better, and they were happy to be part of it.

At the end of their first week back in Lisbon, Ção surprised Ed by getting out of bed as soon as they woke up.

'What's going on?'

'Demo!'

'Come back to bed. I want to make love to you before breakfast.'

'I don't think we've got time for sex, you know, or even breakfast. We've got to get this demo up and running, so we can't just lie in bed.'

'We?'

'You, me and the other true revolutionaries.'

'Er, who are these true revolutionaries?'

'The MRPP, of course.'

'The who?'

'The Movement – oh, let's just say the Maoists. Come on, darling, get up!'

'I'm not sure I want to associate myself with Maoists, my love. I've heard they have a rather different idea of loyalty to mine. The Maoists in China, anyway.'

Ção slipped back under the covers and placed her naked body over part of Ed's.

'OK. Compromise. I'll suck every last drop of sperm out of you, and then we'll go.'

Coming from Ção, it was an offer Ed could not refuse.

When they got down to the docks, the demo was in full swing. Ed had expected to feel out of place among hordes of hard-looking, rough-clad peasants, but most of these Maoists were young and dressed with casual care. Ed and Ção fitted in pretty well. The youngsters managed to be tough and uncompromising in the words they addressed to the targets of the demo – conscript troops being shipped off to the colonies.

'But I thought the wars were going to end.'

'So did we. Yet the National Salvation Council says we've got to negotiate an agreed peace, not just withdraw our troops, so here we are sending these boys off to replace other kids whose tour of duty in Africa is coming to an end. It doesn't make sense!'

'Well, actually, you know, I can sort of see the point.'

'Oh, Ed, don't be so naive, it isn't funny. Most of these kids are younger than you. Some are even younger than me. And some of them won't be coming home.'

Ed was not going to argue. He just wanted to keep Ção out of harm's way, so he gently but unrelentingly manoeuvred her to the sidelines, well away from the potential points of contact between the soldiers and the demonstrators. The youngsters on the boat looked back blankly as their counterparts on the quay called them murderers and urged them to desert, while the vessel slipped its mooring and took them into the broad estuary, seawards, away from everything that was familiar.

*

'There was an awful lot of noise,' Ed said to Keith, the day he paid out on the bet he had lost, 'but it never looked as though anyone was going to get hurt.'

They were sitting outside the Suiça café in Rossio Square, the city's heart.

'That's par for the course. Let's hope things stay that way. I expect they will, you know. Now, since you're paying, you can order for us both.'

Ed perused the menu, conferred with the waiter and asked for a series of choice items.

'Hmm. Your Portuguese has improved. It's come on leaps and bounds since we last spoke. To what shall we attribute that, eh?'

'Necessity. I've been using it more.'

'One of my teachers has just published an article called *Language Learning in Bed*. A title like that, anyway.'

'Could be on to something. But I've been using Portuguese for business, too. Outside the cities, where hardly anyone speaks English or French.'

'Ah, business. Getting difficult, isn't it?'

'A mere blip, in my opinion. People are waiting to see what happens. With this civilian government that has just come in, I think people will really go for it. All that untapped potential for enterprise. Keith, it's a dream coming true!'

'I just hope you don't get a rude awakening.'

The strong afternoon light reflected off the metal edges of the tables. Ed let the sparkling wine tickle the back of his throat and stimulate the taste buds that the bland food had failed to arouse. He opened and closed his eyes to create a strobe effect, and felt glad they were sitting down, and under an awning. Tomorrow he would go out and drum up business, but this afternoon he was going to enjoy the southern lifestyle and the northern company, and in the evening he would let love rule. It really was a perfect way to live.

Rarely had the world so readily and so whole-heartedly endorsed a military coup as it did Portugal's bloodless 'Carnation Revolution'. International approval was cemented by the installation of the civilian government, which included members of all the major political forces outlawed during the dictatorship. People believed that Utopia was around the corner. To judge from their words, they were willing to die for it. To judge from their actions, they were not willing to bet on it. This was particularly baffling, and galling, for Ed.

'What are they waiting for? Don't they know that the early bird catches the worm?'

'Maybe,' said Hélder, when they next met, 'they think that the early bird will be the hunter's first target.'

Ed was not afraid of hunters. He had a car to earn, a wife to maintain, a shining future to build, and he threw himself into his business with boundless optimism and renewed determination.

His optimism was contagious. Although the supermarket chains refused to commit themselves, small independents began to put pen to paper. The day after the government brought in a minimum wage for the first time in the country's history, two large grocers in a dreary suburb of Lisbon signed up with Ed for RSS's loyalty card scheme. Back in the city centre, he went straight to the Sussex School, where Ção was having her German lesson, to break the good news to her directly. He joked with the secretaries at the reception desk as he waited for the lessons to end.

'See if you can cheer up your fellow-countryman,' said Laura, wiping tears of laughter from her eyes. She pointed to a black-haired man with a straggly beard who was resting his thin, lengthy frame in a chair against the wall and gazing at the ceiling with a sombre expression. Ed went over and introduced himself. The man looked steadily at Ed through his stylish glasses.

'Oh, yes. I've heard of you.'

'Yes, I'm the bloke who's just got married. It's an open secret around here.'

'I'm married, myself. Waiting for the wife now, actually. She teaches French.'

A bell rang. The classrooms emptied and the reception area filled. Ção appeared by Ed's side.

'Darling. What a lovely surprise!' She kissed him for long enough to raise a few eyebrows. The thin man got up and greeted, with a light kiss, a woman whom Ed recognised as Simone, the French teacher he had met several months earlier. He introduced Ção to her as his wife. She, in turn, introduced them to her husband, Mark.

'Won't you come and eat with us?' Ed offered. 'We're celebrating.'

'What are we celebrating, darling?'

'I'll tell you in the restaurant.'

The restaurant was full, so they had to wait for a table. As they stood at the bar drinking aperitifs, Ed told them about his successful day. Ção was thrilled; Simone was pleased; only Mark could not produce a smile.

'Sometimes you get lucky,' was his comment, 'but it doesn't last.'

Ed wondered why Mark was trying to rain on his parade.

*Must have his reasons, I suppose.*

He decided to thaw him out with wine and good cheer. It was hard work. What did the trick was Simone bringing up the topic of families. Not the ones they had, which was still a sore point with Ção, but the ones they were going to have. They were united in a desire for plenty of children. As they savoured their caramel dessert, they also relished a feeling of being together on a path toward personal fulfilment.

*

A late Spring downpour that freshened the evening caught Ed and Ção on their way home. Once inside, they helped each off with their clothes. Ed sat his wife on his lap, facing him, and dried her hair with a towel.

'You do know who that was, don't you?'

'I've run into Simone a few times. Had a nice long chat with her in French, once. She's Joséphine's best friend here.'

'No, silly, I meant her husband.'

'Mr. Face-ache? No.'

'He's the trading stamps man. His name's Mark Rotherfield. You know, your rival in business.'

'No reason for his nose to be out of joint. He's got the same great opportunities here as me. Should be better placed, in fact, since he's been here longer. More contacts. Talking of contact, can you just move up and … over? Aaaah, yes!'

*

Ed was going through his paperwork in the 'party room' the next morning when Mark rang him.

'Look, I'm sorry about last night. The thing is, I've been frightfully down ever since this so-called Revolution came along. It's made things terribly difficult for us business-wallahs.'

'Are you sure, Mark? I used to think that stability was the be-all and end-all, but, honestly, I'm more optimistic now than when I arrived.'

'Yes, you're doing jolly well. Congratulations. Really. Sorry I didn't offer them in the restaurant. You show 'em! It's just that … things are not going so well for me.'

'Hey, come on, it's early days yet. If you were the type who threw in the towel at the first sign of trouble, you'd never have come here in the first place.'

'That's true enough. But one man's throwing in the towel is another man's cutting his losses while he still can.'

'Look, personally, Mark, I'm here to make money, but I'm not here to ruin your business. This may be a small country, but it's big enough for both of us. Don't you agree?'

'I hope so, Ed. Let's just see how it pans out. If I can help you, let me know. As long as you don't need money – mine is evaporating.'

'I'm on a salary, fortunately. Aren't you?'

'No. I'm my own man. Living on an inheritance, as it happens. Sadly, it's rapidly running out.'

'Well, let's keep in touch, and help each other if we can.'

'OK, old chap, jolly good. See you soon, I hope. Toodle-oo.'

*

June was a hot month, much hotter than Ed was used to. The mercury rose way above Stevenage levels. It was hot in Ed and Ção's bedroom. It was hot in the streets, where militants of political parties old and new, mostly left-wing, vied to outdo each other with the biggest, noisiest demonstrations. And it was hot in the nation's workplaces, where the new right to strike was wielded like a blunt instrument by workers who had never had the chance to acquire dexterity in its use. Landlords, except Ed's, came to realise that their days as darlings of the establishment were over when people previously confined to slums and shanties started to occupy flats kept empty by speculators, and nobody sent the police in to expel them. In the countryside, especially in the south, where the inheritance system had created enormous estates farmed by armies of landless labourers, often for the benefit of absent landlords, the words 'land reform' started to be uttered, first hesitantly, then with burning insistence.

Negotiations to end the wars in the colonies started, but the wars continued at a lower intensity. The independence fighters were not willing to lay down their arms in return for vague promises when they clearly held the upper hand, and Portugal's new rulers were not willing to abandon the Portuguese settlers. Nevertheless, settlers felt the winds of change on their necks, and many feared what those winds might bring. They began to trickle 'home', where they were not always welcome. It was one thing to bring your sons home; it was quite another to have to find room for distant cousins who blamed you for their present discomfort.

The momentum of Ed's business scheme slowed. People were optimistic, even wildly so, but not many were prepared to put hard cash towards fulfilling their vision of a better future. Investment and innovation sunk even lower on the list of priorities for businesses. Ed did not mind swimming against the flow; he did it with some success, but it was hard.

If June was hot, July was scorching. There was conflict among the new rulers, between the Armed Forces Movement, which had physically ousted the fascist régime, and the civilian government, which sought to include all sectors of society. The soldiers were flush with the moral authority of having restored civic freedoms that had been suppressed for nigh on fifty years, and it was they who prevailed. The first 'provisional government' resigned. The departing Prime Minister alluded to military interference as the reason. Three days later, the

President, General Spínola, appointed a soldier as the new Prime Minister.

*

Ed increasingly sought refuge from the heat, hard work and uncertainty in his wife's arms and charms. She never disappointed him. They took to staying in bed until late in the morning, luxuriating in love-making. By associating it with sloth, they gave their sexual activity back something of the spice of sinfulness that it lost when they wed.

Telephone-induced coitus interruptus was not a method of contraception that Ed was prepared to contemplate. One morning, however, a particularly insistent caller rang yet again while they were in the afterglow of orgasm, and Ed unhurriedly got out of the bed, pulled on his underpants and went into the party room to answer it. The caller was James Towsey.

'Are you sitting down, Ed? I would if I was you.'

'Good news or bad?'

'Bad, I'm afraid. Though the dark cloud has a silver lining.'

'Let me guess. The car is going to be a Renault.'

'No. It's worse than that. Are you sitting down?'

Ed wished he were still in bed with Ção. He yawned and sat on the table that held the phone.

'Yes, I am. Out with it, James.'

'Well, the company is really happy with the work you've done over the last few months.'

'That doesn't sound so bad.'

'No, that's good. But the outlook has changed.'

'James, I keep telling you, the outlook here is great! Portugal is ripe for innovation and crying out for investment. More so than it's ever been. My figures aren't bad now. Imagine what they'll be like once things settle down. Believe me, it's going to be plain sailing.'

'Yes, I believe you, Ed. I do know exactly what you mean. It isn't Portugal where the problem lies.'

'So where is it? And what is it?'

'This is it. England! At this point in time, the company does not discern a success scenario for loyalty card schemes in the United Kingdom. On the basis of results and feedback to date.'

'Portugal is not the United Kingdom, James. You know that.'

'Well, the bosses feel they could do the United Kingdom without Portugal, but not Portugal without the United Kingdom. They're pulling the plug, Ed.'

Ed felt glad he was sitting. His neck hurt as though someone had just landed a rabbit punch on it. Words forced themselves out of his dry mouth.

'Where does that leave me, James?'

'The company doesn't want to lose you, Ed. They want you to do a year's management training here in Croydon. Paid. There'll be a decent job for you at the end of it. Oh, and a small car.'

Ed knew James was being kind, but it sounded like a life sentence.

'I see. Tell you what, James, I'll talk to my wife about it.'

'Your wife? I didn't know –'

'Best thing that's ever happened to me.'

'Congratulations. Join the club.'

'I'll talk to Çāo and get back to you.'

'What?'

'I'll talk to my wife. When we've made up our minds, I'll let you know. Thanks for your support, James.'

He felt stupid, as well as angry. He had not seen that coming. He felt betrayed. He had been ready to ditch Retail Support Services, but the company had unwittingly got their retaliation in first. Going back to England was not an option. He would rather starve.

*Might have to. No, I'll pull through. Got to. For Çāo's sake. For both of us.*

Ed went to the bathroom and took a long, cold shower. The water refreshed his mind as well as his body. His neck no longer ached. Saliva formed easily in his mouth, and he spat it out together with his disgust.

Life was good. Without Retail Support Services, it could be even better.

Ed went back to the bedroom and forgot about loyalty cards for the rest of the day.

## 7 THE PLUG IS PULLED

What Ed hated more than the imminent prospect of losing his income was having to tell the grocers and supermarket managers who had signed up with him that Retail Support Services had pulled the plug on the loyalty card scheme. He told them in person whenever he could, travelling on ramshackle buses in sweltering heat to provincial towns that he had first visited in the comfort of a battered Renault. He consoled himself that visiting was generally less expensive than phoning them, and time was something of which he now had plenty. His clients tended to see this as a sign of personal loyalty towards them, and few made a fuss about being arbitrarily dumped by RSS. To each and every one, Ed mentioned the idea of trading stamps, and provided them with Mark Rotherfield's address and phone number. He got some very sceptical looks.

Ed gave Mark an annotated list of his retail contacts throughout Portugal. He reckoned that since RSS was pulling out, he might as well make his contacts of use to someone. Mark needed all the help he could get, and Simone probably deserved it. Ed and Ção saw them often, even though regular classes at the Sussex School had finished until the autumn, when Ed did not envisage a need to re-enrol for Portuguese lessons. Mark had become half-hearted in his attempts to push his trading stamp scheme, despite Ed's continued insistence that the time was ripe. At such moments, Ção abandoned her Maoist slogans and backed Ed up. Simone seemed bemused. Ed wondered whether she was fully in the picture regarding the parlous state of her husband's finances. With Simone's income also disappearing over the summer, Ed was surprised, and impressed, by their outward lack of concern. They always insisted on paying their share, and were excellent company.

Ed himself was reluctant to contemplate a return to England. It would smack too much of quitting, and that was a habit he was determined not to start. Besides, he liked Portugal, especially its colours and the warmth of its climate and people. The person who mattered most to him, Ção, was not someone he saw easily or joyfully adapting to an unfamiliar, foreign society. Nevertheless, he suggested a short holiday in Stevenage that would give her the opportunity to meet his parents and to see how she reacted to the country and the possibility of moving there. She surprised him with her enthusiasm.

'Ed, my love, that's a wonderful idea! Why didn't you suggest it sooner? I'm longing to meet your Mummy and Daddy. How soon can we go?'

That summer, the notion of rights and freedom found some unexpected takers in Portugal. A group of former secret police agents, incarcerated in Lisbon's most secure jail, staged a riot and had their complaints about the conditions in which they were being kept aired repeatedly on national television, provoking much bitter laughter. Moreover, the well-paid workers of the national airline, TAP, which Ção said stood for 'Take Another Plane', were savouring the right to strike, so Ed and Ção had to wait until they could get a pricier flight with British Airways.

Once ensconced in the vicarage in Stevenage, they were surprised at how far off people's radar Portugal had fallen. Acquaintances listened to their tales of tanks in the streets, demonstrations in every city, a world turned upside down, with detached interest, but soon changed the subject to headaches and parking fines. Ed's parents were exceptions to this. Their interest in every detail of their son's new life, new wife and new country was heartfelt and unfaltering. They gave Ção the warmest of welcomes, as Ed had anticipated. The way Ção took to them exceeded his hopes.

'You have such lovely parents, Ed. You're so lucky! We must see them more often!'

'If we move to England, we will.'

'Move to England, you say? I haven't seen much of it yet. You know, it's nice and all that, but this town, Stevenage, is it typical? I mean, all the houses look the same, and nothing much happens. Don't you find it a bit, um, boring?'

'More than a bit. That's one of the reasons I left. If I stay with RSS, we'll be living in Croydon. That's a little like Stevenage, but nearer to London. Let's spend some time in London before you write England off as boring.'

'London? Now you're talking!'

Day trips to London did wonders for Çāo's mood, and helped her take a rosier view of England as a whole. She showed a passing interest in the major tourist sites, galleries and museums, but fell immediately in love with its shops. Ed accompanied her, and began to feel that he had seen enough shops that year to last him a lifetime.

'I've got Daddy's cash to splash. I'd better make the most of it before you make him angry with me again.'

'You didn't tell me you were his darling daughter once more. Is your mother with him on this?'

'Yes, of course she is. I told you they could never stay angry for long with their little conception. Especially not Daddy. They're still very angry with you, though. Very, very angry.'

Ed pulled a wry face. He did not want to make it clear to his wife how little that bothered him. Her parents' hostility and condescension motivated him even more strongly to stay in Portugal and do whatever he could to make a decent living there for his wife and himself.

On the train for their final visit to London, Çāo gave Ed a Maoist run-down of the evident evils of English capitalism. He saw no point in contradicting her.

'I guess when I was living here, I couldn't see the wood for the trees.'

'All the more reason not to live here again, then, don't you think?'

In fact, he had long since made up his mind.

'We'll live wherever you want us to live, my love.'

'Really? You're so sweet, Ed. You know, you're everything I've always dreamed of!'

She nuzzled up against him and kissed his neck, giggling.

At King's Cross station, Ed left Ção to make the most of her last shopping opportunity in London. He had an appointment with James Towsey in Croydon. Ção already knew her way around and, anyway, was resourceful enough to get by on her own.

James had a copy of the *I Ching* placed strategically on his desk when he ushered Ed into his office. He nodded at it.

'Book of Changes. Want a consultation?'

'I don't think so, thank you, James.'

'I've become quite a master at it. It's done me a power of good. At this moment in time, it could point you into the right strategic orientation, Ed, if you understand the direction of my thought.'

'No. James, I've made my decision, together with my wife.'

'Where is the lovely lady? Afraid I'd steal her from you, were you?'

'Not really, James. She's in London, spending her father's capital before the wrong type of socialists get their hands on it.'

'Sounds like she could have fun here with you.'

'Look, James, you've been great with the two months' notice and holiday pay, and your offer, and all the time to think it over, but Ção wouldn't be happy away from her family, and I'm committed to her. And to Portugal.'

James sighed.

'I thought that was what you'd say, somehow. What did you call your wife?'

'Ção. Short for Conceição. Maria da Conceição. Just nasalise the vowel.'

'Oh, right. Well, good luck.' James picked up the I Ching and held it out to Ed with a raised eyebrow.

'No, thanks, James, really. I'd rather rely on my own reasoning. And instincts.'

Ção didn't keep Ed waiting long in the buffet at King's Cross, where they had arranged to meet. They missed another train while he told her about his meeting with James, but it didn't matter: Ção was overjoyed that Ed would not ask her to uproot.

On the journey back to Stevenage, Ed felt light-headed, as though a weight compressing his brain had been removed. He looked at his wife: she was radiant, like a Madonna in a Renaissance painting.

*The first child might have to wait, though.*

Ed's parents were far from overjoyed at his news. Nevertheless, they respected his right to make his own decisions and learn from his mistakes. His father, the vicar, made another attempt to give his son some money.

'You know, I can't leave my house to you when I go to meet my Maker, like a normal father could, but having a vicarage to live in has saved us a bob or two, and I'd like to pass some of that on to you now, Ed, when you really need it, I imagine.'

'Dad, you're too kind. Look, I'll be all right. I'm happy making my own way in the world. I never wanted it to be easy.'

'But your wife? Your future children?'

'You've got a point there, Dad. Listen, if I ever need money for them, I'll ask you first. I promise.'

He grabbed his father in a Portuguese-style hug, that drew itself out. He could feel individual bones in the older man's rib-cage. Ed wondered if he himself would ever lose his physique to that extent.

At Lisbon airport, both Ed and Ção had their luggage meticulously searched. Ed was glad the customs officers restricted themselves to stripping his wife with their eyes. They were smaller than him, and he was not always able to hold his temper in check.

When they finally came into the Arrivals hall, Ed noticed tears on Ção's cheeks. He thought she was feeling humiliated, but he was wrong.

'Oh Ed, England was nice, but I'm just so happy to be back in my own country. Just look at these tears of joy.'

Yes, thought Ed, *England is 'nice', but Portugal is the place for us to be, the place where it is all happening.*

In that late summer, Portugal started to do something about the main cause of the revolution: its colonial wars. First, it recognised its colonies' right to independence. Then it signed an agreement with Mozambique's liberation movement paving the way for that country's actual independence. The very next day, Portuguese settlers, including some calling themselves the 'dragons of death', staged a 'white rebellion' in Mozambique's capital. It was put down in short order by the local police. The day after that, Portugal recognised its small West African colony of Guinea-Bissau as an independent country, which the local liberation movement had already declared it to be a year earlier. Angola, where oil had been found in quantities large enough to whet the appetites of the industrial nations, was tougher to decolonise, because it had three major independence movements jostling for power.

All this progress was welcomed by most of the colonised people, and internationally, but it was deemed too much too soon by some at home, including the President himself. General Spínola had been installed as a figurehead on the day of the Revolution, when the besieged Prime Minister of the old régime, Caetano, had insisted on handing power to him personally so that it would not fall into the hands of 'the street'. Spínola, however, then found himself constantly outflanked and out-manoeuvred by the more radical officers who had planned and carried out the coup. In an attempt to halt the momentum of change, he now appealed to a 'silent majority' to take to the streets and show its strength and its support for him personally. Its strength, though, proved to be far less than that of the radicals, who set up barricades around Lisbon that prevented Spínola's supporters from marching on the capital. Nor did he succeed in mobilising his many backers within the Armed Forces effectively. Recognising his defeat, he called off the march. Instead, it was the radicals who staged a massive march, to celebrate their victory and the failure of what they termed an attempted coup.

Ção and Ed persuaded Simone and Mark to take to the streets with them. Simone, a veteran of the 'Paris Spring' of 1968, was enthusiastic;

Mark came along 'for the tour'.

'Yeah, I'll be your guide,' Ção told him.

They joined the demo when it reached the park near Largo do Andaluz. Although the air was warm and humid, the purposefulness of the marchers and the rhythmic unison of their slogans sent shivers of anticipation down Ed's spine. Together, they strode down the Avenida da Liberdade, alarming the swans on its waterways, past the square named in honour of the long-dead heroes who had freed Portugal from Spain and into Rossio, the city's main square. Ção told Mark the history of the place: how it had once been the favoured spot for public executions and autos-da-fé.

'Portugal's gift to the English language,' Mark asserted.

'The Holy Inquisition's gift,' Ção corrected him. 'We should burn counter-revolutionaries here.'

Mark turned paler.

'You don't mean that.'

Ção looked at him as though he were a heretic.

'Just you wait!'

They strode on through the city's commercial district, Ção chatting amiably with Mark about its history, how the Marquis of Pombal, the power behind the throne, had had it rebuilt after the great earthquake of 1755, the first earthquake to be studied scientifically, laying the new city centre out in a grid pattern so that the King's horsemen would be able negotiate it easily whenever they had to put down revolts by the people.

'We'd better keep an eye out for the cavalry tonight,' commented Simone.

The various strands of the demo coalesced in the enormous square by the river where, on the day of the Revolution, ship's captains and tank commanders had refused to fire upon the rebels. The humidity was intensified by the river air, the heat by close-packed bodies. They linked arms as the marchers set off along the riverside toward the President's palace. Ed made certain that his stronger arm was firmly linked with Ção's, so that she would feel protected, if she gave it a thought.

The mood was again celebratory, tinged with anger. The Revolution had survived its first serious challenge. It could now remove people who were holding it back from positions of power. From now on, the going would be smoother. But first, the message had to be delivered to the President in no uncertain terms.

The noise was deafening as thousands of demonstrators moved westwards. Stretches of cobbled road surface slowed their progress. Ed thought of the Alentejo miners he had heard on the radio in the Algarve, crunching over gravel before bursting into song. He wondered if some of them were here this evening to support this new 'land of brotherhood', as a line in their song expressed it. The Alentejo was already cementing its reputation as Portugal's most radical region by taking the lead in land reform. Today's developments would gave that a boost, too.

By the time they reached their destination, hours had passed since they set off. The President's Palace was near the rowing club where Ed had met Lourdes, almost next to the medieval Jerônimos monastery. Luckily, there was plenty of open space in front of it, so the risk of people getting crushed was slight. Nevertheless, Ed kept an eye out for revolutionaries trying deliberately to press against Ção in the crowd.

President Spínola was the butt of the slogans, which soon targeted his perceived henchmen, too. As passions rose, and the demonstrators' sense of righteousness increased, the content of slogans degenerated into calls for the execution of the Silent Majority ringleaders. Ção took these up enthusiastically; after a while, Simone joined in, too. Ed looked at Mark. Mark shrugged, smiled and shouted louder than his wife. Ed swallowed, took a deep breath, then added his voice.

Their passion spent, the demonstrators dispersed peacefully. Most of them went in search of late transport home.

Ção was energised and impassioned in her lovemaking that night. She fell asleep straight afterwards, but Ed lay awake re-living the march.

Towards dawn, his turning over awoke his wife.

'Ed, what's wrong? Can't you sleep?'

'No, my love. I keep thinking about yesterday.'

'About me?'

'Yes. And about the demo.'

'It was a good one, wasn't it? We showed them all right!'

'I can't help thinking about those things we were shouting. Calling for people to be killed. It's not right, but I did it, too.'

'Oh, don't worry about that. Nobody really meant it. This is Portugal. They were just mouthing off. That's all. Fancy a quickie, darling?'

Ed did, and the waking dream of making love with Ção was followed by sleep in which the dreams were too deep for him to remember the next day.

The day after that one, President Spínola resigned. He was immediately replaced by Costa Gomes, the more radical general whom the revolutionary officers had wanted to fill the post back in April. A few people were arrested. Nobody was executed.

Ed caught his first glimpse of the new course the following Sunday. He went down to the street for a newspaper from the kiosk and found all the shops open. He bought a few supplies at his local grocer's and asked what was going on.

'Everyone's at work today – a day's work for the nation. It's not a bad idea.'

'A very good idea: action not words. If I had a job, I'd do it as well.'

*So would Ção and Mark, he thought. I wonder whether Simone is doing extra classes for Keith today.*

\*

The lack of a steady job, and the dwindling of savings, was a worsening problem for all of them. Only Mark acted unworried by it, although his financial crisis was the most acute. With no work on the horizon, Ed decided to put his free time to good use by completing the course he had enrolled for at Britain's new Open University soon after it opened. He had completed the foundation course in short order, but it was not challenging enough to hold his interest, and he let it slide. Still, they had not kicked him out, and now he would go back and finish it. In Portugal, it was a big thing to possess a university degree: people called themselves 'Doctor' as soon as they had one. He could learn useful stuff and boost his status at the same time. Moreover, his new determination gave him the chance to enlist his father's help without asking him directly for money. What he asked was for the vicar to record the Open University broadcasts for Ed's course from television to tape, and to send him the tapes. He explained how to use a timer for this, so that his father would not have to get up in the middle of the night. Ed heard the pleasure in his father's voice when he agreed to do this.

As long as Ção stayed on good terms with her parents, Ed knew he did not have to worry too much about supporting her. He would supply the basics, and they would satisfy those whims of hers that demanded an outlay he could not afford. When she went on a shopping binge, he knew that Daddy or Mummy had coughed up. He kept out of their way, so that the living evidence of their daughter's adulthood should not tempt them to stop spoiling her and her mood.

His living arrangements with his wife received an unexpected boost from Joséphine. His landlady complained endlessly about how shopkeepers and workmen no longer treated her with due deference. A taxi driver even reduced her to tears. One evening she turned up at the flat and announced to Ção and Ed that one of her French boyfriends had finally left his wife. He had invited her to live with him near Toulouse, and she was leaving Portugal for good at the end of October.

'That's marvellous news, Joséphine, marvellous! Congratulations! I'm sure you'll be very happy. We really hope so. Since you're going, can we take over the lease?'

'But of course. I will tell the owner you are the perfect tenants.'

Ed knew from the start that Joséphine did not own the flat; she just sub-let rooms, illegally but with the connivance of the owner, who did not care as long as she got her rent and few demands for maintenance. Now Ed and Çāo had the chance to become proper tenants.

Ed had a pleasant surprise when he met the owner. The rent she asked for the whole flat was only a little more than Joséphine had charged him for a single room when he moved in. Moreover, Ed was getting a legal contract, which he knew was likely to be rent-controlled. Ed concealed his haste to sign, but did so as quickly as the bureaucratic procedures allowed. When he put pen to paper, he thought how much he would enjoy doing the flat up, to Çāo's specifications. As soon as he could get some money together, which meant finding a job. He had no capital yet for a business of his own.

Ed carried Joséphine's luggage down for her on the day she left. It was a fine Indian Summer's morning. Ed thought he could detect aromas of roasting chestnuts and *água pé* in the air. He packed the taxi with her cases while the driver waited.

'Goodbye, Mr. Scripps. Wish me luck. I have left that beautiful poster above my bed, so you both can remember me. You will look after it, won't you?'

'Of course,' Ed lied.

## 8  FINEST OLD COLONIAL

Mark stretched his legs and sat back in the armchair in Ed's party room.

'I'll tell you one thing, Ed, I'm jolly glad that courses at the Sussex are back in full swing again. It's a shame that dumb blonde Joséphine left Keith in the lurch, swanning off in mid-term like that, but now Simone is officially Head of French, and doing a lot of the classes that her skeletal compatriot walked out on.'

'Plenty of money coming in, then.'

'Coming in to Simone, there's plenty. I haven't got a penny left, myself. Even worse, old bean, I've got debts. Up to my eyes. So it's a really specially jolly good thing that Simone is prepared to support us both.'

'All the same, don't want to live off your wife if you can help it. Do you?'

'Damned right I don't. But what's a fellow to do?'

He furrowed his brow and fixed half-closed eyes on Ed.

'How are you placed, old chap?'

'Me? I need work. Soon. Was thinking of taking up Keith's long-standing offer.'

'Can't see you as a teacher, somehow. I think you'd need a bit more patience.'

*I'm patient enough with you, aren't I?*

'Well, I enjoyed it when I did it in Wimbledon, and the people I was teaching seemed to learn. It's more that Keith and I … well, we're kind of rivals, as business people. I'd sooner buy him out than work for him.'

Mark laughed. Ed heard a key turn in the lock and rose to embrace his wife as she came through from the hall. Çāo's face was flushed, her eyes shining as she threw her arms around Ed.

'Ed! Mark! I've got a job! I really have. I've gone and done it. I've got a job!'

'Darling, that's wonderful!'

'Clever girl,' said Mark. 'Spill the beans. Tell us all about it.'

'It's simple. Someone in the Movement owns a travel agency, and now that the Revolution is coming into its own, he's planning to expand. His big idea is to offer affordable holidays to workers who never earned a decent wage before. And since I'm a language girl, and ideologically sound, he wants me in his team. I'm starting next Monday.'

'Fabulous! Let's have a drink to celebrate. There's some fizz in the fridge, I think.'

'Oh, I say, let's go out and celebrate. Simone can pay.'

'Give her a ring for us, will you, Mark? But this evening, this lady is going to pay. I've got an advance!'

Ed was proud of Çāo for rescuing their finances by venturing into the world of work. However, he was abashed at the prospect of becoming a kept man. His aim was to provide for Çāo, not have her provide for him. He thought that with his experience and drive, he was the one who should make things happen.

On Monday morning, Ed accompanied Çāo to the travel agency, wished her well and took the underground to the Sussex School to ask for work. Keith was apologetic.

'I'm sorry, what I need right now is another French teacher. I've got all the English teachers I need. There might be a few private lessons to fill in the New Year, but nothing full-time.'

'Aren't you expanding, then?'

'Not at the moment. We will be, though. I'd love to give you a job next autumn, but until then I simply can't. Not unless one of my teachers gets the heebie-jeebies about the communists coming and decides to run away.'

'Or does a Joséphine.'

'Quite.' Keith gave a wry smile. 'Both are possible. Keep in touch.'

\*

Çāo made light of her job at the travel agency. There was little actual work to do other than plan for the coming expansion, and that left plenty of time for chatting and sorting out the country's ideal future political direction. Her co-workers were similar to Çāo in outlook and background, though some of them had been to university, including her boss, Fernando, who interpreted 'learning from the masses' as listening to his half-dozen employees on all matters regarding his and their work. He attributed the success of his agency to precisely that.

One evening, as rain washed the windows of their flat, Çāo took a call from Estrela. They had seen little of each other since the wedding, and their conversation outlasted a chapter of Ed's Open University textbook. When Çāo came back into the room, Joséphine's former bedroom now cleared and converted into a study, she crept up noisily behind Ed and placed her hands over his eyes.

'Guess who!'

Ed reached behind him, located Çāo's right knee and slid his hand slowly up the inside of her leg.

'Well, judging by the fine texture of the skin on this delectable thigh, I would say it belongs to a certain Mrs. Scripps.'

'Right!' She giggled, moved her legs further apart. Then her voice turned serious. 'Ed, do you like studying?'

'Well, I like learning. So if studying means learning, it's okay. Especially when it gets interrupted by a sexy little beast called Conception!'

Ed swivelled the chair to face her. She brought her thighs together over his hand. Ed rose and thought of lifting Çāo to his shoulder to carry her into the bedroom, but he wanted neither to hurt her nor to remove his hand. Instead, he drew her close. Çāo lightly bit his neck, then stood on tiptoe and whispered in his ear.

'Just slip a couple of fingers into my vagina and keep them there while you gets us both into the bedroom and naked. If you think you can.'

That was the kind of challenge Ed relished.

Çāo still had sperm on her lips when she resumed their earlier conversation.

'What if I were to make these delectable thighs belong to a certain Mrs. Dr. Scripps?'

'Meaning what?'

'That was Estrela on the phone earlier. You remember her, the witness at our lovely secret wedding. She told me the University is going to run evening classes for working people. She's just enrolled to study law. I think I might do the same.'

'Wow! That's quite a commitment, you know.'

'Not really. I can ditch it if I can't cope, or if I get fed up. No problem.'

'You'll be burning the candle at both ends.'

'What?'

'Working all day and studying all night. Whenever would we make love?'

'Never again! So we'd better make the most of our time together now!'

She turned her attention to restoring Ed's erection.

Later in the week, Çāo got the morning off work and took the bus up to the Old University to enrol. It was not yet too late in the year to do so. She tried to get Ed to stay at home with his textbooks, but he insisted on going with her, to keep her company. At her request, he sat with a textbook in the Department of Literatures café while she dealt with the bureaucracy in the Administration Block.

'My goodness, you shouldn't read Samuelson in this place, young chap. They think that old Yank leftie is a capitalist lackey around here. Spit in your coffee, I shouldn't wonder.'

Ed looked up. The speaker was a florid-faced man at least twice Ed's age. He was chuckling, so maybe he had been joking.

'Are you serious?'

'Not entirely, though you never know. Patrick Harte, by the way.'

'Ed Scripps. Glad to meet you. Care for a – ?'

'Thank you. Already got one.' He held up his glass of amber liquid. 'Mind if I join you for a minute, before I rush off to my class? Got the clever kids today. If they show up.'

Ed pulled up a seat for him at the small table.

'What brings you to this august seat of failure to learn?'

'My wife. She's enrolling for Law.'

'Oh, serious stuff. Preparation for the real world. Here on this side of the campus we only prepare people to be over-educated housewives or underpaid teachers. Goodness, not a student, are you? Or a teacher?'

'Not here. I'm in business. Or I was. But I'm doing an Open University degree so I don't waste my unexpected free time, and I may have to become a teacher sooner or later.'

'Well, you can have my job if you want it. Been here twenty years, nigh on, but they don't appreciate me any more, so I'm darn well buzzing off. Sod 'em.'

'What is your job?'

'Teaching English to the rich and privileged. These young things you see flitting around you. I'm yesterday's man to them, so I'm getting out while I've still got a few tomorrows left.'

'Must be hard to get a job like yours.'

'Was. Was indeed. Had to be damned well qualified when I got in. Now they'll take anyone. Desperate, they are.'

'Why?'

'They're letting virtually anyone in to study. Haven't got room for them. Haven't got teachers. Just apply for a job, and you'll probably get elected. Native English speaker, aren't you? Must be, with that dreadful accent. No offence, old boy.'

'It's the normal way people speak in Stevenage.'

'Yes, sorry. Look, I'll find someone to propose you, if you want. Can't do it myself, for the reasons I've given. Past my expiry date here. Sorry, got to go and pretend to teach these buggers something. Here's my card. Give me a ring next week, and I'll give you the details. You'll regret it, though.'

'Thank you. That's very kind of you.'

'You won't thank me in the end.'

He put down his unfinished drink on the table, got to his feet, nodded to Ed and ambled to the exit, looking around him with detached amusement.

*Did he say 'elected'?*

Ed was pondering how best to grab this unexpected opportunity when Ção arrived. She was miffed because she would have to return the following week to do more paperwork, but she cheered up when Ed recounted what Patrick Harte had told him about the chance of a job.

'He said I had to get elected to the post. That can't be right, can it?'

'Yes, really, that's how we do things now. New teachers have to be publicly elected at a meeting of all the teachers and students in the Department. It's direct democracy in action.'

'Do you think I can get them to elect *me*?'

'Of course you can, Ed my darling. I'll use my contacts. With any luck, I can get all the comrades to vote for you.'

'All the Maoists? I'll have to confess that I'm a businessman.'

'I know, Ed, but you're *our* businessman.'

Ten days later, Ed was back on the campus of Lisbon's Old University, which was adjacent to that of its bitter rival, the Classical University. This time he sat in a very large lecture hall in the Department of Literatures, next to Xavier D'Silva, a scion of an ancient Portuguese family that had helped colonise what became Ceylon, long before the British arrived there. Xavier's English sounded to Ed even posher than that of Patrick Harte, who, true to his word, had put Ed in touch with Xavier because he was a language instructor at the Department who could plausibly propose Ed as someone worthy of joining them.

The lecture hall was more than half full. On a dais facing the assembled students and teachers sat the luminaries of the Steering Committee that now ran things in place of the formal bodies discredited by their association with the fallen fascist régime.

The meeting was into its second hour, and the matter of potential new teachers had yet to be raised. In the new order, 'Any Other Business' came at the start of the agenda, not the end, and it was still in full swing. The student body seemed split three ways: supporters of the Soviet-influenced Communist Party; the Maoists, who referred to the former as 'social-fascists'; and the 'revolutionary left' followers of the military architect of the April coup, known to all by his exotic first name, Otelo. This group considered both the others to be beyond-the-pale reactionaries. Whenever members of one of these factions took the floor, they were interrupted by their antagonists, who, if they failed to shout them down, took the floor immediately afterwards to rebut what they decided had just been said. Progress towards the agenda was slow, but Ed found the demonstration of academic democracy fascinating.

Xavier sat next to him, doodling on a sketch pad and making occasional ironic comments. Ed leant across to see what he was drawing. It was a series of sketches of the Chair of the Committee, an attractive, dark-haired, olive-skinned woman in her forties, whose energy and beauty leached out of her in each successive, time-numbered sketch. Several of the previously vocal students, though few of the Maoists, left the hall when 'Any Other Business' concluded; others arrived shortly afterwards. Ed calculated that dusk had fallen outside when they reached the item that concerned him.

Xavier was called upon to introduce him, which he did in glowing terms, highlighting his commitment to the new Portugal and, at Ed's prior insistence, his idea of running courses on business English to broaden the employment scope for language graduates. Xavier did this in Portuguese. Then Ed himself was called upon to speak, in both Portuguese and English, to show that he could. He repeated what Xavier had said, making it more factual and less glowing, then said that he would like to teach evening classes so that his students would be working people, to whom business English could make a real, practical difference. This drew a round of applause, even though the majority of those present were daytime students.

'Nice one, Ed,' said Xavier, 'it's in the bag.'

The vote was by a simple show of hands. A visible majority voted 'yes', half a dozen opted for 'no', and a score or so raised their hands to abstain. The meeting moved on to the next item on the agenda.

'Is that it?' Ed asked.

'That's it. Welcome, O Language Instructor. I'll fix you an appointment to see Pretty Polly there.' He tilted his head in the direction of the subject of his sketches. 'She can give you all the details. She's a bit full of herself, but she means well.'

'When can I start teaching, do you think?'

'End of January, maybe. After the Christmas holidays, anyway. Don't worry, there's never any rush around here.'

Ed, however, was in a rush to get an income flowing. When he met 'Pretty Polly', Deolinda d'Almeida, he was disconcerted at how modest the salary was, and astounded at how few teaching hours he was required to do to earn it: twelve a week. He persuaded Deolinda to let him enrol students before Christmas, launch his classes early in January and start getting paid at the end of that month. She was very complimentary about his willingness to do evening lessons and to teach business English, yet he came away from their meeting with a feeling that she had not told him everything he needed to know.

*

Christmas was miserable. Ção wanted to spend it with her parents, and they would not invite Ed, so he flew to England to spend the holiday with his own parents. He hated being away from Ção. They phoned each other every day to compare the cold rain of Stevenage with the warm rain of Portugal, though what was important was the warmth in each other's voices. Ed's parents were proud of their son's becoming the first member of their respective families to teach at a university, and Ed used the long hours without his wife to learn what academics considered to be business English and to plan his courses.

Back in Portugal and reunited with his wife, Ed spent days tending to Ção's sexual and emotional needs, making up for the time he had spent away. He looked forward to being able soon to fulfil her financial needs, too. He also got in touch with his friend Mark.

'Still looking for a job, Mark?'

'Oh dear me, yes. But as much as I look, there is nothing to be seen. I eat thanks to Simone, and I drink and occasionally make merry thanks to a loan from my dear sister, Harriet.'

'Could you see yourself teaching English at the University?'

'I'm one of those who can. I do. I don't teach.'

'It's better than living off your women, surely?'

'You do have a point there, old bean, but why would they employ an unemployed businessman?'

'To teach business English. They've taken me on to do just that.'

'Well, I'm sure I'm more qualified than you are, with my degree in Modern Languages. '

'Precisely. Together, we'd make a great team. We could really help the students!'

'OK. Tell me more.'

Mark, too, was less impressed by the salary on offer than by the light workload. Ed gave him the phone numbers of Xavier and of Deolinda, then phoned them to explain that another potential language instructor would be getting in touch with them. He also got Ção to see Simone and talk up the job opportunity that was landing on her husband's doorstep.

On a warm, wet late afternoon in mid-January, Ed caught a bus up to the edge of the university campus. As he walked up the avenue that led to it from the bus stop, he felt the thrill of anticipation which a new venture brought him. Three pieces of imposing fascist architecture stood at the top of the avenue, as though defying the population to enter.

Nevertheless, Ed did climb the steps of the one to his right, push open the heavy glass doors and enter the large atrium. No classrooms were assigned, so he had arranged to meet his students outside the main lecture hall. Before Christmas, he had enrolled two groups of forty each. Xavier had told him not to expect all of them to show up, yet at least forty faces greeted his arrival with expressions ranging from eager to sceptical. Together, they then began what was to become a ritual: searching the building for an empty classroom. Ed explained that the class at this time would be general English and the one starting two hours later, when the proportion of working students would rise, was to focus on business English. Thirty-five of the enrolees had shown up, together with twelve newcomers. Only twenty-eight students showed up for the eight o'clock lesson, of whom seven were newcomers. When Ed said that he would focus on business English, a few of them asked to move to the earlier class.

For the rest of the month, every time Ed arrived to teach a class, new faces added to the mix. Turning people away was against the new ethos of the University, so, when they could not find a large enough classroom, some students would stand behind those who found seats. Ed squared the circle by creating a third group, although this meant that each group would get only four hours' tuition a week instead of six. His training had not prepared him to teach such large classes with so few resources – he even had to bring his own chalk, in case there was a blackboard – but he saw this as an opportunity to carve out an area of expertise for himself which might one day have monetary value.

In response to popular demand, Ed made two of his classes general English and only one business-focused. He asked Xavier about the higher demand for general English.

'It's a matter of status, Ed. Business English sounds like vocational training, whereas general English, what I call ENOR, English for No Obvious Reason, is deemed a fit study for high-fallutin' minds, for the élite.'

The working students he asked, though, told him that they had enough contact with business English during office hours, and preferred a change in the evenings. Ed resolved to find a way to square that particular circle, too.

He phoned Mark to ask for advice. Simone took the call.

'Mark's not here. He's out drinking.'

'What, alone?'

'Yes, he said he wanted to drown his sorrows without me around to cheer him up.'

'But he's about to get a job at the Old University!'

'No, Ed. They had the meeting this morning. The vote went against him.'

'What? But that's crazy! I can't believe it!'

Simone sighed. 'They said he had no training or experience. And that one English businessman doing capitalist indoctrination was more than enough, even if the students liked him. Especially if the students liked him.'

'That's awful. It's so unfair!'

'In the end, it was close. If they don't get teachers, students graduate later. But the Maoists voted against him as a block. I guess he has the wrong wife.'

Ed thought he heard a sob.

'I'm so sorry, Simone. Of course it's not your fault! Look, please ask Mark to phone me when he comes in, no matter what time it is.'

'He won't. He blames you for his humiliation.'

*

Towards the end of the month, Ed thought that Spring had arrived. A warm wind scattered the clouds above him as he strode, as best he could, up the avenue to the campus. He was on his way to the Administration Block, to sign the chit that meant, as Xavier had told him, that he would get his pay a few days later.

He eventually found the right office, with a clerk whose eagerness to chat he would have welcomed on another occasion. The clerk shuffled through a stack of papers.

'I can't find a Scripps on the list. What is your full name?'

'Edward Clement Scripps.'

'Let me see. Definitely no Scripps. … No Edward … Clemente, yes, several: Araújo, da Costa … Rodrigues, Soares. No Scripps. I'll double check.'

Ed's stomach felt as though he had not eaten all day, after an evening's hard drinking.

'No, I'm sorry, you're simply not on the payroll. Hang on a minute. I'll get your file.'

The clerk disappeared into a back office. Ed found a chair and slumped into it. Winter assailed his mind. The clerk returned, looking glum.

'I'm sorry, you don't have a file. We have no record of you. As far as we know, you are not an employee of this university. Not yet, at any rate.'

Ed pushed himself up and made for the exit.

The clerk noticed Ed's limp.

'I'll keep looking, Doctor Scripps. See you tomorrow.'

'Thank you.'

Ed let the warm wind dissipate the winter inside him. After all, worse things had happened.

As he walked unwillingly towards the bus stop, a red Ferrari thundered past him, then hit the brakes. Ed smelt burning rubber as it reversed sharply until the car was level with him. The driver got out, came over to the pavement and embraced Ed. It was Paulo. Ed had not seen or heard from Lourdes' younger brother for months. Paulo opened the passenger door.

'Ed! Let me give you a lift home. Or wherever you're going. You don't look too steady.'

'Home. Thanks, I appreciate it.'

Paulo's glance was still quizzical. Ed outlined his situation.

'That's tough,' said Paulo.

'And you?'

'Oh, I'm doing all right. Trading like mad with the ex-colonies, while we've still got them. Doing very nicely. You should grab a piece of the action. I can cut you in on a deal or several.'

As music to Ed's ears, it was even better than Mozart.

*If he means it.*

Ed changed the subject to Paulo's new car.

Paulo put it through its paces as well as he could inside the city. Ed was impressed. Paulo halted the Ferrari in Largo do Andaluz. He reached into his jacket and pulled something very small, wrapped in aluminium foil, from an inner pocket. He handed it to Ed.

'Try our product. Then let me know what you think.'

Ed took it and lifted it to his nostrils. The intense aroma reminded him of parties.

'Thanks. I will.'

'Finest old colonial,' said Paulo.

# 9 MONEY MATTERS

The hardest part was convincing Ção.

'You just can't cut your ties with that scrawny, ancient hag, can you? How do you think I feel with you fraternising with her baby brother?'

'I don't have any ties to Lourdes, my love. Paulo's a nice guy. And he's giving me an opportunity I don't otherwise have: the chance to provide for my wife and maybe our future kids.'

The product was good. That helped convince Ção, or helped Ed to convince her. It did no harm, either, when Paulo showed up at the flat with flowers for Ção, with more product for them to sample, and insisted on their coming with him as he put the Ferrari through its paces on the coast road.

Alone with Ed, Paulo was business-like.

'This is essentially a short-term opportunity. Thousands of settlers are coming back from the colonies. They don't like it that the biggest colonies, Angola and Mozambique, are already under transitional governments. They can't see anything halting the run-up to independence and majority rule.'

'Yes, I heard about the agreement on Angola. All the factions coming together. Unbelievable!'

'Right. It won't last, but now there are limits on what people can take out of the country if they leave. You can't take a block of flats or a suitcase of cash, but you can fill a container with top-grade marijuana and bring it here. If you're clever and have the right connections. Or buy them.'

'What, they just let them do it?'

'Officially, no, of course not. But money still talks over there, and here too.'

'I see. So why is it just a short-term opportunity, then?'

'Two reasons. First, our guys still run things over there at a day-to-day level. We have the connections. When independence comes, that won't be the case any more. The new guys in charge will be Marxist puritans. They are bound to try and stop the flow of grass. Second, before that happens, the mafias that run the international drugs trade are going to want their cut. Which tends to be one hundred per cent.'

'But that hasn't happened yet?'

'No, not yet. I reckon we have a few months' grace. Interested?'

'I have to be. But why do you want me in? Anything to do with Lourdes?'

'Nothing to do with my sister. Your equity is your knowledge of retail, distribution channels and three international languages. Also, you're above suspicion. So hold on to that university job, even while they're not paying you.'

Ed arranged another appointment with Deolinda d'Almeida to find out why the University was not paying him. She looked at him coolly, as though disappointing eager young men was something she did every day.

'Well, strictly speaking, you aren't really employed by the University yet. Your election needs to be rubber-stamped by the official authorities. That takes a while.'

'How long?'

'A month or two. Can you wait that much? We really appreciate the work you're doing. You'll get back-paid to the month you started to teach. January, right?' She smiled. 'We're all making sacrifices to build a new Portugal.' Her smile wilted, and she sighed.

Ed kept up his classes. He thought they were going well. Ed's evening students were, in most cases, determined to take full advantage of the higher education they had been denied before the Revolution. They were also interesting people, drawn from many walks of life and rich in experience. Ed started to develop a personal dedication to them in addition to his more abstract dedication to the country's future.

Xavier introduced Ed to some of their fellow instructors, ones who had classes at a similar time to Ed's. Carolina Isfahan was a local girl with Scottish roots who had converted to the Baha'i faith when she married an Iranian devotee. Her husband had suffered persecution in Iran, but was longing to return, with his wife and future children, if and when the Shah's régime fell under the pressure for real democracy. Rupert Harley-Davidson was an ethereal figure, a gentle man of few words. Xavier told Ed that Rupert had published two books on Portuguese wildlife. Ashley Beecroft, a rotund, humorous man who claimed to be a citizen of the world but travelled on a United States passport, supplemented the meagre pay by reporting for various foreign newspapers on Portuguese football. They took to having a coffee together before or between classes, or a beer afterwards. Ed got the impression that his business background made him seem like a creature from another world to them, but they were curious about such creatures and accorded him respect for getting elected to their ranks on a near-unanimous vote.

Ed told them a good deal about supermarkets and his ideas for improving them, but nothing about his new business venture. When he next spoke to Simone, he told her he had an offer to work with Paulo, but did not go into any details as to its nature. The fewer people who knew those details, the better. Nor did he tell his mother, though her practical support was crucial. He phoned her at a time when he knew his father was likely to be out on parish business, and took her up on her own private offer of financial help, explaining the pay situation at the University and asking her to lend him the minimum amount he deemed necessary to keep a couple going for three months. She sent him enough for six months.

His next task was to persuade Ção that they would have to turn their flat into a meticulously marijuana-free zone. He did not want its distinctive smell floating down the stairwell and prodding civic-minded neighbours into alerting the police. He convinced her by cooking a very aromatic curry for them with the kitchen windows open, then closing all the windows in the flat and retreating to the bedroom, where he lit several joss-sticks, shredded half a dozen cigarettes, rolled enough joints to contain every last shred of their private marijuana stash and made sure that Çāo smoked more of it than he did, to the accompaniment of Rimsky-Korsakov.

Ed was surprised to wake up the next morning fully clothed and lying on the floor. He was relieved that Çāo was on the bed, though outside the covers, also fully clothed, and still asleep. He did not disturb her as he went to wash and then to make coffee in the cold kitchen. In fact, he let her sleep all morning. When she finally came to and realised what had happened, she asked whether she had overdosed. Ed reassured her that you could not kill yourself with marijuana, but was pleased to hear her say softly, 'Never again'. It was better that way for both of them.

Ed realised he did not have enough contacts he could trust to run a whole marijuana distribution network. His solution was a pyramid structure. He first sounded out and then recruited three of the most enterprising, but discreet, of his supermarket and grocery contacts, and made each one responsible for a given area: the inner city; the suburbs; and the south bank of the river and beyond. Each was to sub-divide his territory among three trusted lieutenants, who could, in turn, sub-divide further. Ed insisted on vetting, indeed on knowing, only the people in the two layers of the pyramid below him. That kept down the number of people who knew him and his role. Paulo dealt with the returned settlers, found storage sites, which he changed constantly, and employed what he called 'quality control officers' to grade the product.

Everyone else in the pyramid was forbidden from sampling the marijuana. Paulo himself only indulged when he wanted to check the work of the 'quality control officers'. Sometimes, he would invite Ed to help him with the task. Occasionally, Ed met settler contacts of Paulo's at these sessions. The accounts they furnished of their lives in Angola and Mozambique left Ed impressed with their entrepreneurial flair and disgusted at their blind racism. He foresaw that they would have difficulty in adjusting to the mainstream European business context, in which skin colour was deemed irrelevant and where, when this axiom was ignored because of inherited irrationality, having Mediterranean colouring was rarely an advantage. To those who sought it, he offered whatever advice he could. The ones who asked for it were willing to heed it. Many, though, expected blithely to transfer settler culture to the 'motherland' and were appalled at the hostility which their ideas aroused in the new times.

Unlike Portugal's conscript soldiers and junior officers, most of the settlers had hated General Spínola when he first advocated negotiating an end to the wars in its colonies. Now, however, they saw him as their best hope of turning the clock back. Although no longer President, he had not given up hope of an eventual return to power. Increasingly, he had to scrape the barrel to find backers among the dregs of the former régime. With these behind him, he launched a coup attempt in mid-March.

The attempt was fairly pathetic. A rebel plane strafed an army base on the outskirts of Lisbon. It shot up the soldiers' canteen, but the canteen was empty and the attackers only managed to kill one recruit, who was setting the places for lunch. Other rebel troop movements were easily contained. Spínola himself fled to Spain, where a fascist régime still ruled the roost.

The left was triumphant. It had beaten off every political and political challenge to its authority, to its leadership of the revolution. Now it would deal with the economic challenges. Portugal was in recession and scapegoats had to be found. It was easy to berate 'capitalist saboteurs', especially when they instigated failed coups, but the public wanted concrete evidence of economic sabotage. Now they got it. A major bank in the country was called the 'Espírito Santo' Bank, not out of religious devotion to the Holy Ghost but because that was the surname of the family that owned it. Now the bank's workers had the run of its archives. They uncovered evidence which suggested that the family had siphoned off money allocated to providing jobs for demobbed troops, and that it was funding right-wing political parties. Three days after Spínola's failed coup, the government nationalised Portugal's banks. Land reform intensified, social housing became a priority and decent wages drew nearer. On the other hand, foreign investment dried up.

Ção and her fellow-Maoists, however, were not content. They felt marginalised as power consolidated in the hands of the Communists and the 'revolutionary left'. Increasingly, they saw these as the real barrier to their aspirations, and the hostility they showed towards them at times exceeded that of the die-hards nostalgic for the old régime.

Ção's mood soured. She became less inclined to euphoria and celebration. Worse still, from Ed's point of view, her aroma of cinnamon dissipated. If anything, she smelt now of citrus: pleasant, but not devastating to his senses. He asked her about it.

'I changed my perfume. It's no big deal.'

At the end of the month, the University bureaucrats again denied Ed's presence on the list of their employees. He didn't want to live on his mother's money now that he was supposedly earning his own. He phoned Paulo.

'How's the business doing, Paulo? Are we making a profit yet? If so, I'd like a few bucks because the University still isn't paying me.'

'Good Heavens, Ed, I'm so sorry. Yes, of course. I'll be round at your place first thing tomorrow.'

Paulo did as he promised. Ção had already left for work, but Ed was making a pot of coffee when he arrived.

Ed took the pot into the spare room and as they settled over their small cups, Paulo pulled out two thick wads of banknotes and pushed them across the table to Ed.

'Some dollars and some escudos. You'd better spend the local stuff first because its value is going to drop, very fast and very soon.'

'What's this? A year's advance? I don't need this much.'

'This is your share so far. Don't turn it down. Make the most of it while it lasts. Just don't make a big show of it, not in this political climate.'

Ed accompanied Paulo down to his car. He had come in the Renault, not the Ferrari.

'Still going strong, you see. Like my sister, actually. No big show of wealth, all right, Ed? And please be a bit more bloody careful what you say on the phone.' Paulo's mouth was smiling but his eyes were not. His words rang in Ed's ears together with the clashing of gears. The smell of burning rubber overpowered that of the square's Spring flowers. The sounds and the smells were strong enough to make Ed sure he was not dreaming.

Ed had another visitor that morning, an unexpected one: Mark Rotherfield. When Ed opened the door, Mark was scratching his thin beard.

'Hello, old chap, can I come in?'

'Sure. Step right in. If it's too early in the day for a proper drink, I'll make you some tea or coffee.'

Ed did not want Mark to see the pile of cash, so he led him to the kitchen, opened its outer door and set out a couple of chairs on the top platform of the fire escape, which he and Ção used as a balcony.

'What brings you here?'

Mark blinked behind his expensive lenses.

'Look, I'm sorry I've been a bit of a rotter, blaming you for that fiasco up at the University, but really I felt so bad I just wanted to keep out of people's way.'

'So what's changed?'

Mark's face brightened.

'I've got a job. At the English Council. Teaching English there.'

'Mark, that's fabulous news! Congratulations!'

'It's only part-time, but even so they pay more than you'll be getting at the University.'

'Wow! And they gave you work in the middle of term. How did you manage that? Hang on, I'll fetch the tea.'

When he came back out with the two full mugs, Mark was resting his feet on the 'balcony' railing. He took a mug from Ed with one hand and stroked the thick knot of his tie with the other.

'Oh, I see,' said Ed. 'Where did you go to school?'

'Tonbridge.'

'Where on earth is that?'

'Little town in Kent, actually. Got a river, a jolly old castle and an association football team known as the Angels.'

'Must be looking after you.'

'Yes. Damned good school, Tonbridge, though I say it myself. Tough but fair.' His smile flickered.

'And the trading stamps?'

'Oh, I've forgotten them already. I've darned well had my fill of supermarkets and grocers.'

'Yes, but between us we could've shaken 'em up, don't you think?'

'By George, yes!'

As they downed their tea, they traded ideas. Ed did not think much of Mark's vision of supermarkets with carpeting and decorated in pastel colours, but he warmed to the thought of check-out staff in well-designed uniforms they'd be pleased to wear, and was impressed by Mark's fantasies of maxi-supermarkets built on cheap land outside towns, with ample parking space and selling stuff you'd now have to go to several kinds of store to find. He was glad to have his friend back, and sorry when Mark rose to leave.

'Thanks for the tea, old bean, almost as good as the real thing. Now I really must go and prepare some lessons. Oh, I almost forgot. I've brought you a little something to put in our pipe of peace.'

He pulled a small transparent bag from his jacket pocket. Ed glanced at the marijuana and ushered Mark into the kitchen. He shut the door to the fire escape behind them, and spoke to Mark in a low voice.

'That's very kind of you, Mark. But I've given that up. No, really. Won't even have any in the house. I'm not kidding. Wouldn't be good for the baby.'

'Oh, I say, is Çāo – ?'

'Not yet. But she will be soon.'

'Oh, jolly good! Maybe we can have a christening party all together.'

'Let's hope so. Meanwhile, if you want to do me a favour, next time you come, bring me some real English tea.'

After seeing Mark out, Ed went into the party room. The pile of money was still there. He counted it again and reached the same amounts as before. He started to believe it was his. Theirs. The moment Çāo arrived, he took her by the hand and led her to it. Her eyes widened.

'What's this?'

'The fruits of enterprise. To put it another way, my love, the security we need to start a family.'

'Oh Ed, let's start one now, right this moment. It's just about the best time of the month.'

She ran into the bedroom, pulling Ed with her. Çāo slid off her jacket, then unbuttoned her blouse and let it fall. She pulled Ed to her and attacked his trousers as he kissed and nibbled her neck. Ed stepped out of his trousers, removed his briefs and then could wait no longer. He pushed Çāo backwards onto the bed, reached his hands up under her skirt, pulled down her panties, moistened her vagina a bit more with his tongue, then eased his penis into her and began moving rhythmically in the way he knew would bring her to orgasm soon.

'No, Ed, darling. Don't make me come, make me pregnant!'

Ed wondered briefly about his wife's sex education, but absorbed the message and thrust harder and faster, imagining himself going so deep inside her that when he came, the spermatozoa would have only the tiniest of journeys to make. With that thought, he climaxed, and felt fatherhood calling in his ear.

Çāo stroked his hair as he lay still on top of her. After a few minutes, she whispered into his ear.

'Ed, my darling, let's do it again. Maybe we can have twins.'

## 10  THE POINT OF SEX

Çāo's next period came as regular as clockwork. Ed was disappointed, but there was plenty of time. He knew that her first pregnancy would happen sooner rather than later.

'Must try harder, Ed,' was Çāo's only comment.

Try they did. Çāo's passion for innovative positions and alternatives to vaginal sex gave way to a focus on positions deemed to offer the best statistical chance of conception. Reading her legal textbooks took second place to studying the publications of Masters and Johnson and other fertility experts. At night, she repeated that she could only be satisfied with Ed inside her, deep inside her. Ed remembered his father's sermons about procreation being the purpose of the sacrament of matrimony, and attended to his wife's wishes whole-heartedly. He buried the memory of his mother's wry asides about copulation's no longer necessarily leading to population, and the implications thereof. Love plus sex equalled the joy of children: he knew that.

Now that he had learned the ropes of the marijuana trade, Ed redoubled his efforts to make his equity useful to the business. He took a more proactive role with the returned settlers, offering them the contacts and the knowledge he had acquired while criss-crossing the country during his short career in the legal retail trade. He did it out of gratitude to Paulo, but he also calculated that some of those he helped would eventually regain both wealth and status, and could be in a position to help him in the future. Or help his children, for he would love to bring them up in Portugal. Paulo appreciated Ed's growing contribution, and made a point of handing him wads of dollars and escudos at regular intervals.

Ed came home one afternoon with his jacket pockets full of them, to add to their 'baby fund'. With the University in full swing, and its discontents in effervescence, Ed did not expect to find his wife at home; yet Ção was there, in the party room, slumped in the armchair next to the telephone, her head resting on her arm, the sleeve of her blouse wet.

'My love, what is it?'

Ed's first fear was medical. Instead of answering, Ção began to sob. Ed moved quickly over to her, knelt beside her and wrapped his arms around her, holding her and rocking her gently until she felt able to speak. It was minutes before she did.

'Oh, my poor Daddy. Poor, poor Daddy. And Mummy. I can't believe it.'

'What's happened? Are they all right.' Ed felt a premonition of disaster.

'They –' Ção relapsed into sobs, which grew louder, then trailed off. She looked at Ed, pain breaking through the tears in her eyes.

'They're getting a divorce. They've told me they're getting a divorce. A divorce. My poor, poor Mummy and Daddy. But it can't be true, can it, Ed?'

Ed tried to make Ção feel his love, to console her with it through words and caresses and holding her in silence. He had expected the news to be worse. He saw no reason to believe it was not true. Civil divorce had been possible in Portugal even for Roman Catholics since mid-February, and if his in-laws were prepared to put up with the enduring stigma of it, then, he imagined, they had good reasons to want separate lives, reasons that were unlikely to be new. But he said none of that to Ção.

Later the same evening, Ed phoned his own parents. He insisted on speaking to both of them, and drew comfort from finding them at home together. He did not mention the demise of his in-laws' marriage. Nor did he mention his new wealth, let alone its source. When he put the phone back in its cradle, he wished he had less reason to hide things from them, or from anyone. He returned to the bedroom and slipped in between the sheets. He took Ção in his arms.

'Ready for some family therapy of our own?'

He read puzzlement in her face.

'Let's get this family started!'

'Oh, Ed, not tonight, please. Not tonight.'

Ed fretted over the several following nights when they did not make love, wasting potentially fertile opportunities. Ção was distracted. She spent hours talking on the phone to her elder sister, Agonia, to whom her parents' split came as less of a surprise, less of a trauma. Ção asked Ed for marijuana, to calm her down. He brought some home for her, but insisted that she close all doors and windows before smoking it with joss burning and something aromatic on the stove. The marijuana calmed her.

Ed decided that his wife was in mourning for her parents' marriage and, even less consciously, for the end of her own childhood and her social innocence. The cocoon in which she was raised had split open, and she felt weak and vulnerable. It was a comforting explanation, because it meant that he could do something about it, namely show Ção that he could protect her better than her parents had, and help her grow and become stronger. Which also meant that her current weak and vulnerable state would not last.

For the time being, though, it got worse. Ed's lovely, bubbly wife lost her thirst for knowledge as well as her hunger for motherhood, lost her exuberance at work and at the Law School as well as in bed. Not even politics could rouse her passion.

At the same time, the fizz went out of the Revolution. The Communists and the revolutionary left miscalculated badly. They thought that that their popular support and military backing meant that they could attack their political opponents literally as well as metaphorically. But physical attacks on right-wing party activists and meetings, and even on each other, were seen as harbingers of a return to the bad old days in which having a discordant political opinion could get you persecuted and tortured.

The leftist military leaders overplayed their hand disastrously. They forced the political parties to sign an agreement that enshrined them in a leading political role for the next three years. Instead of freedom's heroes, they started to look like petty dictators.

On 25 April, exactly one year after the overthrow of the fascist régime, elections took place to elect not a Parliament but a Constituent Assembly entrusted with drawing up a new, democratic Constitution. Misreading the mood in the country, the military leaders called upon the people to boycott the election as a mark of support for their own continued leadership. Their hubris got its just desserts: people turned out in unprecedented numbers for their first-ever chance to express a meaningful vote. The results, too, disappointed the extremists: the centre-left Socialists came first; the centre-right 'Popular Democrats' came second; the Communists and their allies came third; the far right came a distant fourth; and the extreme left came nowhere, perhaps because their people had heeded the call not to vote.

Ção brushed off the electoral demise of her Maoists as a foregone conclusion.

'Our struggle is in the streets, not in a pathetic scramble to stuff ballot boxes.'

Ed had read or heard no evidence of electoral irregularities.

'Our aim is to win people's hearts and minds, not their here-today, gone-tomorrow votes.'

She did not sound convinced. Nor even perturbed by her party's failure to achieve either aim. Ed wondered how he might inject some life back into her words.

He went to see her parents. He found her mother at home, alone. She invited him in, offered him something to eat. Remembering the effects her cooking had last had on him, he declined.

'Oh, that.' She understood. 'I'm sorry about that. You see, I was desperate not to lose another daughter. I knew that when Ção left home, I'd be so alone, so terribly alone. I just wanted to punish you in advance for taking her away, or stop you if I could.'

'No chance. And it's water under the bridge now. You look a lot better than when I last saw you. A million times more relaxed.'

'Thank you. Shall I tell you why that is? Because I've finally summoned the courage to break free of my husband's domestic fascist régime, and now I'm building my own life. Not that it's easy, mind you, not in any way at all.'

'Ção is the one who is desperate now. I can make her better, believe me, but it'll take time. It'll be quicker if you help her, too. Let her know that she's still part of your future.'

'You know, you're not a bad man. Actually, I never thought you were. I really liked the way you tucked into my food.'

*

With the cooperation of his reluctant mother-in-law pledged, Ed turned his attention to the father. Dona Maria das Dores did not know where her husband had gone to live, and he would not take Ed's calls to his office. Ed knew where he worked, and collared him one afternoon as he emerged with a group of colleagues. Senhor Cunha saw the determination in Ed's face and did not want to risk a scene.

'Excuse me, gentlemen. This here is my no-good foreign son-in-law. I'll have to buy him a drink or else he'll beat my daughter.' His colleagues snickered as he detached himself from the group and ushered Ed to a nearby café. Ed did not care about the insults. He came straight to the point.

'Do you know how much you mean to your daughter?'

'Next to nothing, since she married you, against my wishes, my better judgement and my express command.'

'You couldn't be more wrong. Do you realise how upset she is over your divorce? Have you any idea what a gap there is going to be in her life if you disappear from it?'

'I hadn't looked at things in that light, in truth – from my daughter's point of view.'

'Well it's about bloody time you did! The phones still work, and you know the number.'

Ed slammed a handful of small coins on the café table and pushed his way through the throng of customers. Along with anger, unfamiliar emotions passed across Afonso Cunha's face as Ed stormed out.

Having done what he could to get his in-laws to think about their younger daughter as well as themselves, Ed looked at what he could do himself to help his wife emerge from her mourning. He could flash his new cash, but at the moment, he reckoned, Ção needed security more than frivolity. He went to see his landlady.

The widow Esteves was not a greedy person, though she was canny with her money. As the years advanced, she paid less attention to the swirl of events outside her windows and thought more about eternity. She had labelled Ed a man of the world, and was ready to listen when he pointed out that with rents frozen for the foreseeable future and other events unpredictable, it might be to her advantage to sell her properties now. Ed made her an offer for the flat in Largo do Andaluz.

'I shall certainly think about it. I will contact you again after I have spoken to my lawyers, and to my dear nephew who gives me such good advice.'

Two days later, Ed was poring over a map of Portugal, planning the further expansion of Paulo's marijuana enterprise, when Senhora Esteves rang. After ritual, warm greetings, she came to the point.

'Dear Julião would certainly like the chance of a little more cash to play with, but my lawyers tell me that the housing market is in a dreadful state, which I presume is why you offered me so little, and that it can only go up.'

'Well, they are right that it's in a bad way. That's one reason why I didn't offer you the earth for a small flat. But it's not going to recover until the economy as a whole does. And if your lawyers have any evidence of that happening soon, I'd really like to see that evidence. I can't see house prices doing anything but fall for the next year. At the very least. For my part, I have a personal reason for buying now.'

'I understand your point of view, Mr. Scripps, and I shall not enquire as to your personal circumstances. I shall give your words, and your offer, due consideration.'

*

Çāo did not tell Ed directly that she was back in close touch with both her parents, but he could tell from the way her mood improved, the way she screened incoming calls, and the length of time she spent on calls that included the words 'Mãe' and 'Pai'. She began to smile again, from time to time. She was tender towards Ed: affectionate but bereft of lust. He felt she was treating him like an overgrown child. He wanted to make that change, to get their life together back on track.

Ed got back into the habit of getting up early. If he could not have sex, he could keep himself fit by jogging around the park. He would buy bread and pastries on the way home, and make coffee to complete their breakfast. He graded the kisses Çāo gave him before she left for work. They were affectionate, but the temperature was low. Soon after her regular departure time, Paulo was likely to call him for a business conference, so Ed was caught off guard when his landlady beat Paulo to it.

'Look, Mr. Scripps, I have half a mind to accept your offer, in principle at least. But the amount you mentioned is simply too low.'

Ed reiterated the arguments he had used to convince her she was getting a good deal, then offered her a slightly larger sum. She procrastinated. Ed played his trump card.

'I'll pay you in cash. US dollars.'

Ed had made a small fortune, by his standards, in the brief period he had been working with Paulo, but it was not enough to buy a flat. He made up the shortfall by touching his partner in crime for a loan. Paulo produced the money immediately, but with a warning.

'Remember, Ed, our little scheme is time-bound. It cannot last forever.'

Ed's mind was focused on the present and on his immediate future with Çāo. The first thing he did after he completed his purchase of the flat was to change the lock. He knew Çāo would go straight from the travel agency to her evening classes, so he phoned her at the office and said he would collect her after class. He ended his own class early to allow himself time to cross the campus, without making her wait. Ed stood just inside the entrance of the Law School. When he caught sight of Çāo, she was walking with her eyes lowered, her shoulders weighed down by two bags. She looked up as she heard the doors creak, caught his eye and smiled briefly. She kissed him on the cheek. Ed added her bags to his own, took her hand and led her down the long avenue towards the main road, telling her about the things his students had said during his classes. When a taxi approached, he hailed it.

Although he was weighed down with bags, Ed felt like running up the stairs to the fourth floor. He held himself back, and pretended the climb had tired him out.

'You open the door, could you, while I get my breath back?'

In silence, Çāo extracted her key and put it in the lock. It would not turn.

'What's wrong, my love?'

'It won't turn. It doesn't even seem to fit. Maybe I'm using the wrong one.' She took it out and scrutinised it.

'Here, let me have a look.'

She passed Ed the key. He glanced at it.

'No. This isn't your key.' He took one of the new keys from his jacket pocket and handed it to her.

'This is your key. Try it.'

Çāo inserted the new key and opened the door. Ed dropped the bags, embraced her from behind and pushed her into the flat.

'That was your new key, and this is our new flat. I've just bought it. It really is ours.'

Çāo's eyes lit up. 'Oh, Ed, that's marvellous!' Pleasure warmed her voice.

*Her old self is coming back!*

Ed slipped his hands inside the front of her blouse, and under the waistband of her skirt. He imagined them making love there in the hall, against a wall or on the floor. Then Çāo noticed the pots of paint stacked up along the corridor. She removed Ed's hands from inside her clothing.

'What's all this?'

'Well, now that it's ours, we can paint and decorate it the way we want it.'

'That's wonderful, Ed! Let's talk about what we're going to do, right away!'

They got to bed hours later than Ed intended.

'What a day!' said Çāo. For a moment, they lay on their backs, side by side. Then Çāo took Ed's hand and placed it on her breast. She arranged it so that her nipple lay between two fingers. She pressed the fingers together, arched her back, moaned, turned her face toward Ed, reached for his erect penis with her free hand, closed her eyes and forced words out of her lips.

'Make me come, Ed! My darling husband, make me come!'

## 11  Senhor Doutor

Ed and Ção had fun decorating the baby's room, erasing from it every last trace of Joséphine, its previous decorator. Ed had no colour scheme preference, so he asked Ção to choose.

'White! All white! So that our lovely little brat can learn to scrawl Maoist graffiti all over the walls. What, did you think I'd go for some stupid colour coding based on whether it's a boy or a girl?'

'Well, er, no, of course not. You know that. But maybe we should decide on a name well in advance. Have you got any favourites?'

'Something revolutionary!'

'Perhaps we should wait until we know whether it's a boy or a girl.'

'If we call it something revolutionary, that won't matter.'

'Hmm. An English name or a Portuguese one? OK, I know your answer, but it had better be something revolutionary that sounds the same in both languages.'

Ção laughed and Ed kissed her, then surprised her with a swift move he had once learned in judo that threw her off balance. He eased her to the floor and hitched her skirt up. Later, when he had climaxed, emptying his seed deep inside her, he began to laugh.

'What is it?'

'Let's call our baby after you, when you've had a few drinks: Çhão.'

'But that means floor!'

'Conceived on the floor. It also means ground, doesn't it, and what could be more grassroots and Maoist than that?'

'And the way you ground into me! I like it!'

No matter how often Ed ground into her and emptied his seed, whether on the floor, on tables, in bed or anywhere else, signs of a revolutionary baby failed to materialise.

Ed embroiled himself in his work, both in the marijuana trade and at the University. He spent less and less time at home. When he was there, he focused his attention on procreative sex, when he could persuade his wife to cooperate, which he mostly could. In business, he was keen to expand his distribution network further and further from the capital, but Paulo held him back.

'The further out we go, the less protection I can guarantee. We mustn't overstretch ourselves. I don't want to tread on the big boys' toes. They're not boys, anyway, they're snakes. Or alligators.'

Ed wanted to learn the security side of the business, too. Everything could be grist to his mill; but Paulo refused to teach him.

'It's too dangerous, Ed. Besides, you've got enough on your plate as it is.'

That was true. Turnover kept growing, fast, so that storing the cash itself became an issue. Paulo warned Ed not to keep too much at home, and offered him several hopefully safer alternatives, which he accepted. Yet despite the risk, the joy of walking home with a cash-lined jacket kept its shine.

When he went to teach at the University, Ed felt he was entering another world. Academia had always struck him as an artificial place, its concerns unworldly and alien to his own practical focus. But his evening students were living in the real world and, what's more, in many cases working to improve it. Increasingly, he came to identify with their individual and collective struggles, though he wished he, or someone else, could inject a dose of business efficiency into the University bureaucracy. They had yet to pay him his first salary.

The summer was heating up in more ways than one, and the students were keen to wrap up their classes and head off to make or break the revolution in the streets, to escape to a beach resort or to another country, or simply to spend more evenings with their families. Ed wished there was more time to teach them, to get their English up to a decent level, but he could use the extra free time himself, so he agreed to their request to finish everything in June.

Ed pushed open the huge double doors of the Department of Literatures, which his English-speaking colleagues dubbed 'the Deli' , marvelling that such a monstrous example of fascist architecture had yet to be earmarked for physical destruction. Well, much of its interior was falling apart of its own accord. He looked for his group of forty or so students. Instead of them, he caught sight of the distinctive figure of Carolina Isfahan, her wavy red hair falling to her slim waist. She approached him, clutching a set of rolled scrolls.

'Peace, Ed. I was waiting for you. I thought you might need these.' She handed him the scrolls.

'Do you know what they're for?' she asked.

Ed unrolled them. They were lined and embossed with the University crest. Nothing had been written on them.

'Is it a holy text that's visible only to believers?'

Carolina's smile froze.

'Ask your students.'

'Carolina, I didn't mean –'

But she had pushed past him and out into the warm June evening.

Ed located his students, and together they found an empty classroom for their end-of-year assessment. Under the new dispensation, teachers and students assessed each other. Ed's students were kind to him. They praised his commitment and his methods. Their only complaint was that he had dragged the classes on too far into the summer. Marks had been abolished, to avoid stigmatising less academic students: they could award either a pass or a fail, based on continuous assessment. Ed was at ease with continuous assessment. He had kept meticulous records and used them to report on each student's performance on individual and group assignments, and on their participation in class. His students were taken aback: they had not expected such thoroughness.

'Look, Ed, thanks for all that, but just tell us whether you think each of us should pass or fail, and then we'll discuss your suggestion and put it to a vote.'

Ed was happy to pass most of them, but a few had made little effort or progress, and he thought they should be made to repeat the course, and try a bit harder next time. That was not a popular idea, especially to those he named and who had shown up for the assessment. Ed thought of the interminable student and faculty meetings, and decided to impose democracy.

'OK, I think we've discussed things long enough. Let's put the assessments to the vote.'

Everyone present was voted a pass, which was denied to those who had officially dropped out during the year, and to two of those whom Ed had deemed inadequate and who had not turned up that evening.

Before they left, Ed asked them about the scrolls Carolina had given him.

'Those? Those are official forms on which you have to register our end-of-year results, in triplicate. And don't make any spelling mistakes in the names, or else you'll have to do them all again. How come you didn't know?'

Ed's spoken Portuguese was now excellent, but he didn't have much cause to write it often. Portuguese surnames were relatively few, but most people seemed to have at least four of them. Getting over forty such names right, down to the last accent, three times for each of his three classes was a daunting prospect. A couple of students saw him turn even paler than normal, took pity on him and offered to help. By the time they finished, his next class had located the room and filed in. This time, Ed got help with preparing the official record sheets before starting the assessment. These students were more interested in the details of his evaluation of their learning, and more critical yet more appreciative of his own performance, but the result of the assessment was the same, as indeed it was two days later, when Ed wrapped up his third and final class. This was the class to whom he taught business English, and he was pleased when they told him how much they had come to appreciate its usefulness.

The next day, Ed took a taxi up to the University to hand in the assessment record sheets. The clerk accepted them with thanks and without demur.

*Now let them tell me I'm not on the staff!*

Ed felt that he had unloaded a weight from his shoulders. He strolled across the campus to celebrate with a beer in the café where he had met Patrick Harte. The café was less full now that classes were ending, but Carolina and Rupert were there, drinking milky coffees together over a stack of forms. Ed queued to pay, queued for his beer, then took the bottle over to join them.

'Carolina, you saved my life! That was really kind of you! Whenever you need a favour … Right now, would you both like a real drink?'

They each asked for more milky coffee, with a brandy chaser. Ed put down his beer bottle and went to queue again.

Rupert gestured to the pile beside him when Ed came back.

'Thank you. How come they never told you about these things?'

'They just assume you know,' said Carolina. 'They know, and you're a teacher, so you must know, too.'

'They assume their way is the universal way, and dead obvious,' said Rupert.

'That's the same in any organisation. There are always things it's assumed that you know. You just don't know that you don't know them. What I needed was a proper induction.'

'Induction courses for new teachers?' Rupert looked at Ed with a raised eyebrow. 'In fifty years' time, maybe.'

'Anyway, cheers!'

They shared a taxi into the city centre. Ed insisted on paying for it. He wanted to take them somewhere posh for a few more drinks, but they both had more work to do on their student records. Instead, he went up the hill to the English Council and had a quick bevvy with Mark between his friend's classes. Mark was happy to be earning a regular salary, but he resented Ed's long and early holiday.

'You lazy, work-shy so-and-sos! No wonder there's an economic crisis.

I've got to work all bloody summer, special courses and all that. Even though it's only part-time. They don't think I'm good enough to teach full-time!'

Ed was unsure how far Mark was joking. After he had left for his next class, Ed ordered a snack of spicy sausage with bread, olives and goat's cheese. He washed it down with a single glass of red wine from the barrel. His taste buds told him that the wine had been doctored with local firewater, and he resolved to stick to bottled wine in future, whenever he had the choice.

To get home, Ed walked across town in the clear, warm evening. He relished the mixed scents of the flowers, both temperate and tropical, that were abundant in the city's many small parks and public gardens. By the time he reached home, his shirt was wet with sweat and clinging uncomfortably to his torso. Even so, he took the stairs two at a time, eager to see his wife. Her keys were on the hall table, but she was not where he expected, in the party room, nor in the kitchen, the study or the baby room. The bathroom, too, was empty. Ed took off his drenched shirt and rinsed his upper body, then went quietly to their bedroom. Ção was in the bed, asleep. A T-shirt and a pair of trousers lay draped across a chair. Ed preferred his wife to wear skirts because he found them sexier and they gave him easier access to what was underneath. These trousers were not even of the thin, bottom-hugging kind that could look so enticing. Ed bent over his wife to kiss her neck. She stirred.

'Is that you, Ed? You smell of wine.'

As he kissed her neck, Ed noted that the citrus aroma that had replaced Ção's scent of cinnamon was no longer on her. He removed the rest of his clothes, eased his naked body between the sheets and snuggled up to Ção, cupping her smooth, firm breasts in his hands and moving her legs apart with his own.

'Oh no, Ed, please, not now. I'm so … tired. I'm just … exhausted, really exhausted. The baby can wait. She'll come when she's ready.'

The next morning, Ed sent Carolina an enormous orchid, with a note explaining precisely why, lest her husband misconstrue his gesture of thanks.

The political scene to which the University's students and staff of a political persuasion could now devote their attention was as hot as the streets on which it was played out. The mass media were a battleground, with a Church-owned radio station occupied by dissident staff, and a top newspaper editor forced out by the paper's workers, who claimed he was a mouthpiece for the centre-left Socialist Party. The Socialist Party did not take kindly to that, and launched a series of well-attended rallies in his support. In July, as the revolutionaries sought to consolidate their grip on power, flying in the face of popular support for a more moderate approach, the far right came out of hiding, orchestrating violent attacks on left-wing party offices, a break-out by imprisoned former secret policemen and thefts of weapons from Army warehouses. It was also reputedly behind the formation of an Azores Liberation Front on a series of wind-swept islands under Portuguese jurisdiction in the mid-Atlantic. Meanwhile, another wind-swept mid-Atlantic archipelago, the Cape Verde Islands, officially became independent of Portugal, as did tiny São Tomé e Príncipe and the vast territory of Mozambique.

Ed got away from the heat and pressures of Lisbon. He went to London for an Open University summer school. Paulo assured him that Ed had set up his distribution networks and procedures so well that they could withstand a month without his direct supervision.

Ed hoped to get through his course as fast as possible, in case his lack of a degree was the undeclared reason why the University authorities in Lisbon had yet to ratify his appointment. Back home, his teaching, business and reproductive duties took up most of his time, but in London he was free to study as much as he liked. Those who needed accommodation, as he did, were housed in a student residence in Camden Town, a lively and central location. He found the courses interesting, well taught and far from onerous. His fellow students were a disparate and engaging bunch, as eager to socialise as Ed was to study.

He received a lot of personal attention from female students, most of them older than him. At their social gatherings, when his wedding ring failed to dissuade them, he took to praising his wife's many virtues and talking about babies, which a few of them were there to get away from, before leaving the company with an abrupt 'My books are calling!'

In truth, Ed missed his wife desperately. Ção had refused to accompany him. Although her Maoist rhetoric had faded, she was ever ready to denounce 'the imperialist powers', which still included England, in her opinion. She had enjoyed the shops and sights of London, but she scorned the country as a whole.

'England! Hah! Too expensive and no food! And such a male chauvinist culture.'

Whenever he could do so without interfering with his studies, Ed invited a group of his fellow students for meals or drinks. He did not want to act like Lord Bountiful, but he knew that most of them were making sacrifices to be there which he no longer had to face. He explained his cash-happiness with the lie that he had played the foreign exchange markets and won, backed up with the refrain 'Easy come, easy go!'

Ed's days were full, but they passed slowly. He was happiest when Ção was on the other end of the phone line, chatting about how wonderful the weather was, or her boss, Fernando, and colleagues at the travel agency, or the quickest way to overthrow the military oligarchy, the patriarchy or the university hierarchy. Ed tried to make her hear the love in his voice, and strained to hear it in hers. Even when she was too distracted to let it be evident, he relished the lilt of her words in his ear.

Ed had left Portugal with rather more dollars than he was allowed to take out. Luckily, neither he nor his luggage had been searched, and Heathrow did not live up to its nickname of *Thiefrow*. On his first weekend visit to Stevenage, he paid his mother back the money she had lent him, and added a good deal more beside.

'For you both. For a rainy day.'

He explained how now that he had a regular job at Lisbon University, his financial problems were a thing of the past. He could not tell whether his mother believed him, but she accepted the cash, and for once Ed felt dutiful rather than prodigal.

England seemed unusually colourless to Ed, though he welcomed its coolness. The start of the English summer had been marked by a cricket match between Derbyshire and Lancashire falling victim to two inches of snow. By the time Ed arrived, it had turned into one of Britain's hottest, driest summers of the century. There were so many baking hot days that the tabloid press had to find alternatives to 'Phew! What a Scorcher!' as their lead headline. In Lisbon, Ed kept out of the sun; here, he could enjoy walking in it. Yet those around him wilted in the heat, and complained bitterly. They also complained bitterly about double-digit inflation and interest rates, and a double-dip recession. Unlike Portugal, no-one had any great plans or vision for making things better. Outside wartime, they had always muddled on through, and until the next war, they would continue to do so. The flurry of interest in the overthrow of fascism on the edge of Western Europe had long since dissipated, and to get news of events in his adopted country – Ed caught himself using that expression – he called Paulo regularly. Sometimes Lourdes answered, coldly, rebutted Ed's attempts to make friendly small-talk and passed him over to Paulo at once. His friend and business partner let Ed know what was happening in the country, as he saw things, and also assured him, though not in so many words, that the business was carrying on just fine. It occurred to Ed that Paulo's pessimism as to the longevity of their joint venture might be unjustified.

Paulo told him that in Portugal things were coming to a head. The two biggest political parties, in electoral terms, had left the government, which they had become unable to control, and a fifth provisional government had taken power. It was pushing through a series of measures dear to the Communists and the revolutionary left, as though it might have the time and the means to implement them, while the soldiers who really ran the show were themselves divided between extreme revolutionaries and moderate revolutionaries, divisions which were becoming sharper and more bitter. Meanwhile, said Paulo, those nostalgic for a return to the bad old days bided their time and collected weapons.

'What about the Maoists?' Ed asked him.

'What Maoists?' Paulo laughed and said goodbye.

Ed's diligence at the summer school paid off, in part. He got very high marks. However, everyone who had made the slightest effort, between sessions in the pub and rocking the night away, passed.

*Bloody hell,* he thought, *it's just like Lisbon. Well, I've learned a lot. I'm just no nearer to getting that damned degree than any of the others.*

It was raining when Ed returned to Lisbon. The rain took the dust out of the air, and as he stepped out of the plane, he breathed in the reassuringly familiar mixture of maritime and chemical breeze that wafted up from the estuary.

Ed hoped Ção would meet him at the airport. Instead, he found Paulo waiting for him, in the company of a tall, thin African man a bit older than them, wearing a bright green shirt and tailored red trousers, and carrying a leather briefcase. Paulo gave Ed a long, brotherly hug, took his suitcase and introduced the man as Moisés. Lourdes' battered white Renault, minus Lourdes, was parked right outside the Arrivals entrance. Paulo slipped a ten-dollar bill to the squat, ruddy-faced man looking after it and opened the back-seat door for Ed.

'I know you can't wait to see your wife, but honestly, Ed, we have some business to attend to first. You'll both be glad we did, believe me.'

They drove into the city centre and Paulo parked outside a self-proclaimed luxury restaurant. The head waiter gave Ed and Moisés a disdainful look as they entered, but became effusive as soon as he saw Paulo behind them. The delicate taste of the fresh lobster and the smoothness of the white wine from nearby Colares on his palate helped Ed, who had forgotten such treats, to put up with the chilly air-conditioning. Their business, Paulo said, was steady. He coaxed Moisés into talking at length about his home country, Mozambique. Ed complimented Moisés on his English.

'Thanks. I've spent some time in South Africa.'

*That accounts for the accent.*

'In Africa, you know, we pick up languages easily. We learn our mother tongue, then a colonial language, maybe a couple of our neighbours' languages. It's normal for us to be multilingual.'

Ed thought of his Lisbon University students and the trouble they had with English, and the problems he and his fellow-countrymen had learning anyone's language but their own.

A waiter came to clear their coffee cups. Paulo asked him to put a clean tablecloth on. When he had done so, Paulo gestured to Moisés, who carefully placed his briefcase on it.

'Now,' said Paulo, 'we come to the main business of the evening. It's your birthday soon, Ed, right?'

'November the First.'

'I have a little early present for you, then.'

Moisés opened his briefcase, drew out a sheet of parchment, smoothed it, turned it in Ed's direction and pushed it across the table to him.

Ed read the embossed lettering: *Universidade de Lourenço Marques.* Below it: *Edward Clement Scripps.*

'Congratulations, Senhor Doutor Scripps, you now have a degree in Economics!'

'Wow! This thing looks genuine.'

'As far as anyone here can tell, it is entirely authentic. Now, shall we have some fine malt whisky to celebrate?'

Paulo dropped Ed off outside his flat and roared away with Moisés. Ed felt stone-cold sober, but his heart was beating fast as he went up the stairs, and not just because he had done little physical exercise in London.

The flat was empty. Ed's head swam. He sat on the floor, let his head clear, got up, went to the phone. Beside it was a note from Ção.

*Staying with Mummy. She needs me. See you soon. xxxxxxxx Your little*

*Conception xxxxxxxx.*

Ed reached for the phone, then thought better of it. He unpacked the clothes, shoes, cosmetics and trinkets he had bought for Çāo in London and arranged them where she would see them if she came home while he was out. Next, he put his papers in order. Then he phoned Xavier, who told him that the University would not be starting classes until the following month, October, at the earliest. After that, he called Mark, whose classes at the English Council had started, and arranged to meet him for a few drinks after Mark finished work the next day. He was sweating, so he went around the flat, opening windows. The rain had long since stopped; the wind had died. Exotic flowers and petrol fumes fought for control of the night air. Ed took deep draughts of it and wished the moment could last for ever.

## 12 A MAN OF PROPERTY

In mid-September, the political tide turned when a sixth provisional government was sworn in. It was more moderate than its predecessor, although it was headed not by a civilian but by an admiral, and it focused initially on power struggles within the armed forces. Although it was more business-friendly than its immediate predecessors, nationalisations continued, and the revolutionary left sought to demonstrate people's power in the streets.

Portugal's neighbour, Spain, had also fallen under a fascist yoke decades earlier, and had not freed itself. Portugal got a reminder of the nature of such a régime at the end of September, when the Spanish government used a police firing squad to execute five Basque nationalists. Portuguese opinion had already been enraged by the earlier garrotting of two young anarchists in Spain. In Oporto, in northern Portugal, hundreds of demonstrators broke through a cordon of troops and trashed the Spanish consulate, burning its contents in the street outside. In Lisbon, the protestors went a step further and burned the Spanish Embassy down. The Portuguese government apologised profusely to the neighbouring régime and paid for a new embassy to be built. Paulo told Ed that everyone believed that the burners had been led by Spanish exiles. In any case, the senile dictator in Spain was on his deathbed and his régime's days were numbered. He had just fancied one last thrill from exercising the power of life and death.

The Portuguese government had long complained of an economic boycott, instead of the increased support it had expected, by the countries of Western Europe and North America. Not even with the new, moderate provisional government did the economic crisis show signs of relenting. Ever the optimist, Ed decided that state of affairs would not last. He resolved to take advantage of the crisis in the housing market by borrowing money to invest more heavily in real estate now, while the market was at its lowest level. He approached Paulo for another loan.

'Are you sure I'm the best person to be your personal banker, Ed?'

'You're the only one I trust.'

'Hold on. I'm the lender. It's more a question of how far I trust *you*.'

'Don't you, Paulo?'

'Sure I do.'

'Didn't I pay you back the loan you made me?'

'You did indeed. Well, Ed, if I lend you this money, I guess I can consider you my long-term security.'

'Let's drink to that!' The loan was made.

When Ed mentioned his real estate plans to Mark Rotherfield, his friend suggested Ed buy a place in a seaside village called Azenhas do Mar, where whitewashed houses nestled above a tiny inlet in the cliffs facing the Atlantic. When they visited the village, Ed loved the view, and was sure that Ção would love the place too, but the houses for sale were too small for his purpose and the village too far from the city and too poorly connected by public transport. His idea was to become a landlord himself, so that he would have an income from the property while its value appreciated, or stagnated.

It was Ção who suggested Cascais. She liked its upmarket status and its relative peace and quiet. The fall in house prices there had been particularly steep. It was at the end of the railway line that ran along the estuary coastline from the city, and the trains were frequent. Moreover, her Daddy knew some houseowners there who were looking to sell. So did Paulo. So did Hélder. Ed was spoilt for choice. For once, he ignored Ção's preferences and took the empty property at the lowest price his drug dollars could elicit, a three-bedroom flat on the lower floor of a semi-detached house in a nondescript but leafy street set back from the sea and off the tourist beat, but within easy walking distance of the station. Then he set about finding tenants.

Ed put up notices at the University, the Sussex School and the English Council. He also launched messages on the foreigners' grapevine. Plenty of potential tenants phoned him. Some balked at the rent he was asking, others were put off by having to leave a room for Ed and Ção to use occasionally, and by having to share with another tenant in any case. Most, however, were eager to rent the place. Ed interviewed five people and settled on two teachers from the English Council. Both had a foothold in the media world. Len Hoffman described himself as a Rhodesian. He was as tall as Ed, blond too, though chubby and with a baby face. He had nurtured a posh English accent, in which he reported occasionally for the Voice of America on Portugal and on Southern Africa. Seamus King was a short, dark, thick-set biker from Liverpool who acted as a stringer for a news agency. By all accounts, including their own, they got on well together. Seamus had been living in a windmill in the countryside, and relished the chance of a winter that might be wet and windy outside his bedroom but not inside as well. Len's current flat was frequently rendered dark and dangerous by unreliable wiring which the landlord refused to fix. He carefully examined the electrical set-up at the Cascais flat and gave it the thumbs-up. They would both move in at the end of the month. Ed offered each of them the materials to paint and decorate his own room as he saw fit, and promised to consult them on decorating the shared rooms. They volunteered their labour for that, too.

Ção made it clear to Ed that she would rather live in the quiet of Cascais than in the bustle of the city, but Ed was deeply attached to the flat in Largo do Andaluz, above all because it was the place where they had met. It was to please her that he kept a room reserved for them at the flat on the coast instead of renting it out to a third tenant. He also promised that they would raise their children there. One big advantage of renting to foreigners was that they were not likely to want to stay for ever.

The fact was that living in the city was convenient for both Ed and

Ção. It made it easier for Ção to pay a quick visit to one or other of her parents, and it meant that they could both be home before midnight after a late evening class. And Lisbon was the centre of Ed's distribution network. Ção pointed out that buying a car would make Cascais a more viable option.

'I fancy something chic and French. A nice Peugeot, for instance. What do you think?'

'You know I have to keep a low profile. I can't run around in a brand new car.'

'Well I can! Do you think you're the only person in this couple? Do you think women can't drive?'

'My love, as far as I know, *you* can't drive.'

'Well, my brain is as good as any man's, so I can learn, can't I?'

'Of course you can. Look, here's what we'll do. You take driving lessons. When you pass your test, I'll buy you a second-hand car, and we can both use it.'

'Well, that's a start, I guess. But if you really want to show your love, you'll buy me a new one.'

Ed handed over some cash for the lessons and forgot about the matter. He wanted his wife to have everything she desired, but he did not want her splashing cash in a way that might draw attention to its likely source. On the other hand, he wanted his money to be hers, too, which meant that she should have an equal say in how it was spent. *Within reason.*

Ed was also glad that Ção was making him think about the division of labour within the household. He noticed that she had stopped doing the washing up, and realised that it was something to which he had paid little attention. Without saying anything, he took it upon himself to do it, as well as any other piece of housework he realised needed seeing to. After all, Ção had been willing to help with the decorating, although paint cans still lined the hall walls because they had not yet found time to start on it. Ed did not want to press her. He could see that his wife was tired, with the emotional strain of her parents' split, the physical strain of work at the agency, and the mental strain of her law degree, all of which would get worse when her classes resumed. To cap it all, Ed had not yet made her pregnant, and this had diluted the passion of their love-making, which was now concentrated into the days in the month when she should be most fertile.

Ed had had little recent contact with Rui, the fan of Woody Allen and Philip Roth, so he was surprised when Ção's friend phoned specifically to speak to him.

'Happy birthday, Ed! It is today, isn't it?'

'What? No. Bloody hell, hang on, it's tomorrow. Bloody hell, I'd forgotten.'

'And Ção didn't say anything. Must be planning to surprise you. Not giving you a hard time, I hope?'

'What? No, not at all!'

'Back to the birthday boy. I was hoping you'd be having a party. Hoped I might get myself invited. You didn't do anything last year, I know, but this year it's twenty-five. A quarter of a century! You've got to do something.'

'Damn it, you're right! Of course you're invited. I'll let you know what I manage to arrange in twenty-four hours.'

'And I promise to get very drunk. It's what I'm good at.'

Being a Saturday, the First of November would have been ideal for a party, but Ed was wary of alienating the neighbours with noise, and Ção did not like the idea of a mass of people tramping through what had become her home. Ed also welcomed the chance to splurge on taking his friends out. Saturday night restaurant reservations were hard for large groups, so Ed booked the whole of the Índia Antiga, one of the city's few ethnic restaurants, for Monday evening, and passed several hours phoning around to fill it. He spent his birthday itself at home with Ção, who cooked soup and roast chestnuts for him. Ed restricted himself to drinking *água pé*, lest anything stronger impede his reproductive powers. He felt responsible, and hopeful.

Ed felt less like a family man, and more like his old self, on the

Monday evening. The aroma of curry wafted over his shoulders as he welcomed his guests. It reminded him of London. The cadences of sitar and tabla on the restaurant's sound system added to the cultural mix. He had invited friends from the University, the Sussex School and the English Council, as well as friends he had made through his former legitimate business. Paulo came, too, fortunately not with his sister but with Moisés, who complained that the music was tuneless and the food not spicy enough, but in a good-natured way that made people laugh. Çāo was not in a laughing mood, probably because she had been working all day. She had been quick to erase from the guest list the names of those she deemed *persona non grata*, such as Calvin, with whom she had fallen out over politics and now described as 'Stuttgart's last Stalinist', Lourdes and Paulo, though Ed had reinstated his business partner. She had invited Estrela and a couple of colleagues from the travel agency, and they sat together chatting intensely until Ed came over and regaled them with his best badly-translated jokes. Xavier spent a lot of time talking to the Goan staff about the Portuguese legacy in the sub-continent, which they agreed was reflected nowadays mostly in names and religion. The evening itself showed that in food and music, the influence was more in the other direction.

Ed was in his element, introducing people he felt sure would get along, and keeping apart those he did not, like Mark and the University crowd. He wallowed in the conviviality, and ordered copious quantities of wine to keep it going. Rui lived up to his promise, and found someone who could match his drinking capacity in Seamus, who was in fine fettle, rattling off anecdotes of his recent career as a debt-dodger. This had involved climbing a tree to escape from a grizzly bear in the Canadian outback. In illustrating this, Seamus brought down a wall hanging and overturned a table. The waiters cleaned up the smashed glasses and broken plates without batting an eyelid. As he rushed over to help them, Ed heard Çāo's voice.

'Stupid boy children! Who wants them?'

Her companions giggled.

Before they left, Deolinda d'Almeida paid a visit, clutching a baby and looking flustered. Keith stared at her fixedly. He was not the only one. She gulped a glass of Ed's champagne, wished him a long life, explained that she had to get home to put the latest addition to her family to bed and slipped out into the warm evening. Ed was touched by her visit. Keith sidled up to him.

'Been batting on a sticky wicket, have we?'

'No, no time. I mean, of course not!'

Keith chuckled and went to talk to Simone.

Around eleven, engulfed by animated conversation on all sides, Ed took pity on the waiters and asked for the bill. The head waiter asked him if he really meant to leave such an exorbitant tip.

'Just don't expect it every time I come here.'

It was partly a present to himself. He did not know whether he would be so cash-laden the following year, or indeed ever again. It had been worth it, seeing his friends relaxed and in such good form. Only Ashley Beecroft, his portly, silver-haired, young-acting colleague from the University had disappointed him, teasing Ção with sexist comments and provoking her into feminist diatribes that had her companions nodding at her wisdom and the men within hearing range rolling their eyes, snickering or looking disconcerted. Ed hoped it was not Ashley's eccentric way of getting Ção interested in him. Glancing at the sultry student he had brought with him, who gazed at her mentor with devotion and crossed or uncrossed her long legs whenever Ashley turned to her, Ed decided that was unlikely.

As they emerged from the restaurant, the damp air smelled more of the river than usual. One of the English Council teachers, Pauline, suggested going to a disco. Ed thought that a fine idea. Paulo and Moisés announced that they were going instead to a club.

'A place where you can sit down and talk.'

Len and a couple of others tagged along with them. Keith, together with Xavier, Rupert, Simone and Mark, decided to call it a night and head home. Pauline, the acknowledged disco expert, lead a couple of dozen people eager to dance to a place called Grey's, whose magnificent sound system Ed knew had been purchased with drug money. He felt glad the people who ran it disdained anything so light as marijuana; it meant they would not recognise him.

Ed was enchanted by Ção: she danced with such energy and enjoyment, her short body a concentration of voluptuous sensuality. She danced once with him, then pushed him away, telling him to pay attention to the others while she concentrated on her companions. Ed loved being on a dance floor, where his slight limp was not apparent even to himself, and he was happy to put his friends through their paces. They were not alone, and Ed could not resist dancing with a group of three women who were contorting their bodies enticingly while their faces bore expressions of pure bliss and minimum presence. Ção and her group were dancing together nearby; they too were wrapped up in the music. Estrela backed into one of the women dancing with Ed. The woman turned slowly and jabbed her cigarette into Estrela's arm. Estrela screamed and leapt at her. The two women clawed at each other, going for the hair and eyes. Ed moved in to separate them, but Ção was there first, with a bottle. She struck Estrela's assailant a glancing blow on the side of the head. It was enough to send the other woman crashing to the floor. Ed grabbed hold of Ção and rushed her to the exit. Ed welcomed the chill in the early morning air outside. Someone shouted his name. He turned. It was Seamus, carrying their coats, which he handed to them.

'Oh, thanks, mate.'

'Least I could do, wack. I'll settle your bill. Don't you worry about it.' He turned and went back inside.

Ed took Ção's improvised weapon and tossed it into a rubbish collection bin. He forced Ção to move quickly down the hill towards the city centre and was relieved when a taxi approached.

In the taxi, Ção's reaction surprised Ed.

'Oh, Ed, that was such fun! Didn't I hit that bitch? You saw me, I knocked her flying! Ker-pow! And you were wonderful, my darling, so wonderful. You saved me from I don't know what. Something nasty! So wonderful!' She raised her mouth to his and kissed him passionately.

Ed hoped they could re-ignite their sex life as soon as they got home, but Çāo's adrenaline rush passed quickly. In the flat, she collapsed into bed half-dressed and fell asleep. Ed undressed carefully, got in beside her, failed to shake her into wakefulness, lay back and relived the night's events.

The next morning, a warm, damp feeling between his legs roused Ed from a deep sleep. It was Çāo. Her tongue was pressing the tip of his penis against the back of her palate, as though she wanted to swallow it. Instead she coughed, ejecting it, and giggled.

'I think I'll just try that again.' She did. Ed ejaculated into her throat.

'Don't worry, my love. There's plenty more where that came from.'

'Oh, Ed, my darling, you were so wonderful last night. Now I'm going to show you that I can be wonderful, too.'

Ten minutes later, she was sitting on top of Ed, holding his penis firmly between the outer lips of her vagina. Ed tried to move it so that he could enter her, but she increased the pressure, preventing him.

'No, Ed. No procreation panic today. This isn't for the baby. It's for us.'

'OK.'

'I want you inside me, but if you can stop your willie from spitting just there, I'll make it spit in any other orifice you care to name, just like old times. Deal?'

'Deal.'

Neither of them went to work that day.

A week later, Portugal's biggest, richest and most tragic colony, Angola, became independent. The peace accord there had unravelled, and its Independence Day was just a blip in the civil war which ensued as the world's power blocs armed their proxies to the teeth.

Tiny Portugal itself looked to be heading in a similar direction, a prospect which cast a grim shadow over the future of all those who lived there.

Workers had occupied a radio station that belonged to local bishops The Catholic Church put pressure on the government to take action against the workers. The government had sealed off the station, but the workers continued to broadcast. Now the government sent in troops, who cleared out the workers and blew up the station.

The north and the south of the country differed sharply from each other in climate, history and other significant ways. Their contrasting land inheritance systems had profound repercussions. In the south, the eldest son inherited everything. This resulted in vast estates, often with an absentee landlord, and an army of landless labourers, fertile terrain for collectivist ideas. In the north, land went to all children equally, so that everyone and their dog owned a tiny patch that they would defend to the death against their closest neighbours, never mind a distant government. The far right saw this potential army of smallholders as its ideal conduit back to power and started to scare them into mobilising against a 'red menace', with considerable help from local priests. Left-wing party offices were attacked and burned, and bombs were placed in offices of the land reform agency, with the blame being attributed to 'the Cubans' or local Communists.

The left-wing forces did not take this lying down. Building workers demonstrated outside Parliament and locked its Members inside. Soldiers swore their loyalty to the flag with clenched fists raised.

On the same day as the Revolutionary Council sacked Otelo, the architect of the military coup, from his post as chief of the Lisbon military region, the government itself went on strike, saying it could not do its job in safety and therefore would not.

Everyone, even an incorrigible optimist like Ed, could see that things were coming to a head.

## 13 SILENCE OF THE WOLVES

The left once again overplayed its hand, this time within the ranks of the armed forces, where the paratroopers and the military police were deemed sympathetic to the revolutionary left. When a thousand paratroopers were forcibly demobbed, the remainder rose to the bait and occupied six air force bases. Troops loyal to the leadership forced them out and arrested them. The following day, the leadership sent commandos in to arrest the military police *en masse*. They did so, this time with fatal casualties on both sides. The blood-letting stopped there, thanks to a strange agreement between the President, General Costa Gomes, and the head of the Communist Party, Álvaro Cunhal. Cunhal promised not to call upon the militants whom his party controlled, and the many more workers whom it influenced, to take to the streets in support of the radical soldiers. In return, Costa Gomes promised the Communist Party a continued place in the country's politics. Thereafter, every step back that the country took from continuous revolution was followed by a step further back. The revolution never got the chance to devour its children. Nor did the far right.

Ed asked Paulo, whose judgement he trusted, what he thought lay behind Cunhal's apparent renunciation of any hope of seizing power.

'I guess after all those years in prison and in exile, he likes being a free man on the streets of Lisbon. I don't think he wants to be locked up for years or kicked out yet again.'

'Yeah, I see what you mean. But, you know, he seemed so keen on running the show.'

'I think he's realised how hard it is to dictate things when you're a pawn in someone else's Cold War games. This way, he'll always be a player in our politics, and so will his party.'

What Ed did not expect was Ção's reaction.

'Thank goodness those so-called revolutionaries have had their teeth kicked in! The Army should put them in the Bull Ring and shoot them!'

'But aren't you one of them any more? The revolutionaries, I mean?'

'Yes, of course I am. We are the *real* revolutionaries, Ed, don't you understand that yet? We're rebuilding the party of the proletariat, and that takes time. We don't want the Communists to grab power and stop us.'

'So you're ready to ally with the bourgeois parties if they stop the Communists?'

'Sure, if they stop the Communists and the far left. We want to be able to organise in the light of day. That's what José Manuel says we should do.'

'Who's José Manuel?'

'One of our student leaders. He really understands how things work. He's going to be President one day, you mark my words.'

'If you say so.'

'Meanwhile, we're going to smash the patriarchy.'

'I'm with you there. This country will never get rich as long as it treats women like second-class citizens.'

Ção gave Ed a look he could not decipher.

The government decided it was safe enough to resume work. It marked the new course by mollifying the landowners whose estates had been expropriated as part of the land reform programme. It was busy looking the other way when the military régime that ran Indonesia invaded Portugal's former colony of East Timor and set about massacring the population. The régime had got away with genocide against its own people of Chinese descent ten years beforehand, and correctly surmised that nobody in the world would stop a little bit more genocide in its back yard.

East Timor is one half of one island in an enormous archipelago. The other half, and most other islands in the archipelago, are part of its giant neighbour, Indonesia. The Indonesian generals did not take kindly to having a tiny neighbour with a different official language, religion and culture to their own. When the Portuguese moved out and a leftist liberation movement took over, the Indonesian generals decided to move in and erase the anomaly with the heaviest of hands and the tacit agreement of the US Secretary of State, Henry Kissinger. The Portuguese government protested, when it found time, but no-one listened.

Ed Scripps spent another lonely Christmas in Stevenage, away from his wife, who thought the festive season might be a good occasion for bringing her own parents back together, especially if Ed was not around. However, they were already launched on divergent pathways, and their two daughters' joint efforts failed.

When Ed returned to Lisbon, Mark and Simone invited Çao and him over to celebrate the New Year, even though it was already a week into 1976. Mark had just bought a large television, and insisted on their watching a very slow-moving Brazilian soap opera. Mark and Çao tried to guess what the characters were going to say before they actually spoke. After they had finally got their words out, Simone and Ed shouted out their version of what the characters really thought. The soap opera was followed by a game show: money for nothing was coming back into fashion. Mark and Çao generally beat the contestants to the answers, and neither Simone nor Ed was far behind.

'Do you think they'd let us take part in one of these?' Ed asked. 'We could clean up.'

'It's probably all a fix,' said Mark, wiping his spectacles.

'I don't see why. It's better television if it's genuine, if they're really trying, not just acting.'

A news bulletin followed the quiz show. After reporting on the day's activities by the Army chief, General Eanes, it made a brief mention of East Timor. Simone turned pale.

'You know, French radio is reporting that the Indonesian army has already murdered eighty thousand Timorese.'

141

'They don't hang about,' said Mark.

'That's one tenth of the population,' Simone added. 'What does the BBC say about it?'

Mark looked at Ed. 'You were home at Christmas.'

'Nothing that I heard. You don't get a lot of foreign news at Christmas.'

'The Indonesians murdered five Western journalists on the border there in November, even before they invaded. I guess the rest have taken the hint.' Simone stared at the floor.

Mark put his arm around her shoulders.

'Hey, come back to us, darling. We're in Lisbon, with friends, it's a new year and life is good. And things are going to get better.'

'Everywhere,' added Ed.

Mark moved to top up their glasses. 'Or I could roll a nice fat joint or two?'

'No, thanks. We don't, these days.'

'As you like.' Mark poured.

Ção was tipsy when they got home. Ed had to help her out of the taxi and then to carry her up the final flight of stairs. He shut the flat door with his foot and took her straight into the bedroom. Ção was giggling.

'Oh, put me down, Ed. Put me down, strip me naked, do it again!'

'Don't bring me down, you pretty thing!'

'Do whatever you like to me, Ed darling. Just … no penetration.'

'What?!'

'I've had too much of it, and now I really fancy a little change. Don't you? You know, I'm awfully good at making you come in different ways … in different places. I know you like that. Come on, you love it, don't you, my little Teddy?'

Ed thought there was no point arguing with Ção in her present state. Besides, it was her body. He would just have to be patient, once more.

When Ção drifted off into sleep, Ed got up and went for a shower. Back in bed, he lay awake worrying about his friend, Mark. Before they left, Mark had asked him for a rather large loan. Far from taking Mark on full-time, the English Council was giving him fewer hours to teach. Simone's job was secure, but did not make her rich enough to maintain a spendthrift husband. Ed had promised Mark the loan – he had more than he needed, but he knew how much asking had dented Mark's pride, and he wondered what else he could do to help his friend.

Seasonal rain made the following afternoon feel colder than it actually was. Ed set out on foot to take Mark the money he had asked for. The cold drops sluicing off his umbrella started to find a way inside his mackintosh, so he hailed a taxi. Mark was waiting for him inside the tearoom, a vestige of Portugal's love affair with its 'oldest ally'. When they had finished their scones and attacked a second large pot of Earl Grey tea, Ed handed Mark a thick white sealed envelope.

'Thanks a lot, old chap. This is really helping me.'

'I wish I could do more for you, Mark. Actually, come to think of it, if it's a job you need, I might have something for you. You see, it's getting to the stage where I could use some help with my accounts.' This was plausible, though not strictly true.

'Really? You know, I'm more than willing to do that, but I'll have to talk it over with Simone first. You know, she's a very moral girl.'

'Moral? What's that got to do with it?'

'Well, we never mention it to you, but we know where your money comes from. Not the University, but d-r-u-g-s.'

'M-a-r-i flipping Juana, Mark! Which does no harm to anyone. Unlike the booze that you and I consume vast quantities of.'

'OK, you have a point, but Simone would say that it leads to other things, like heavy drugs.'

'Not if people know the difference, and not if they can get a bit of grass from ordinary people like those in my teams, instead of organised crime gangs that want to push the high-profit alternatives.'

'Well, Simone would say that it's illegal.'

'Well, Simone is right, for the time being. Look, until two years ago, less than, it was illegal to speak your mind in this country. Do you think the law is never going to change? A rational government would take over my distribution networks, make it all above board and tax the stuff. With help for all kinds of addicts, on the national health service, paid for from the taxes.'

'Look, don't think I'm not grateful, old chap. I really appreciate your offer. And as I said, I'll talk it over with Simone. That's the decent thing for me to do. Shall we get some teacakes?'

When they came out into the twilight, the rain had lifted, but a fog hung low over the river, its tendrils drifting up the hills. Together, they walked down into it to the nearest underground station. Before they went their opposite ways, Mark gave Ed a slip of paper with a phone number written elegantly on it.

'That's the number of the guy who runs that quiz show. Frightfully nice chap. We've met him. Simone and I might both be going on it. You should give him a ring. Çao too. Fifteen minutes of fame, and maybe oodles of escudos. Nice, eh?'

'Thanks, mate, but I like to keep a low profile. I'll pass it on to Çao, though. You never know with her. She might fancy it.'

Çao was not at home. Ed watched a couple of quiz shows on their small, under-used television, and tried to picture her lighting them up with her intelligence, high spirits and beauty. She woke him up the next morning, rummaging around in their bedroom and pressing what she found into a canvas grip.

'Oh, Ed, I'm going to spend a few days with Mummy. She's depressed.'

'What? *I'll* be depressed if you leave me on my own, my love, even for a few days.'

'You, depressed? You don't know the meaning of the word, my sweet. I'll be back soon.'

'How about coming back here to sleep?'

'Because you won't let me sleep, you naughty boy. But I will if I can.'

Çao straddled Ed on the bed, placed his hands on her breasts and gave him a long, amorous kiss. Then she moved slowly off and away from the bed, zipped up the holdall, put on her coat, gave him a long, sultry look and was gone. Ed was glad of one thing: she was using cinnamon perfume again.

Ed's antidote to Ção-deprivation was teaching. He was again doing evening classes, one of which he devoted partly, but not exclusively, to English for Business. Continuous assessment was still in fashion, though the pass/fail option had been nuanced with the introduction of A, B and C pass grades. He often met Carolina and Rupert in the café there, before or between lessons, and they forecast a swift return to the old grading system of 0 to 20, with 10 being a bare pass, marks over 14 deemed exceptionally generous, and anything over 17 unheard-of. Ed tried to take this in.

'Perfection leaves much to be desired.' Ashley Beecroft was also doing evening classes this year, and he, like Ed, was new to the old system and less indulgent towards it. 'And it is only for the gods, not mere mortals, not even students of this august seat of learning.'

'Amen, as my Dad would say. But since we've worked out a better system, why can't we just forget the old one?'

Ashley laughed and clinked bottles with Ed.

Outside the University, the country stepped up its pace in the new, reverse direction. The editor of the newspaper taken over by its workers was reinstalled. A big foreign company locked its workers out. The major political parties signed a revised agreement with the Armed Forces Movement; the Communist Party did not sign, but an allied party did. Otelo was thrown into jail, accused of having incited a far-left coup back in November. Most ominously, a far-right organisation calling itself the 'Portuguese Liberation Army' launched a bombing campaign. Ed soon learned to distinguish, when woken at night by his building shaking, the vibrations caused by a bomb near the city centre from those generated by the earth tremors to which Lisbon was prone, built as it was on the ruins of the city flattened by the great earthquake that Voltaire immortalised in *Candide*.

One evening in March, Ed came home from the University cheered by the news that Otelo had been released from jail with no formal charges against him. He saw Otelo as a man of vision, independence and action, and liked him for it. He imagined him, in other circumstances, as being a dashing entrepreneur, one on whom Ed might well model himself. Ção was spending as much time at her mother's as with Ed, so he did not expect her to be waiting for him when he arrived, much as he hoped she would be.

Ed certainly did not expect the scene of devastation that met his eyes when he let himself into the flat. It had been attacked systematically. Soft furnishings and clothes had been torn apart and used to line floors onto which drawers had been emptied. Documents and papers had been ripped up and added to the heap. What unhidden money he had in the house had been thrown into the toilet bowl but not flushed. On top of a torn pillow on his ransacked marital bed, a picture of Queen Elizabeth II was held in place by twin syringes poked through each of her eyes. The wall behind the bed bore a painted message: *Goodby mister Scripps*.

Ed phoned and left a message with someone at Ção's mother's for his wife to call him at the Cascais flat. Then he took a taxi to the station at Cais do Sodré and caught the last train to Cascais. It was after three a.m. when he let himself into his flat there. Seamus emerged from his room, ensconced in a thick black dressing gown, to see what the noise was.

'Ah, Ed. Can you tip-toe or something? Marjorie is asleep.'

'Marjorie?'

'Yeah, you know. Pale face, long blonde hair, wants to be an actress. You've met her.'

'All right, if you say so. None of my business.'

'You look dead pallid yourself. You seen a ghost or summat?'

'Worse than that. Any whisky in the house?'

'Nah, mate, but there's plenty of firewater.'

'Fancy some?'

They went into the kitchen and shut the door. Ed set out a couple of glasses. Seamus produced a bottle of white liquor and filled them from it.

'Cheers, wack. What's up?'

Keeping his voice low, Ed recounted what had happened to his flat in the city.

'Looks like someone has really got it in for you. Have you stepped on someone's toes recently? Offended anyone?'

'I guess I must have.'

Ed emptied his glass. Seamus gave them both a refill. Ed changed the subject to soccer. Seamus followed Liverpool's other team, Everton, and they had a hushed but animated discussion until the bottle was empty.

It was just before noon when Ed woke. Judging by the silence, he was alone in the house. He found some bread in the kitchen and made himself tea and toast. It helped settle his stomach. His head felt fine and his mind was clear. He called Paulo.

'Looks like the day you warned me about has arrived.'

'Save the details, Ed. I'll be right over. Where are you?'

Before he arrived, Ed showered and put on some clean clothes. He realised that the clothes he kept there were now his only clothes. It was lucky that Ção still had plenty of her own stored at her mother's.

Paulo showed up in a blue Volvo. It looked almost new, though it sported a few scratches.

'Nice motor, partner.'

'I got it cheaply. People are keen to sell. Let's go and see the flat. Give me the details as we drive.'

Paulo's face was grim as he surveyed what had been done in Largo do Andaluz.

'Nothing stolen, nothing smashed. This was personal. I would say it was an attempt to humiliate and frighten both of you.'

'You think Ção could be a target?'

'No, not really. Just a means to get at you.'

'Well, it doesn't humiliate or frighten me. I'm not even a monarchist.

But if anything were to happen to Ção …'

'I think these people are serious, Ed. You're my long-term security, remember, as well as my friend, and I want to keep you alive. I'll find out who did this, and why, though I think it's obvious. Right now, I'll help you to get the lock changed and clean up the place.'

They worked solidly, focusing on the task in hand. A locksmith came and did his job. They painted over the message on the wall. They took down a dozen bags of what was now rubbish. They flushed the toilet. They left the flat looking spartan but clean. Paulo drove Ed back to the flat in Cascais before going on to his family's place in the hills.

Ção phoned him late in the evening. She was quiet as he told her about the break-in but grew hysterical as she realised the extent of her own losses.

'I hate you, Ed Scripps! It's you they were after, and it's me who has to suffer. I trusted you so much! I hate you!' Ed heard the phone bounce out of its cradle. At the second attempt, she cut the connection.

*Bitch!*

Ed was ashamed at thinking it. He would go to her mother's the next day and comfort his wife. He would find ways of making her feel better. He always would.

## 14  ALL RIGHT FOR SOME

Neither Ção nor her mother answered the door when Ed went around, early the next morning, intending to talk to Ção before she went to work. He listened outside the flat door, but he heard no sound within. He walked through the city, hoping that the cool Spring breeze and the morning light would clear his mind of dark thoughts. When he reached the travel agency where Ção worked, she was not at her desk. Nor had she called in sick. Ed recognised one of the secretaries from his celebratory dinner at the Índia Antiga. It seemed a long time ago. He spoke to her.

'Oh, I shouldn't worry if I were you. Ção often does this. She'll probably drop in later, like she usually does. Shall I ask her to phone you?'

Ção's scant regard for office hours was news to Ed. He phoned her father's house, but no-one answered. Ed did not have Mr. Cunha's office number. He left the agency and headed back to Largo do Andaluz. It occurred to him that he should check whether he was being followed. He stopped, started again, doubled back, scrutinised reflections in shop windows, looked carefully at people around him. As far as he could tell, nobody was following him. *Let's not get paranoid.*

His flat was as he had left it. He started to make a list of the things he would have to replace. It was long. Well, he was still rich. *Relatively.*

In the late afternoon, he phoned the agency. Ção answered.

'Don't ask. You know I was with my mother. She needs me so much, much more than you do. She isn't strong like you. What have you got us into, Ed, eh?'

'That's what I'm trying to find out.'

'Well, don't expect me back at Largo do Andaluz until you've turned it into a proper home again. One that we can live in, in peace.'

'Look, my love, we can stay at the flat in Cascais. There's everything we need there.'

'Do me a favour, Ed, just get off my back, will you? I've got enough things to deal with as it is.'

'What? Tell me, Ção, please.'

'You wouldn't begin to understand.'

'OK. When you're ready to tell me, I'm here.'

This time, Ed put the phone down. Gently. So this was what married life was going to be like, after the first year. No, it wasn't! He would talk some sense into her, sooner rather than later.

*

Ed received a quick reminder that he, too, had other things to deal with. Paulo phoned, and then, not wanting to go into details over the phone, came to Largo do Andaluz and straight to the point.

'It's bad news, Ed, I'm afraid. The big boys have noticed us, and they say we're infringing on their territory. They want you out.'

'What, me in particular?'

'Yes, you in particular. They don't take kindly to an English amateur doing what they see as their job. What's worse, in their eyes, is that he's making a success of it.'

'Thanks a million. It's good to be appreciated.'

'So they've warned you, gently, as they say, and they want you to know that their next warning will be more ... *incisive* was the word.'

'They seem to think I scare easily. I don't.'

'After that, they say they'll shop you to their friends in the police.'

'I see you've had a good long chat with these guys, Paulo.'

'Yes, they weren't hard to find. I got the feeling they were expecting me.'

'Your pretty little face looks unmarked to me. How come they weren't *incisive* with you?'

'Cool down, Ed. I warned you that this would happen. I was prepared for it, what do you think? I managed to convince them that my skills and my knowledge were worth more to them than my blood.'

'You did a deal with them?'

'Let's say that their hostile takeover bid was successful. I'm now a manager instead of my own boss. I can live with that, as long as my heart keeps pumping and the money keeps flowing.'

'Bloody hell, Paulo. What about our network?'

'Anyone who wants to can stay in it, for the time being. On probation, as it were. The stakes will be higher, though. As will the rewards.'

Ed stared at him, but the face in front of him betrayed no emotion. This was not Paulo his friend. This was another creature entirely. Ed felt sick.

'How could you?'

'Self-preservation. Like a cypress, I bend in the wind so that I don't break. It's a good strategy, Ed. You should follow it.'

'I think you'd better leave, Paulo. Now.'

'OK, Ed, no problem. By the way, one of their heavies asked me to give you this.'

He took a sealed, unaddressed envelope from a pocket of his light jacket and handed it to Ed. As soon as Paulo left, Ed tore the envelope open. Inside was a key and a sheet of paper. The addresses of Ção's parents and of the travel agency were written on the sheet of paper. The key would have opened his flat door before he changed the lock.

*

On the day that Portugal's Constituent Assembly completed its work and passed the new, democratic Constitution which guaranteed civil liberties and workers' rights, Ed set out on a round of meetings with the people he knew individually in his marijuana distribution network. Three of them formed the layer of the pyramid below him, and each had three others under them. Ed explained that he was bowing out, and why, outlined what he saw as their options, answered their questions, thanked them for their work and wished them well. He got a mixed reception. However, nobody assaulted him physically, and a couple of them expressed relief at having an excuse to concentrate on legitimate business once again. Ed shrugged off the complaints, and felt glad that he had found twelve business people whom he could trust. He might need them, or be able to help them, in the future.

Paulo kept phoning him. If he did not find Ed at Largo do Andaluz, he tried Cascais, and vice versa. He said he could not stand there being bad blood between them, and that he was in no hurry to call in the loans he had made to Ed.

'You're my long-term security, Ed. I mean it: long-term.'

Ed was no longer sure he could trust Paulo, but he needed to hear those words. He had plenty of cash, but a lot less than he owed Paulo, and no income other than the low rent that he charged Seamus and Len. As he devised and discarded schemes which might improve that state of affairs, he put his cash to good use preparing both his flats for Ção's return. It involved a lot of shopping.

Ção was elusive. Neither she nor her mother could be found. He went to the agency; she had stopped coming in. He could not find her at the Law School on evenings when she had classes scheduled. Ed again collared her father when he left his office. Mr. Cunha was less hostile this time, but said he had not seen his daughter for a month and did not know where she was: he had assumed she was with Ed, and expressed concern over her mental state.

'Don't worry too much, young man. I'll find her, if she doesn't find me first. She still needs her Daddy, like any girl would.'

Ed was sprucing up the kitchen one morning, feeling bereft, when Ção phoned out of the blue. He had the windows open to let in the air and the April sunlight. The level of street noise meant that, at first, he did not hear the telephone ringing in the party room. However, Ção insisted.

'Did you see it?'

'Çāo, my love! How are you? Where are you?'

'Never mind. I'm fine. Did you see the programme?'

'What programme? Even your father is worried about you!'

'The quiz!'

'Çāo, my love, you know I don't have time to watch such things.'

'We all watched it together, Ed, you must remember, and then Mark went on it, and he won! He won lots and lots of money! He's even richer than you are now!'

'That isn't difficult, my sweet. My career as a rich man is enjoying a little hiatus. But I'll soon get it back on track, with your help. When can we meet? I need to see you, to touch you.'

'You will see me, Ed darling. Just be patient until we come to the end of this little hiatus.'

She made the sound of a long sloppy kiss and hung up, gently. Ed stared at the receiver, took a deep breath and placed it in its cradle.

*Well, good for Mark. At least someone's happy.*

Ed phoned Mark to congratulate him and arrange a celebratory drink or several. Ed suggested a café near the English Council, so that he could visit the library afterwards, but Mark ruled that out: he had become such a local celebrity that they would not be left in peace. Instead they met in the Café Suiça, in the city centre, where Ed had paid his wager debt to Keith. This time the drinks were on Mark. He was radiant.

'How d'you like my new suit, old chap? I had it made to measure by a super little tailor, just around the corner from here. You should try him.'

'I'm not the suit sort, these days. Anyway, I've already got a couple.'

'You can never have too many suits, you know. Oh, I'm going to buy so many things for Simone, too! She really deserves it!'

'It's a good job you like shopping.'

'When it's for her I do. She was so good when I was out of work after those silly soldiers spoiled my plans!'

'So tell me about your show.' Ed sat back and raised his glass.

'Oh, it was easy really. I have all this useless general knowledge, and at last it came in handy. And I'm not the kind of person who'll freeze under the cameras, or any sort of pressure actually: cool, calm and collected. Well, you know me.' Mark scratched his beard and smirked. Ed nodded and smiled. He was happy to see his friend enjoying life again. 'And then there were the specialist questions. And my topic was ecology.'

'Ecology? What's that when it's at home?'

'The environment and stuff. While you lot have been prancing around with Marx and Mao and Movements, I've been looking at the world's long-term future, if it's got one. Have you read *Silent Spring*? Well, you should. Anyway, I've become quite an expert on environmental issues, though I don't go on and on about it. I dare say I know more than the people who wrote the questions, they were so easy!'

'My, you are a dark horse, Mark. Good for you! What else are you an expert on?'

Mark looked over his spectacles and chuckled.

'What are you going to do with all the dosh, Mark? Have you thought?'

'First of all, I'm going to get you and I drunk on G and T.' Mark signalled to a waiter for two more gin and tonics. They arrived promptly.

'Well, apart from the frivolous stuff, of which there will be plenty, and in which I hereby invite you and your good lady wife to partake, I mean participate, I think I shall take the good advice which I once dispensed to you.'

'That clifftop village?'

'Azenhas do Mar! I'm going to buy up as much of it as I can, and then do something with it. I haven't decided exactly what yet, but it'll be something that makes me even richer. Cheers!'

'Cheers! Here's to you!'

\*

On the evening of his anniversary, Ed came home from the supermarket to find his wife sitting at the top of the stairs outside his flat door. He saw her legs as he turned the corner midway up the final flight. For a second, he thought he was hallucinating. She thrust a bunch of carnations at him.

'For you.'

Hearing her husky voice made him realise she was real. All of her. He took the flowers.

'My key didn't work in the lock. I guess you must've changed it, is that right, Ed?'

Ed put down his groceries, pulled out his own key, opened the flat door and went in. Çāo followed him in. Ed walked into the kitchen, put the flowers on the table and started to put his groceries away.

'Haven't you got anything to say?'

'Plenty. I'm not sure where to start. Why have you come here? Why now?'

'It's our anniversary, silly. Two years of happy marriage.' She slipped her jacket off.

Ed's head began to swim. He sat down. Çāo stepped out of her shoes. She eased her short skirt to the ground, then bent and rolled down her panties. Looking Ed straight in the eyes, she straightened up, unbuttoned her blouse and shed that, too. Without breaking eye contact, she reached behind her and unhooked her bra, then shook her shoulders so that it fell to the floor. She moved to Ed and rubbed her breasts in his face. The aroma of cinnamon filled his nostrils. Ed got to his feet, clasping Çāo and lifting her as he did so. His head cleared, he carried her down the hall, into their bedroom, where the smell of fresh paint battled with Çāo's scent. Ed placed his wife on the new counterpane. She tugged at his belt and unzipped his trousers. While he focused his senses on the feel of her skin below his hands, she thrust her hand beneath his briefs and pulled out his stiff penis. She guided it inside her, crying his name. Ed's orgasm was furious and fast. He stayed inside her for the minutes it took for him to get hard again. Çāo was crying. Her sobs touched his heart, and comforted him. He took his time, and made sure Çāo came before he did. Then he cleaned up, took off all of his clothes, and again made love to his wife, slowly and silently. After each orgasm, he rested inside her until his penis swelled and she asked him to make love to her once more. They drifted into sleep. In the small hours, Ed woke and realised that he was alone.

*

Three days later, Portugal marked the second anniversary of its Revolution by holding a general election. Again, voters were eager and the turnout high. Despite the upheavals, there had been no big shift in people's preferences since the year before, and party representation in the new Parliament was similar to that in the Constituent Assembly, which could now disband. The task of directly electing a President was scheduled for the summer. The Monarchists, like Çāo's Maoists, were among the tiny parties who failed to get anyone into Parliament.

Mark Rotherfield found his flash of celebrity extending beyond its allotted span. Advertisers saw his louche, increasingly dandified appearance, coupled with a few words of posh English, or Portuguese with a heavy accent, as just the job for giving their products a competitive advantage, now that he was associated with success. Commercial offers poured in. Mark used some of the money they generated to bolster his image and have a good time, but he poured a far greater amount towards fulfilling his dream of buying up the village on the cliffs. Although he became surrounded by leeches, he did not forget his few friends. He took Ed to lunch at the Trindade beer hall. They sat below elaborate tiles in praise of trade and industry, replete with Masonic symbols. Mark insisted that they indulge in the fresh seafood. He had shaved off his beard and bought contact lenses. He now looked directly at Ed.

'Ed old chap, you were so good to me when I was broke. Even before then, when I was being a stupid silly snob towards you. No, let me finish. Don't think I've forgotten. Last time, down at the Suiça, I was so full of myself and my win that I forgot to ask about you. Well, I've heard about you since, and I'm really sorry that you've lost your business and then your wife.'

Ed, the vicar's son, was moved to profanity.

'My wife? The fuck I've lost my wife!'

'I'm sorry, that's what I heard.'

'The fuck I've lost my fucking wife! Are you out of your mind?'

'Sorry. Just what I heard.'

'What other fucking shit have you heard?' Ed felt like hitting his friend, but he wanted an answer first.

'Well, that you'd been forced out of the drug business by the Mafia. It doesn't seem terribly clear which Mafia. And that you were in need of remunerated employment, the University being not entirely punctual in paying its employees. Which is where I come in.'

Ed brought his temper under control, so that he could answer with words rather than punches.

'Well, it's common knowledge about the University. But what the hell did you mean about Ção?'

'Never mind Ção, for the time being. I don't know where on Earth she is, or what she's doing, or why. Nice kid, but not my concern or responsibility. Let me tell you my plans, and what I can do for you.'

Ed looked at the spider crab claw in front of him and felt like vomiting. He took a deep breath, blinked, took a swig of the dark beer and looked at Mark.

'OK. Now tell me something I can believe.' He still felt sick.

Mark seemed oblivious to the danger he was in from Ed's temper.

'Look, I've realised there's no way I can buy the whole of Azenhas, but I'm already in the process of buying enough to make my voice the loudest that can be heard in the village. I can decide its future, if I grease enough palms, which I'm happy to do. Spread the love.'

Ed had his breathing under control.

'Sure. I know the scene. Go on.'

'What this country needs is a casino. One for real people and serious

157

gamblers. Not that cardboard replica at Estoril, where poor little rich kids go to look at each other, but a place for serious gamblers. What better than a tailor-made casino in a romantic location, with no distractions, for serious gamblers, even if they're not upper-class prats like me?'

'Whatever turns you on, Mark. What's it got to do with me?'

'Ed, you are the ideal person to run it! You're a business man, you're smooth, you're suave, you're even honest. Especially honest. I'd trust you with my wife; better, with my life. You know languages, you're numerate, down-to-earth. People trust you. You're the best person in the world I could find to run my casino.'

'You're very kind, Mark, but there's one major problem: I don't want to run a fucking casino. Look, I believe people should earn their money, not get it for nothing, and I especially believe they shouldn't be lured into losing the money they've earned in the pursuit of money for nothing.'

'Wow! Mister High And Mighty. Think about it, Ed. Are you really in a position to refuse such a chance?'

'Look, Mark, I wish you well, and every success, in this venture and in whatever you do, but I've had enough of offers I can't refuse. Yes, I am in a position – I'd rather starve.'

'Ed, damn you, I'll see you don't starve.'

Ed relaxed. Mark was on his side. They moved up to the whole-litre measures of beer served in mugs known as 'giraffes'.

*

Ed waited for Ção to re-appear, as she had on the day of their anniversary. Every time he turned the corner on the last flight of steps leading up to his flat, he expected to see her shoes, her ankles, her calves, her soft knees, the smooth skin of her thighs. Each time he was disappointed.

What he did not expect was a phone call from Mr. Cunha. Ção's father sounded sad, hesitant.

'Mr. Scripps, I've been in touch with my daughter. Have you seen her recently, by any chance?'

'Not since April the twenty-second. How is she? Where is she?'

There was a sigh at the other end of the line.

'She is fine. She doesn't want you to know where she is. I'm sorry to be the bearer of bad news, though I imagine you must have calculated already the way things are.'

'No, I haven't. What do you mean?'

Another sigh.

'Mr. Scripps, I cannot tell you where she is, but I can tell you whom she is with.'

'Who she's with? Tell me!'

'This gives me no pleasure. I would rather she had stayed with you. I know you've done your best to be a decent husband to her. Excuse me. Let me come to the point. The name is João.'

*John the Traitor!*

'João? What's the full name? Where does he live?'

'The full name is Maria João Nascimento Arantes. Known as João. I don't know where she lives. Somewhere near Coimbra, I think. Ção is with her.'

The world closed in on Ed. All that was left of it was the receiver in his hand and the words echoing in his head.

'I see. What else can you tell me? Please!'

'I don't have a phone number, I don't have an address. All I can tell you is that the woman is an unmarried mother. She has a small daughter, of whom the father has custody.'

*Ção the Traitor!*

Ed felt numb, but lucid.

'And your own wife, or ex-wife, do you know where she is? She doesn't answer her phone these days.'

'I think she is still in Canada.'

'Canada?!'

'She went to visit relatives of hers there sometime after Christmas.'

'Christmas?! Please, if you hear anything more, tell me.'

'I will.'

'Thank you.'

Ed put the phone down, and sat down. It rang again, and he grabbed it.

'Yes?'

A woman's voice spoke.

'Edward Clement Scripps? This is the Administration Office of the Old University of Lisbon. Kindly report here at three-thirty tomorrow afternoon to sign your contract and swear the oath of loyalty. You will receive your salary, including all back pay, from the end of this month. Bring your passport.'

## 15  What's in a Name?

Ed went to Coimbra for the weekend, hoping to track down his wife. The train journey north took a couple of hours. Warm rain greeted him as he alighted. He surveyed what he could see of his fellow passengers under a sea of umbrellas. No-one he recognised. Then he perused the people waiting to greet the new arrivals. They did include three women with a small daughter each, but all three greeted men, with whom they left the station. Ed headed for the hotel he used for his business trips there, located in the centre of the small city.

Despite its modest size, Coimbra is Portugal's third city, after Lisbon and Oporto. It houses one of Europe's oldest universities, and students form a large and noisy segment of its population. Ed hoped that his wife's lover, and hence Ção too, would have integrated into this community and so might show up in town for one of its many activities that weekend, even though Mr. Cunha's words had suggested that they were indulging in a life of splendid isolation.

After checking in to his hotel and changing into dry clothes, Ed set out for the University. The rain had stopped, the clouds had cleared and the ceramic tiles that graced many of the city's buildings sparkled. It was a Saturday, near the end of the academic year, so the University itself was almost deserted. Ed found himself admiring its medieval architecture as a tourist might. His spirits lifted slightly.

The sun brought the students out into the city streets. Ed did not know where they had sprung from, but he did know they would celebrate term's end very noisily and very publicly, especially those who were graduating. It was very different from Lisbon, where any such festivities tended to be private. Ção had once told him that students in Coimbra were more independent because they were more likely to come from outside the city and to live not with parents but with other students. There was a tradition of declaring shared student flats to be independent republics. According to Ção, some of them even designed their own flags. *Ah, Ção!*

Ed tramped the streets of Coimbra looking for his wife. His gaze fell upon very many beautiful, short, curvy young women, none of whom was her. There was no lack of women alone with small children, but Ed had no idea what João might look like. A more mature version of Ção herself, or completely different? Someone like Lourdes? Like him? Like Ção's father? Her mother?

As the afternoon cooled into the long evening, Ed sat in one of the city's central gardens and examined the passers-by. Since his marriage, he had not really looked at women. Doing so now, he was surprised at the sheer variety of faces, of bodies, of clothes that concealed or emphasised them. The clothes tended to be smart, formal, the make-up heavy. The concept of casual chic was absent here, even among the students. He recalled the time when he had looked at women as potential girlfriends or lovers. Now all he cared about was whether they might metamorphosise into his wife.

When he caught himself shivering, Ed walked back to his hotel, collected a jacket and set out to tour the bars. He favoured those where he could sit outside and keep an eye on the comings and goings. He snacked on sandwiches and local finger food, and stuck to small glasses of beer that would not blur his vision. The students who made up most of the clientele had no such inhibitions. Ed started to feel the weight of his twenty-five years.

When night fell, Ed turned his quest to the *fado* houses. Coimbra claimed to be the true home of *fado*. So did Lisbon and Oporto. Ed was not an aficionado of the music, but tonight its melancholy nostalgia suited his mood. He sunk into it, he sunk into the beer, and he sunk into himself. He had neither sight nor sound nor smell of Ção.

Ed got up early the next morning and strolled down to the river that passed through the city. The River Mondego conditioned Coimbra's air less than the salty estuary of the River Tagus did Lisbon's, and Ed let the light breeze that lifted off it filter through the cobwebs that clogged his mind. By ten o'clock, the day was already hot, but then clouds gathered above the city and sheltered it from the sun. Ed paused twice to consume pastries and coffee, but continued to examine every female form for signs of Ção. A twinge in his left leg, the one whose slight shortness made him limp, reminded him that he was out of condition now that he no longer frequented the rowing club or engaged in the physical activity of sex.

*This is ridiculous. She's not here, and she's not going to miraculously appear like Our Lady of Fátima!*

Ed continued to search, but decided to do so at a couple of tourist sites: the Carmo church and the Celas convent. The contrast with his father's spartan parish church disturbed him. He wondered when he had stopped believing that gods could be found in buildings, and could not remember the moment. Outside the convent, he looked down at the narrow streets as they tumbled toward the river.

*What can I sacrifice to the god of love to bring my wife home?*

He did not expect an answer, but the next young woman he scrutinised smiled at him.

At lunchtime, the streets emptied. Ed found a small restaurant and dined on trout. The local white wine, full and mellow, helped him reflect on the futility of his quest. When he tired of his own dark thoughts, he moved to a city centre café for a small, strong coffee among a crowd of voluble patrons, and then out to the city's botanical garden, where he sat and watched it fill with families and couples. They were having a good time, but he was not. He was tired and lonely. He even missed Lisbon. When the day's first drops of rain fell, he hastened back to his hotel, checked out a day earlier than he had intended, and caught the first train back home. He stared at his reflection in the compartment window and asked himself what was wrong with him, what had frightened his wife away. Then he watched the countryside pass by: so green in the Spring, so fertile.

When the train pulled in at Lisbon, Ed staggered out of the carriage. He felt that he had abandoned a piece of himself in Coimbra, leaving him no longer whole. At the station bar, he surprised the barman by asking for a dark beer at room temperature. Fortunately, they had one. While he swigged it, he phoned Mark. Simone answered. Hearing his tone of voice, she invited him to come up to their place and have a bite to eat. Ed lurched out of the station and got into a taxi.

He was relieved to be with friends again, though their smiles faded when they saw him.

'You look like you've seen a ghost, old chap. Something the matter?'

'I *feel* like a bloody ghost. Form, no substance. Nothing inside. I left my heart, I don't know where. Must be somewhere.'

'Anyway, come in and have a drink.'

'I think Ed could use some food. I'll rustle up a couple of quick sandwiches and get cooking. Fancy something French?'

Ed did. They sat in the kitchen while Simone cooked. Mark made culinary suggestions that she ignored. Ed poured his heart out and replaced it with beer while Simone and Mark shared gin and tonics. Mark made wife-hunting suggestions that Ed ignored. They let Ed ramble on, though he became less and less lucid. When Simone served the food, Ed shut up and concentrated on that. Simone was pleased to see him enjoying it. She started to tell him about progress on their plans for Azenhas do Mar. She and Mark became animated with their enthusiasm. Ed kept nodding and prompted them with a 'Delicious!' whenever they paused. He finished his plate, emptied his bottle of beer and passed out.

The next morning, Ed felt fine. He woke up on top of the bed in Mark and Simone's spare room, fully clothed but minus his shoes. They had been placed in a corner, next to his grip. *Someone's been looking after me*, he thought.

Ed found himself singing as he freshened up in the bathroom. He changed into some cleaner clothes that he dug out of his grip, and ambled into the kitchen. Mark was there, washing dishes. He smiled when Ed came in.

'You look better than I feel, Ed. Start the morning well and take a look at those photos on the table. Tea or coffee?'

The kitchen table was laden with photos of whitewashed houses in Azenhas do Mar. Next to them were estate agents' brochures and some leaflets emblazoned with the word *PANGAIA*.

'Coffee, please. I'll make it. May I?'

'Be my guest. Same for me.'

'Fancy a run this morning? It is still morning, isn't it?'

'Barely half past ten. You know, I don't mind if I do. As long as we're not in a hurry.'

Mark finished the dishes. Ed dried. They drank their coffee.

'Beautiful photos, eh? Just imagine owning all these and turning them into a gambler's paradise!'

'Not my cup of tea, as you know, but I'm sure you two can make it work. Where's Pangaia? I've never heard of it.'

'It isn't a place, old bean, it's a movement. A jolly interesting one, actually. It can teach us how to live in harmony with everything on this Earth. Here, grab yourself a leaflet. Someone I did the show with put me on to them. I'm really glad she did.'

Ed folded the leaflet and put it in his back pocket. They set out. The morning was hot and dusty, the traffic snarly, drivers incredulous when they saw them running. They reached Praça da Alegria, where Mark had a sneezing fit and called a halt.

'Bloody hay fever! Do you ever get it?'

'Never. Let's sit down.'

'Lucky you.'

They sat on a bench in the garden in the middle of the square, underneath a banyan tree brought over from the colonies. Ed was feeling even better for the exercise.

'Fabulous day, isn't it?'

'A lot better than yesterday, judging by the way you look.'

'Funny how one's mood can change, don't you think?'

'Listen, Ed, Simone is going to ask about Ção and that João among her contacts at the School, in the French community, wherever. Someone must've heard something.'

'*I've* heard something. I just need to know where to find her, then I'll go and bring her back. I know that's what she wants me to do. It stands to reason. Shall we get running?'

'No. I've got to get back indoors, where I won't have to sneeze so much. Let's just stroll back to my place. You've left your grip there, I think. Come on.'

Once Ed was reunited with his holdall, Mark bade him farewell.

'Remember old boy, any time you're short of cash, I've got some for you. Like right now, for instance, have you got some?'

Ed checked his wallet. 'Erm, actually, next to nothing. I can call in at the bank.'

'Don't waste your day in queues.' Mark pressed a wad of escudo notes into Ed's palm. 'Think of me as a time-saving machine bank.'

'Thanks, mate. You know what, that gives me an idea. What if banks used machines instead of cashiers? A machine in the street would take your fingerprints, you'd type in your account number, and if the two matched, the machine would give you some cash. How about that?'

'Then you'd queue up in front of a machine instead of a person. Not a big improvement, I venture to say.'

'Yeah, I see what you mean. But the machines could maybe turn on after the banks close. Anyway, thanks again, pal. Be seeing you.'

Ed soon shed his jacket as he walked home across the city, which had wound down for lunch. Ed himself stopped at a snack bar for a local-style burger – a thin sliver of beef and a fried egg filled the bun. He drank cold fizzy mineral water with it.

At home, he decided to turn his attention to his own students. Those in Coimbra had reminded him that the end of the academic year was imminent at Lisbon University, too, bringing with it the annual assessment ritual, and Ed wanted to be very well prepared for that this year. The teaching had been easier. For one thing, student numbers had stabilised. Although Ed's evening classes were always packed, they now had specific rooms assigned to them, and as often as not these were free of squatters. Moreover, not all the blackboards were damaged beyond use.

At first, Ed had mentally divided his fellow teachers into two groups: those who wanted to change the academic system and the education it offered for the better, and those who wanted to turn it back into a rigid structure geared towards preserving the status quo. Naturally, he placed himself in the first group. Now he saw that the divisions were not so simple. The progressive camp included both independent thinkers and people who were following party doctrine, which changed faster than the seasons, whatever the party. The reactionary camp was starting to find its voice again, and it was flanked by a group of people who felt that tradition had given them a right to command, no matter the underlying ideology. Then there was a large group of people following Paulo's advice and bending in whatever wind rose so as to conserve their job and salary. Ed could imagine himself joining them, once he started receiving a salary: as long as he could teach, he could help his students. He talked these things over with Rupert, Carolina and Ashley when they met in the University café. Ashley was a hardline progressive, though a law unto himself; Rupert liked to have good rules that people could understand, endorse and stick to; Carolina just wanted to keep her job and be liked. That was how Ed saw them, though he tried not to judge them: they were first and foremost his friends.

He found them all together in the café the evening he completed his assessments.

'Same bloody story!' He sat himself at their table, still clutching his pile of forms.

Ashley passed him a full but uncapped bottle of cold beer. 'I saw you coming.'

Ed swigged from it. 'Ace, man! Thanks. I needed that!'

'What's the story?'

'You spend the whole year meticulously grading every assignment you give them, oral or written, you propose grades based on all that, you present it to them in as much detail as there is –'

'And still it's a free-for-all, isn't it?'

Ed was quick to answer Carolina's question.

'Not in my classes. Really. They're happy enough with the grades I give them. They see the logic. They just won't let me fail anyone. At least, no-one who's present.'

'Why would you want to?'

Ed turned to Ashley. 'Personally, I think it's my duty to the Portuguese state, which will shortly be paying my salary, I hope. You know, not to let university degrees go to people who don't deserve them.'

'It's my duty to make them deserve them,' said Carolina, 'so I don't fail anyone.'

'Did you say you were going to get paid?' Rupert asked.

'That's right. End of the month. It's only been two years or so.'

'Gosh, you poor wee thing!' Carolina looked distraught.

'I'll get you another drink. Remember me next month. Same again, everyone?' Ashley took his portly frame to the till.

Ed ran into Carolina in the administration block the next day. They were both handing in their student records. She looked good in a loose-fitting cheesecloth blouse, a silk scarf caressing her neck and inching down her back to meet the top of a colourful ankle-length skirt. Her long red hair was lustrous, and her face was more relaxed than when he saw her at work, but she tightened it briefly.

'It's a disgrace that they haven't paid you all this time. How have you managed to survive?'

'I'm not sure. As much by luck as judgement, I'll readily admit.'

Carolina turned to the clerk who was examining her papers. 'Is it true that you're going to pay this fella at last?'

The clerk smiled.

'We certainly are, at the end of this very month. We're really looking forward to it.'

Carolina turned to Ed.

'Seems you're famous.'

They left the administration block together, emerging from musty coolness into searing heat.

'Are you on foot? I've got the car.'

She drove skilfully and parked below Ed's flat.

'Can you cook?'

'Only when I have no alternative.'

'Even a hopeless wee Sassenach can make coffee, though. Have you got some milk in the house?' Milk was often in short supply in the city.

'Sure. Come on up.'

Ed was glad of the company, and glad that Carolina was a married woman who would never put herself into a compromising position. He made coffee for them and she drank it without comment. Then Carolina asked Ed to show her around the flat. She looked curiously at each room and nodded noncommittally. In the bathroom, she said:

'It's awful hot today. Do you think I could have a quick shower?'

'OK.' He showed her how to get hot water, backed out of the room and closed the door. He was relieved to hear Carolina turn the key in the lock. Ed went to what was now the study and set out his Open University textbooks for some studying of his own. He was delving into Durkheim when he heard his name called. He went to the bathroom and stopped outside.

'Ed, could I have a towel, please. You know, a clean one.'

'Sure, I'll fetch you one right away.' He padded down the corridor and into the spare bedroom where he – they – kept the towels. The towels were all new. He thought a green one would suit her: it would match her eyes. He turned and found himself looking into them. Then at the rest of her, standing in front of him, dripping water onto the floor, with only the scarf around her neck to absorb it. She was slim, less curvy than Ção, perhaps better proportioned. A feeling in his loins told him he appreciated the sight, and he sent words after it.

'By God, you're beautiful!'

169

'You're easy on the eye yourself, Mr. Scripps.' She flipped her scarf over Ed's neck and used it to draw him to her. The feel of her lips and the taste of her tongue sent Ed's mind reeling. He broke off the kiss.

'We shouldn't do this.'

'Do it!'

She took the towel that Ed still had in one hand, spread it on the spare bed and lay on her back on top of it, splaying her legs. Ed could not take his eyes off her.

'Come on Ed. What are you waiting for?'

Ed's mind fought his body, and his body won. He pulled off his clothes and approached the bed, trying to control his breathing.

'Carolina …'

'It's all right, Ed. Honestly.'

'No, I mean, I don't have any condoms.'

'With me, you don't need them. I'm on the Pill.'

The wetness of her body excited Ed even more, but he took pains to bring her level of arousal up towards his own before he entered her. Her vagina was not as tight around him as was Çáo's, but she exercised more control over her internal muscles. She was noisier. As Ed brought her towards orgasm, she shouted words in a foreign language. He could make out something like *Razguarman* and assumed it was her husband's first name. His performance anxiety was smoothed when she came before he did.

Soon afterwards, Carolina eased herself from below Ed and off the bed. She picked up the green towel.

'Now that I can dry myself, I'll take another shower.'

She draped the towel around her pale body. It did suit her. At the door, she turned to Ed.

'That's it. You can get dressed now.'

Ed did so, then waited outside the bathroom door. Carolina emerged fully clothed.

'What was that all about, Carolina, Mrs. Isfahan?'

'I just thought you needed cheering up a little. And indeed you do look more sprightly already. Mission accomplished, I'd say. Now, excuse me, I have to get home. Oh, and thanks, Ed, that was good for me, too.'

He accompanied her down to her car. Carolina gave him a smile full of warmth and complicity, then got in and drove away. Ed felt dazed, but warm too. It was as though a door in a wall had opened on to an enchanting garden. He had long known the door was there, but he had stopped seeing it.

At the end of the month, Ed went to the University to collect his pay. He had already signed the pre-payment form, so he knew the money was there. He had considered splashing as much of it as he could on a blow-out for his friends, but not even the thought of two years' back pay could put him in a mood for celebration. He went in the morning, so that he would have time to put the money into his account during bank hours.

'Good morning, Jaime, what are you looking so glum about? It's my big day. You know you've been longing to pay me, ever since I first set foot in your august office.'

'I have, Professor, I have. And I would love to pay you today.' Ed could swear he saw tears in his eyes.

'What's up? You've spent my money on custard and tarts, I mean custard tarts?'

'We've done something terrible, Professor, I'm so sorry. It's like this: we've paid your money to someone else.'

'Very funny, Jaime. Now just give me my cash. Please.'

'No, look, here.' The clerk pointed regretfully at a form with a long list of names. 'It happened yesterday, while I was away at a seminar. The woman who stood in for me isn't familiar with foreign names, and she gave your money to this colleague from another department.'

He pointed to a line where Ed's name was typed, with an enormous sum in escudos set next to it. Ed deciphered the signature of the person who had received the money: Maria Pia Antunes da Silva Clemente.

'Clemente,' said Jaime, 'my colleague said she paid the money to someone with the same name as you.'

171

'You're joking, aren't you, Jaime? It isn't funny, but you are joking, aren't you? Jaime?'

The clerk averted his eyes and shook his head.

'I swear on my mother's grave that we'll pay you next month.'

'No, don't do that. I'm sorry about your mother.'

'Look, I'm so sorry. I feel terrible about his. If you're broke, Professor, I can lend you some money to tide you over for another month, I think.'

'Thank you, Jaime. One more month won't kill me. I have other sources. I'll survive.'

Ed wondered briefly how he would survive, then curiosity overcame bitterness.

'By the way, Jaime, what was the seminar on?'

'Advanced Public Relations in the Modern University Context.'

Ed had enough loose change with him to pay for a taxi to the English Council. He found Mark between classes, surrounded by a group of students hanging on his every word. Ed signalled urgently to him. Mark excused himself and came over.

'Hello, old fruit. Something wrong? You look agitated.'

'Mark, I need to speak to you urgently. Have you got time?'

'Not right now. I'm about to go into class. If you could possibly stick around for an hour or so, I'll take you to lunch and we can chat all afternoon, if that suits you.'

'Yes, fine. Sure. I'll be in the library.'

Mark took him to a chic new restaurant that specialised in vegetarian food. Ed explained his predicament and asked Mark to lend him a month's salary.

'Oh, sure, no problem. I'm pleased I can do something for you. Actually, we'd better make that two months' whack, just to be on the safe side. I can give you the cash this time tomorrow, if that's all right. Why don't you come over for lunch? Simone'll be at home, and I'm sure she'll be happy to put something together for us. As long as you don't want to eat murdered animals.'

'Er, no. I'm quite happy with vegetarian food. How long have you been – ?'

'Ever since I joined Pangaia. I wish Simone would, too. She hasn't joined yet, even though she admits it makes total sense. Well, it's obvious, isn't it? We've only got one world, haven't we? So we've got to look after it, right?'

'Of course.'

'Omomnos says we're like a spaceship hurtling through the void. If we break the windows, we're done for.'

'Quite. But Omomnos?'

'He's our marvellous, magical guru. The person the world needs as captain of the spaceship. You should meet him, face to face, if you can. Did you read that pamphlet I gave you?'

'Er, not yet. I've been preoccupied with mundane stuff, as you know.'

'Do read it, Ed. Pangaia can change your life, and very much for the better. I was lost before I joined, I tell you, lost.'

When Ed got home, he rummaged around for the Pangaia pamphlet. He found it in the back pocket of a pair of trousers he had put aside to wash. It did not say much, just a few phrases about saving the Earth and finding inner peace, but inside was a glossy picture of its leader. Beneath his bushy beard, the handsome features and brilliant smile of Omomnos reminded Ed of someone, though he could not recall whom.

That night, as he lay in bed, trying not to think of Carolina and to think of Ção instead, he forced himself to recall the night he and his wife had met. It had been at his birthday party: November 1st, 1973. Ção had come with people from the Sussex School. *Eureka!* Ed threw off the sheet and limped into the study, where he had left Mark's pamphlet. He brought it to the light, opened it and scrutinised the face of Omomnos. Yes! It was the man whom the police had removed from his party by force, the man they had known back then as Jorge.

## 16 WHERE THE GRASS IS GREENER

On the last Sunday in June, Portugal went to the polls to elect a President, the first time its people were able to do so freely. Over three quarters of the electorate cast a vote, and a clear winner emerged: the Army chief, General Ramalho Eanes, who stood as an independent. Eanes had organised the previous November's coup or counter-coup, depending on your political standpoint, and the fact that it had not led to civil war stood him in good stead at the polls. His military and now political rival, Otelo, came a distant second, ahead of Prime Minister Pinheiro de Azevedo and the Communist Party's candidate, Octávio Pato. There were celebrations in Lisbon, but they were not wild. Ed knew that Ção and her Maoist friends would be pleased at the defeat of their leftist rivals, even by an Army man, but he did not think she would be overjoyed to the point of coming to the capital to celebrate in the street, so he stayed at home. He, too, was pleased, though more at the event than its outcome. He saw both event and outcome as helping Portugal become a normal democracy open for business, open to people like the person he had been when he first arrived.

Ed and most of his fellow language teachers at the University were concerned about what the normalisation might entail for higher education. Would working students be excluded? Would the old hierarchies be re-imposed? Would public funds be slashed to boost private education? With the academic year over, they were not in a position to organise resistance or put forward alternatives.

The University's bureaucrats did not enjoy the same lengthy holidays as its teachers, and they again called Ed to receive his first salary. This

175

time, he went with low expectations, but Jaime greeted him with a smile as bright as the morning sun.

'Professor! Here is every last escudo that the University owes you! Please sign for it and take the cheque straight to the bank. If they query the amount, or if someone steals it, ring me here and I will sort them out.'

Ed signed for the cheque, took it from Jaime's hand, folded it and slipped it into his shirt pocket.

'Well, seeing is believing. Thank you, Jaime, for this.'

The warmth in Jaime's smile intensified. He shook Ed's hand with vigour.

'Many people promise, Jaime delivers!' he said, adapting one of the new President's election slogans.

Ed was still not in the mood for festivities, but he wanted to show his gratitude to Mark and Simone, so he invited them out for a meal, together with Len and Seamus, now gladly relegated to being his secondary source of a reliable, legal income. They sat on the terrace of a seafront beer house in Cascais, overlooking the bay in the long, post-equinox evening, dining, at Ed's expense, on fresh fish and the house lager. Mark soon removed his tie, which was a different shade of green from his shirt, which was lighter in tone than his suit. He noticed the others staring at his clothes.

'I haven't been able to match them yet. I've only been wearing the green for a few days.'

Seamus looked at him quizzically. 'What, becoming Irish, are you? Nobody will believe it as soon as you open your mouth.'

'Oh, no, it's not that at all, not that I've got anything against the Irish – lovely people, I'm sure. No, it's a physical manifestation of my adherence to Pangaia.'

'Pan who?'

'Pangaia. It's this marvellous movement that's lighting up the world. It's based here in Portugal, and I'm a member.'

'OK, I see, but why all the greenery?'

'It symbolises our dedication to the Earth.'

'The earth is dirty brown in my part of Liverpool, what little there is of it, I'll tell you that for nowt.'

'Didn't Ziggy Stardust say it was blue? The Earth, that is.'

'Thanks, Len. Maybe one of the real astronauts, or cosmonauts perhaps. No, come on, chaps, green for our environment, the life force of Nature!'

There was a silence, in which Ed looked at Simone. She was wearing a green blouse, but her skirt, choker and handbag were all black. Seamus coughed.

'Well, Mark, er, tell us more, would you?'

Mark did not waste a second. He repeated what he had already told Ed, and explained how the followers were divided among those who lived together in the community in the countryside, some way outside Lisbon, and those like himself who followed from a distance. All of them, however, were required to till the land, and his most urgent project was now to buy some land where he could do just that.

'What about the casino project?'

'You know, Ed old chap, I'm going to have to reconsider that. Maybe you were right about the ethics of it being a bit dubious.'

Ed noticed that Simone was looking uneasy.

*Good thing I didn't take up his job offer.*

Mark was in full flow. He moved on to praising his leader, the guru Omomnos. Seamus looked as though he could not believe he was hearing such things from worldly-wise Mark. Len wiped a cynical smirk from his own face. Simone looked embarrassed. Ed tried to get a word in, but Mark stopped for no-one. Ed pulled out the Pangaia leaflet that Mark had given him. He placed it on the table in front of everybody, with the image of Omomnos uppermost.

'Now, who does Omomnos remind you of? Shave off the beard and a couple of years and you have our old friend ...'

'My God! So that's what he's been up to!'

'Bugger me! It's disappearing Jorge!'

'Who?' Simone did not recognise the face.

'Jorge. Used to hang around your School. Boyfriend of Anne the English teacher. The secret police carted him off from my birthday party in '73. Hadn't been seen since. Missing presumed dead or imprisoned. I think we should tell Anne.'

'Oh, Anne left. But we can get a message to her, I expect, and set her mind at rest.'

Mark was unfazed.

'Well, whatever he's done in the past, he's more than made up for since. His message is lighting up our troubled and threatened word, and I wish all of you would listen to it very clearly.'

For once, Len butted in. 'He certainly had the gift of the gab, old Jorge, but he was a lousy lay.'

Seamus looked interested. 'Is that what Anne said, or are you talking from your own experience?'

'Both.'

Simone's hand tightened on her glass. Slowly, she raised it.

'Here's to revolutions and transformations. In Portugal they tend to be for the better.'

They all drank to that.

When Ed next went to Cascais, it was to collect the rent from Seamus and Len. He brought them over a couple of sacks of top-quality charcoal that he had got from a former business connection. He knew that the two English Council teachers were busier than him and would have little time to go hunting for it.

'Just remember to invite me to your next back-garden barbecue.' In truth, it was a concrete patio, not a garden, but Ed had installed a barbecue pit for them.

Len handed over something more than the rent: a slip of paper with the name *Maria João* and an address.

'If she's who you're looking for, that's the place to go. It's near Coimbra.'

'Man, how – ?'

'I asked around. In clubs and stuff.'

'Len, you're great! You don't know how much this means to me.'

He enfolded Len in a bear hug.

'Hey, don't crush my bones. I might need them.'

'Thanks, Len. Now I can get my wife back.'

The following morning, Ed hired a car and set out for Coimbra. The road surface was not in great condition for a major trunk road, but the traffic was light and he made good enough time to allow himself to stop twice to slake his thirst in roadside cafés. He intended to arrive at lunchtime, when he reckoned João and Çāo were most likely to be at home. Because their place was near the Roman ruins of Conimbriga, south of Coimbra, the road signs were quite helpful, and Ed pulled in to his destination not long after one o'clock. The address was that of an old farmhouse set back from the road. Ed parked the car in the shade of trees and walked up to the building. Two dogs tied on leashes greeted his arrival vociferously, and a woman emerged from the front door to see what was going on. It was not Çāo.

The woman shushed the dogs as Ed approached. She shielded her eyes against the sun to see him better. She herself was tall and slim, her light brown hair thick and curly. Ed thought her over-dressed for the season in a work shirt and denim overalls. Was this Çāo's lover or her gardener?

'Good afternoon. Are you Maria João?'

'I'm João, yes, Ed. I guess you've come looking for your ex-wife.'

'My wife.'

'Your ex-wife isn't here.'

'What about my wife?'

'Çāo isn't here. She lives here, with me, but she isn't here at the moment.'

'Will you kindly ask her to come to the door and speak to me?'

'I told you, she isn't here at the moment.'

'I don't mind waiting. She'll come out of her own accord in the end.'

'Look, how many times do I have to tell you?' The woman sighed and continued. 'Do you want to go in and have a good snoop around? Look under the bed, perhaps. Go ahead, but you won't find her.'

Ed moved to enter the house. The woman blocked his way. Ed thought of knocking her aside, but controlled the impulse.

'No, on second thoughts, you're not coming into our house. She wouldn't want that.' João's expression softened. 'She'll be back tonight or tomorrow. You can lie in wait for her, but she won't want to speak to you, I know. If you leave me – leave us in peace, I'll ask her to contact you. Soon.'

Ed weighed up his options, and decided that violence, however enticing, was a bad one.

'I'll thank you to do that.' He turned and left João staring after him. The dogs protested his leaving. He got into the car and drove to Conimbriga. When he had been in the area in the past, he had lacked either the time or the transport needed to visit the Roman ruins. Despite the neglect, they were heavy in atmosphere. He spent the afternoon there dwelling on the past, then the evening driving back to Lisbon, dwelling on the future.

A week later, a letter arrived, addressed in Ção's hand and postmarked the day after his visit. Ed opened it carefully. It was indeed from his wife. It was short.

*Ed, don't be angry with me. I know I've been a naughty girl and a bad wife, but please try and understand why. There is only one reason I left you, and that is love, my love for João and her love for me. It's overwhelming. The rest is just the icing on the cake, the feeling of freedom, finding out who I really am, and just being myself instead of a figment of other people's imaginations. I did love you, Ed, once, in my way, but this love with João is the strongest emotion I've ever felt in my whole life. If anything, it's getting stronger by the day. I hope we can be friends, you and I, after the divorce. Until then, try not to hate João, she's a good person and she means the whole world to me. Kisses from your little Miss Conception xxxxx*

The three letters of her signature below the kisses sliced through Ed's heart strings.

*I know you loved me, and I know you still do.*

He sat down and read her words again.

'If anything' – *so you're not even sure.*

'Divorce'? *Over my dead body!*

*No, I don't hate John the Traitor – she's a nobody who means nothing to me. Once you realise the difference between infatuation and real love, I'll have you back with me in no time.*

Ed did not scrawl an immediate reply. The lines of communication were open once again, and he could await wiser counsel from his brain once it cooled. What he did instead was to phone Çāo's father, paint an unflattering portrait of Maria João and give him his daughter's address. Over the next few days, he did the same with as many of his and Çāo's mutual friends as had not left the city for the summer. He also put the information into a letter that he posted to Çāo's mother at her Lisbon address, with a request to 'please forward'. Some among those people, surely, would talk some sense into his wife.

Len and Seamus held their barbecue on a sweltering evening in July. It was the first large social gathering unconnected with business that Ed had attended on his own for over a year. He showed up early and helped his tenants get things ready. They had plenty of helpers as it was. Ed felt like part of the furniture, and that suited him. The house and the garden soon filled: Len and Seamus knew a lot of people. Ed recognised and greeted several of their colleagues from the English Council, and he supposed that many of the younger guests were students of theirs. He put himself in charge of the barbecue, easing his throat with cold white wine as the heat of the embers fought with that of the falling night and the smell of grilled sardines and chicken snuffed out the scent of the neighbours' citrus trees. Strategically placed, he spoke to everyone who came over for grilled food, and as his tongue loosened, his spirits rose. When he heard the sound of Genesis coming from inside, he could not resist the urge to go in and dance.

An hour later, Ed staggered into the kitchen and took a bottle of chilled wine from the fridge. He looked out into the garden, where Len was competing with the music from inside by strumming through Simon and Garfunkel's back catalogue on his acoustic guitar, to an appreciative audience. His colleague Xavier came in from the garden.

'Ed! Long time no see. Give us a drop of that wine, will you?'

'Xavier, old friend, for you, anything.' Ed found a clean plastic cup, filled it and handed it to Xavier. They started chatting about the University, and their colleagues. Something came to Ed's mind.

'Here, Xavier, you know our Carolina. What's her husband's first name?'

'Firouz, I think. Why don't you ask her? She's out in the garden.'

Ed looked out and saw her immediately. She was alone. The thought of sitting under the stars talking to a charming, lightly dressed redhead appealed to him enormously.

'Yes, I think I will. See you later, Xav.' He took out the bottle and another clean cup, worked his way around the audience and sat on the ground next to Carolina.

'I've brought some balm for that lovely tongue of yours.'

She looked down at him without surprise.

'I've been waiting for you. No more wine thanks, I'm driving.'

'What brings you here all on your own?'

'I've come to give you a lift back to Lisbon.'

'Actually, I'm staying here tonight. I still have a room here.'

'Well, my husband's away, and I have a couple of hours before I need to relieve the babysitter.'

'Let's waste no more time.'

'The car's around the corner in Avenida Navarro. You know it? It's a little way down on the left. Wait five minutes after I've left, then join me.' She went inside to say goodbye to Seamus, waving to Len as she passed.

She would not let Ed touch her in the car, in case they were seen by other people leaving the party, or even arriving for it. But when they parked in Largo do Andaluz, she was all over him. As they climbed the stairs, Ed, for the first time, hoped not to find Ção waiting outside the door for him.

The passion with which Carolina made love to him surprised Ed. Çāo, too, was passionate, but she moved to her own rhythm, whereas Carolina threw herself into his. The warm breeze that blew in from the open window cooled neither their perspiration nor their ardour. Ed was licking Carolina's neck in post-coital languor when a doorbell rang. The sound came from below. Çāo still had the key to the street door. Ed stayed focused on Carolina. The bell rang again.

'Aren't you going to answer that?'

'No. Can you stay a while longer?'

'Yes. As long as you don't bite me or leave any visible marks anywhere else on my body. I get enough of those from Firouz.'

Ed made love to her as gently as he knew how.

After Carolina had left, the phone rang. *That could be Çāo.* Ed answered immediately.

'Hello, Ed? This is Sônia. We met at Len's party, remember? You gave me your number.'

Sônia? Sônia? Sônia! 'Yes.' A lithe brunette, with a lovely voice. Ed had been transfixed by her shapely legs as they danced.

'Ed, are you busy? Can I come over?'

'Yeah, I'm kind of busy right now.' *Not to mention exhausted.* 'But if you're free tomorrow evening, give me a call. Maybe we could –'

He heard the receiver slam into its cradle.

'Lovely talking to you, Sônia.'

On the Sunday evening, Ed was polishing off an Open University assignment when the phone rang. He hoped for Çāo, suspected Sônia, yet answered to the voice of Simone babbling in colloquial French.

'Calm down, Simone. Take it easy. What's going on? Are you all right?'

'No! It's Mark! I can't bear it!'

'Simone, calm down. Take a deep breath and tell me what's happened.'

'Mark … he's gone!'

'Gone where?'

'It's too horrible! Mark, my Mark, he's gone to live in the Pangaia community.'

'What!? He must be crazy! Why on earth would he do a stupid thing like that?'

'He says it's a spiritual thing, getting closer to the heart of the matter. Oh, it's too horrible!'

'Sounds like mumbo-jumbo to me, frankly, that Pangaia stuff.'

'It is, Ed, it is, but he believes it. It was all he talked about. Didn't you notice? And now that 'Omomnos' has got to him.'

'Jorge? He always had a way with people, damn him.'

'And now he's taken over my husband's brain. He makes them believe some awful things.'

'Love the Earth doesn't sound so bad.'

'No? Well, what about this: they're not supposed to love each other, because human beings are bad, so Omomnos tells them. But they are supposed to screw each other, to show their disdain for human flesh or something.'

'And I expect the guru takes the lead in that. It's standard practice.'

'But it's my husband! He can't have my husband!'

'You're right, Simone, he can't. Look, everyone knows that Mark is a one-woman guy, just like I am – like I was when I was married, I mean when Çāo was living with me.'

There was only sobbing at the other end.

'Simone, look, first thing, try not to worry too much. We have to think straight. You must have lawyers from your Azenhas business, right? Get on to them. They'll have ideas about what to do. Stay positive. You're not going to lose Mark.'

*One more person for me to rescue from themselves.*

184

## 17 REVELATIONS

Ed was desperately worried for his friend, but he had already booked a flight and his place at the Open University's Camden residence, where he hoped to learn an enormous amount at the summer school, breeze through his courses with flying colours and then wrap up his degree in double-quick time. Ed had a plan for that, and he had a plan for Ção, but he did not yet have a plan for rescuing Mark. Although he was tempted to stay in Lisbon, devise an ad-hoc scheme and put it into practice straight away, Ed decided that distance, time and fresh perspectives would help him both to avoid the risk of making the situation worse in the short term and to devise a better strategy to act upon when he did return. Besides, he fancied another taste of his homeland. He packed and flew to England.

Ed was happy to see his parents again, to shed a little of the responsibility for ordering his own life, a responsibility he had sought with eagerness and determination since he had hit adolescence, or that of others around him. Stevenage was as bland as ever, but its very blandness relieved him: a place that was impervious to change and progress, and immune from disaster, was useful to have as a fall-back, or even as a temporary respite from a world where the stakes were higher. The rain fell more slowly here, and was colder. He and his father walked under it to the local pub, the We Three Loggerheads, on the evening Ed returned.

The landlord's eyes rose when they walked in. He quickly lowered them, and turned his face first blank, then affable.

'Evening, Reverend. Lad looks like your son Ed.'

'It *is* me, Dick, you twerp. Now pull us two pints of proper bitter, none of your keg rubbish.'

'I think I'd best stick to water. Don't want my parishioners gossiping.'

'They'll gossip anyway. The first round is on the house, Reverend.'

'Like the lad said, Dick, two pints of proper bitter. There's free wine waiting for you every Sunday in St. Catherine's.'

'I hear you're a bit stingy with it, though.'

'At that time in the morning, I have to think of the health of my flock. Ah, thank you, Dick. Your health!'

They took their beer and sat in an alcove by a leaded window through which they could watch the rain fade the remaining colours in the street outside. The beer tasted of malt and hops, and it warmed them. For once, Ed told his father the troubles that were weighing on his heart, and for once he was ready to absorb his father's advice.

'I don't have any easy answers for you, Ed. I have to churn out pat solutions for my parishioners, because that's what they expect and want. But for my family, no. If you do my job, even in a quiet place like Stevenage, you pretty soon realise that things rarely work out the way people plan. Things are nearly always more complex and more complicated than they seem. Not to mention people. I'd just ask you, not advise you, just ask you, not to give up on your wife.'

'Don't worry, Dad, I'll never give up on Ção.'

When Ed bought up the subject of Mark, his father was more forthcoming.

'It's an occupational hazard of mine, coming into contact with cults and sects. England's full of them, as you probably remember. They aren't always entirely bad, but they are always rivals to the Church of England, so we take them very seriously.'

'Dad, my friend's wife is desperate. Even if this Pangaia is not entirely bad, she doesn't want to lose him to it. He's already left their home to live with the sect.'

'Well, you need to get your friend back in his own home before they brainwash him. If they haven't already done so.'

'They've started. How *can* we get him back, though? That's the question.'

'Well, the cults that I've known generally share two features that make them strong: greed and secrecy. The greed – for power or money, usually both – motivates them, and the secrecy stops outsiders from finding out about the greed.'

'That doesn't sound like Pangaia. They put out leaflets and don't ask the public for money.'

'Do their leaflets say that they break up families? I thought not. Where does the money come from that keeps their community running?'

'I don't know.'

'Not from tilling the fields, I'd guess.'

'Isn't there anything we can do, apart from kidnapping Mark?'

'Don't do that. It would put you on the wrong side of the law. Which is where you want to put *them*. There are things you can do, though they won't necessarily succeed.'

'Tell me, Dad.'

'Well, those strong points I mentioned are also weak points. Greed makes people irrational, so they make mistakes. And they usually have a reason for loving secrecy, so if you can bring their dirty secrets to light, you stand a chance of bringing the whole edifice down.'

'I see what you mean. But isn't that kind of a long-term approach? We're losing Mark *now*!'

'Yes, I'm sorry. There's no guarantee that you'll be able to free your friend from his captors – because that's what they are even if he doesn't see it. But there are ways you can try. First of all, keep him in touch with the real world, with the people he knows. Get them to write to him, not asking him to leave the cult, or you can be sure the letters won't get through. Just chatty little letters that will remind him that there is a world outside, there is an alternative.'

'Will it help if people express an interest in Pangaia in those letters?'

'Yes, but without prying. And tell people about the cult, as much of the truth about it as you can dig up. Just don't put yourself in danger, Ed, do you hear me? Cults can turn very nasty.'

Later, well after closing time, they staggered home together. Ed's mother was not best pleased to see her husband under the influence.

'How much has he drunk?'

'Only three pints. I guess he's not used to it.'

'Not any more, he isn't. Help me to get him up to bed.'

'Who's "him"? Is that me you're talking about, Lynne? I've got a name, haven't I? And I can get myself up to bed.'

But he could not, not by himself. Between them, Ed and his mother helped him up, Ed supporting his back and taking the weight, Ed's mother clasping his elbow and guiding them. They left him on top of the broad bed, muttering thanks below the scornful gaze of a crucified Saviour. Mrs. Scripps' displeasure had turned to fury.

'Don't you ever do that again, do you hear? Getting your father drunk!'

'What do you mean, Mum? It was only a few pints! He knows when to say no, if he wants to stop.'

Ed himself felt stone-cold sober. His mother sighed.

'Come downstairs, Ed. There's something I have to tell you.'

They sat in the living room of the vicarage, with its spartan, tasteful mahogany furnishings.

'Ed, before I knew your father, before he entered the Church, David was a registered alcoholic.'

'I don't believe you!'

'He says the Church saved him. Not Jesus, mind you, the Church, with its hierarchies and rituals and guidelines for good behaviour.'

She registered her son's distress.

'I'm sorry, Ed. I should have told you before, a long time ago, probably.'

'*He* should've told me.'

'Yes, he should. You would have understood.'

'Yes, I would. I do. It just puts him in a new light. I don't think any the worse of him for it.'

'Well, let him know that. Never put him in that position again. And, Ed, you might think about your own drinking behaviour, too.'

'I will, Mum. You don't want another alcoholic in the family.'

'No, I don't. It's a good job I prefer cannabis, myself.'

'What?!'

'Yes, I do. Really. I haven't used it for years, not since David became a vicar, in fact, but I love it. Just to let you know I'm not so holy, if you ever thought so.'

They talked long into the night. Ed's mother could not tell him anything more about cults, but she did offer solace and sympathy over Çāo. And she said the words he most wanted to hear.

'I know you'll get her back.'

The next morning, Ed got up early and cooked breakfast for his parents. Çāo had got him out of the habit of eating a "full English" at home, but he still remembered how to make one. His father was shamefaced, but he was jolly. His mother seemed content to see them happy in each other's company.

Ed accompanied them to church. With his new knowledge, the Church of England no longer seemed quite so much the enemy, the purveyor of quaint folk tales underlying an irrational belief system that drove people to self-abnegation and passive acceptance. Now it was also a source of strength, for his father anyway, and that meant he owed it. The least he could do was pay the occasional visit.

His father's evening in the pub was already top of the local gossip charts, but nobody took him to task for it when he greeted each of them after the service, and although he complained of a headache once home, the Reverend Scripps was cheerful over lunch. Ed spent most of the afternoon writing to Simone, passing on his father's comments, asking for news of Mark and urging her to be positive. For once, he was reluctant to leave the vicarage, and it was only after a long and emotionally cosy family tea that he forced himself to grab his rucksack, say his goodbyes and head for the train to London.

No janitor was on duty at the hall of residence in Camden Town, but there was a notice saying whom late arrivals should contact to get their keys. Ed located the room, and knocked. No answer. He put his rucksack on the floor, sat down next to it, leaned his back against the wall of the corridor and waited for F. Callenthorpe to arrive. A few people came down the corridor, offered a 'Hello' or 'Hi' or 'Evenin'' as they passed and walked on. Finally, someone stopped beside him.

'You looking for me?'

Ed had been dozing. He opened his eyes and found himself looking up the short skirt of a young woman. He tilted his head so that he could see her face instead. Whereas the thighs had been chubby, the face was thin. Hollow cheeks sat under slim glasses, framed by a dark mass of curly hair.

'I'm Frances Callenthorpe. I run the logistics of this show. If you tell me your name, I'll give you your keys, assuming that's what you want.'

Ed got to his feet. Now he could look down on her, slightly.

'Yes, it is, thank you. I'm Ed Scripps.' He followed her into the study-bedroom.

'Oh, the man from Portugal. We've been looking forward to meeting you.' She handed him a pair of keys on a ring.

*We?*

'Are you hungry? Thirsty? The pubs are shut but our bar is still open.'

'Er, no, thank you, Frances.' She looked younger than him. Probably a student, earning some holiday cash.

'What do you eat in Portugal? Fanny.'

'Lots of good things, actually. Including fanny. My wife likes it, too.'

'Good, I'm glad.' She laughed. 'What I meant was that most people call me Fanny. As in Frances. Fanny Brawne? Fanny Keats?'

*Ah, an English Literature student.*

'Can I call you Frances? I like that even better.'

'Do you? People tell me I'm especially tasty. Want to try?'

*It's England. I'm alone. No-one here knows me.*

'Sure.'

They dined on each other. Frances was both succulent and juicy. She stripped naked, as did Ed, but insisted on keeping her glasses on 'So that I can see you properly.' After Ed had bought her to orgasm, she said she wanted him inside her vagina. She asked Ed not to put on a condom; instead, to pull out of her well before he reached his climax. When he did pull out, she twisted her body round until he was astride her face, then drew his penis into her mouth, sucking on the tip of it until she could feel that he was ready to explode, when she jerked it out of her mouth and directed the warm spurt of his semen on to her glasses. Then she at last took them off, lay back, held them up and let the semen drop from the lenses into her open mouth, before swallowing it. Ed found the sight so arousing that he was ready for an immediate encore. Frances was happy to oblige.

Ed overslept, in his own room, so he skipped breakfast in order not to be too late for his first class. He located the seminar room, opened the door softly and tip-toed in. Twenty faces turned to stare at the intruder. One of them belonged to Frances.

*Oh, Jesus, I've screwed a classmate before we've even started.*

'Come in, Ed,' she said, smiling at him. 'Everybody, this is Ed Scripps. He normally teaches at Lisbon University, but here he's just a student like all of you. Ed, grab a chair, I'm sure you'll find out everyone's names soon enough.'

*Jesus, Mary and Joseph! I've bedded the bloody tutor!!*

Ed took a seat in the circle between a balding man he deemed twice his age and a shaven-headed girl he thought half his age. When the seminar ended and they all got up to go, the man leaned in to him and whispered 'Teacher's pet!'. Ed looked at the girl, who narrowed her icy blue eyes and hissed at him. He turned back to the man, ready to let his tongue loose, but the man smirked and winked at him. Ed laughed and headed for some fresh air.

A year ago, he had been oblivious to the charms and attentions of the women taking a break from their real lives and eager to try out new selves and new, brief liaisons. This year, he was up for anything, but found himself already marked as off limits. He found it unfair that the property of a distant Portuguese woman should be fair game, whereas the teacher's pet was not even to be stroked or fondled by anyone else.

Frances took his new role seriously. As long as Ed anointed her regularly and as per her instructions, she bestowed special attention on him both in and out of bed. She guided his studies and encouraged him, and made sure the other teachers knew of their bond. She also helped him search for offshoots of Pangaia in England. In the process of failing to find any, Ed learnt a good deal about cults that did exist in his native land. Their modus operandi followed a pattern that became familiar to him.

Frances' pillow talk tended to concentrate on the matter in hand, so Ed was surprised when she asked him, 'Does your wife know you're here?' Frances had insisted that Ed come inside her this time, and stay there until he was ready to make love again. The question tarnished the glow of inter-coital tenderness in which they were luxuriating and deflated his nascent re-erection.

'My wife? She doesn't know and she doesn't care. She's with someone else at the moment.'

'She's left you? Ed, I'm sorry.'

'No, she hasn't left me. She's just taking time off. I'm going to get her back, so don't be sorry.'

'And then you'll be faithful to her.'

'Of course.'

'But in the meantime –'

'I'm not going to play the victim.'

Frances laughed. 'I'm never going to get married.'

'That's easy enough to say at our age. How old are you?'

'Twenty-three. Younger than you, but wiser.' She kissed him tenderly and caressed his testicles, then bit the inside of his lower lip and squeezed the base of his penis. Ed felt her vagina tightening around him as his erection returned.

Frances could persuade Ed to do anything for her in bed. She could not, however, persuade him to come away for the weekend with her, neither to her family home in Harrogate, where he would have to take off his wedding ring and pretend to be single, nor to South Coast hotels, where wearing it would help them to register as man and wife. He was adamant.

'I want to be who I am! I don't want to pretend. I don't want to be single again, and I don't want to be married to you, lovely as you are.'

Frances looked at him scornfully.

'Better get used to it, kiddo.'

'What?!'

'I'm sorry. I didn't mean that. Forget I said it.'

To make it up to him, Frances took Ed shopping. The one thing he really missed in Lisbon was books in English. The only place he had found them there was at 'Holt's Books', where Tinkerbelle Holt welcomed her few customers with tea and biscuits, and gently persuaded them to purchase from her small selection of generously marked-up paperbacks. Ed thirsted for books to read for their own sake, books to help him complete and follow up his Open University studies, and books to help him develop his knowledge of how to teach English as a foreign language. Frances knew the best places in London to find all of those.

Ed saw Frances off on her train from King's Cross before catching his own to Stevenage for the weekend. She cut a forlorn figure as she shuffled up the platform: pale and over-dressed for August, though perhaps she would need the coat in Yorkshire. Ed imagined she would have friends there who would cheer her up, if her family could not. He himself had a hefty bag of new books to keep him company in Hertfordshire, as well as a budding new understanding with his parents.

On the Sunday evening train back to London, Ed searched the day's papers in vain for news of Portugal. He hoped to see a headline like 'Guru Arrested' or 'Sect Dismantled', but if any such event had taken place, its distance from London meant that Fleet Street deemed it as un-newsworthy as anything else in a country experiencing the first month under its newly sworn-in First Constitutional Government. Ed wondered why he expected more of editors who accorded far fewer column inches to the earthquakes that had caused thousands of deaths in the Philippines and in China than to Keith Moon, a rock band's eccentric drummer, who had collapsed and been taken to hospital in Florida. He guessed it was because people like him still bought what they were offered, and wanted to know about Keith Moon. He started to dream of a day when new technology might make it possible to buy English-language versions of Philippine and Chinese newspapers in London as easily as English ones, and to dwell on the distribution issues involved.

*

Frances did look happier after her weekend back home. Ed found himself mighty pleased to see her and to be welcomed back into her bed, where something at the back of his mind came to the fore and landed them in another argument.

'Frances, I was just wondering, do you do this with all your students?'

'Only the ones who want top marks.'

'I don't care what bloody marks you give me!'

'Hey, I was joking. I'm choosy, if you hadn't noticed.'

'I thought I chose you.'

'Think again.'

'You knew I was a student. Don't you have any reservations about that kind of thing?'

'Not many. Besides, I don't think you knew I was one of your tutors, did you?'

'No, but seducing a student is not something that I would do. In my book, it's an inappropriate exploitation of an unequal power relationship.'

'Sure, if you say so, Ed. Look, just leave that mumbo-jumbo in your book for once, okay? I've got a mouth that needs filling with something better than harsh words, if you know what I mean. Please.'

Ed obliged, though it was he who had a bitter taste in his mouth as, afterwards, he lay awake beside her.

Ed had to take some flak from his fellow students for the high marks he got at the end of the course. He pointed out that the marks he received from the other tutors were as high as those he got from Frances. Besides, all the material they had covered was dead easy. He went to say goodbye to Frances. She had already gone: the room was empty. On the writing desk was a sealed envelope addressed to him. Inside was a slip of paper with her address and phone number, and a drawing. Ed recognised himself, naked and erect, ejaculating tiny hearts that had somehow amassed to outline the body at his feet, recognisable by the glasses that sat atop the hearts which covered her body, waiting to be covered in their turn. Ed placed the envelope in his shirt pocket. He could feel his real heart beating against it.

On the last day of his holiday, Ed went to the morning service at St. Margaret's again. He hoped his appearance there would boost his father's standing among his parishioners a little. He could play the returning prodigal son as well as be a real son and his own man.

On the plane home to Lisbon, Ed wondered why Simone had not answered his two letters. He hoped that no news was good news, because he did not think that between them they could do much to dent Pangaia. He did not want salvaging Mark to sidetrack him from the more urgent task of winning Ção back, which he was determined to do sooner rather than later. As northern Spain came into view, he began to contemplate how he might make money by selling English books abroad at a reasonable price. It was probably a question of distribution, logistics and scale. However, by the time Lisbon was below them, he had decided to start small: he would write to the publishers of language-teaching textbooks to persuade them to offer teachers free samples. That would be good for everyone. As he stepped from the plane into the welcome humidity of the Lisbon evening, his heart beat faster against Frances' wistful fantasy.

195

# 18  CONTACT

His flat stank of emptiness and unwashed bedclothes. Ed dumped his luggage on the floor, dropped the wad of mail he had found in his postbox onto the hall table, opened all the windows, tugged the sheets off his bed and shoved them into the washing machine, together with the few of his dirty clothes that would fit in, got the whole thing going, and lit some of the cinnamon-scented joss sticks he had found in Camden Market. Then he pulled a beer from the fridge and enjoyed the cool chemical-hop flavour as it tickled his throat and washed away the journey while he scoured the pile of mail. It was full of bills and bureaucracy, but held nothing from Ção or Mark, nothing relating to Ção or Mark, nothing from Simone. He picked up the phone and called Simone. One of those new-fangled answering machines told him in three languages that Mark and Simone were not at home but he could leave a message after the beep. He asked them to ring him back. Ed was pulling his clothes out of the washing machine when Simone did so.

'Ed, I am very glad you are here again.' Her voice was tremulous.

'Are you alone?'

'Yes. But not in my mind.'

'Of course. Let's not talk over the phone. Can you meet me tomorrow lunchtime?'

'I have classes at the Bank until half past twelve. It's in the city centre, near Rossio.'

'Good. I'll meet you at the Rossio fountain at ten to one.'

He was clutching his new purchase when Simone arrived. Dressed all in black, she looked worn, but happy to see him. They embraced;

then Simone drew back.

'Ow! What have you just stabbed me with?'

'Oh this? Sorry.' He showed Simone the sharp-edged cardboard box holding his brand new telephone answering machine. 'I realised yesterday how much I need one of these. Anyway, tell me about Mark.'

'Mark has not come back. Mark is silent. I don't know if he gets my letters, but nothing ever arrives from him. I've been to the Pangaia headquarters at Vila Abade, but they will not let me in. It's a walled compound, and the walls are too high to climb – even for someone like you.'

'I see. Let's go and get some lunch.'

'I'm not hungry, thank you, Ed.'

'Hungry or not, Simone, you have to eat. You've got to keep your strength up.'

'Well, I don't mind watching you eat. The reason we're here is to talk, isn't it?'

Ed chose a popular restaurant that was crowded and noisy with cheerful lunch-break workers, where they were unlikely to be overheard. He ordered for both of them, then asked Simone about the letters he had sent her.

'Yes, I did get them, Ed, thank you. I'm sorry I didn't answer. You see, I couldn't, I was just too depressed.'

'Simone, you can't afford to be depressed. Mark needs you calm, clear-headed and full of energy.'

'But it all seems so hopeless, just so hopeless. What can we do?'

'Listen, Simone, there's a lot we can do.' He stopped talking as a waiter brought their food.

'At least eat the salad.'

Ed outlined for Simone the main things that he had learned about cults in England, together with his father's suggestions. A little colour returned to Simone's wan features.

'One thing above all you have to remember, Simone: it's not your fault. Don't blame yourself.'

'But I do. It *is* my fault! I'm not a good enough wife! I'm not a good enough person! Otherwise he would have stayed.' She looked on the verge of tears. Ed did not want her to attract eavesdroppers by crying. He poured her some water.

'Believe me, you can't control another person. Not even Jorge can do that, not totally. When Mark comes back to you, he will stay. Honestly, he will, I know it. Let's concentrate on getting him back. We can do that.'

Simone looked down at her plate, nodded without conviction and toyed with her food. Then she started to attack the salad. When he was sure nobody was paying them undue attention, Ed asked if Simone had learned anything new about Pangaia. She shook her head, then, as an afterthought, added:

'There is one thing I already knew, which I don't think I told you.'

'Tell me now.'

'All the people who go and live at the compound take a new name, a Pangaia name.'

'That often happens. The idea is to distance newcomers from the old, familiar lives. Do you know Mark's?'

'Yes, it's Adubo, the Portuguese for compost, or fertiliser, or manure. That's why I didn't tell anyone. '

Ed fought back a chuckle.

'Mark was never keen on self-deprecation.'

'They said it was good, it made things grow, it made the Earth even more fertile. They've told him he is destined to make Pangaia grow.'

'Typical brainwashing technique. Trying to make him feel special. Look, when any of us writes to him, we should use that name, and say how much we like it, how good it will be if he makes Pangaia grow. The last thing we must do is reproach Mark or sound hostile. That would only turn him away from us and deeper into Jorge's arms. Let's get writing, and get all his friends writing, too. We've got to love-bomb him as hard as the Pangaia people are probably doing. OK?'

Simone nodded. Then smiled. She even smiled at the waiter when he brought the bill, which Ed took and paid. He walked Simone to a taxi rank. As she got into the taxi, Ed looked at her dull clothes. She wound the window down to say goodbye.

'Simone, next time we meet, wear something colourful. It doesn't have to be green.'

She smiled again.

'Because I'm not in mourning, right? Yes, I will. If I hear anything new, I'll let you know, and if I don't find you at home, I'll leave a message for you on your new toy.'

She was still smiling when the taxi drove away.

Ed headed for the shady side of the street and looked at the colourful apparel the local women were sporting as he strolled home to his empty flat, where he installed the answering machine and spent the evening with the books Frances had helped him find in London.

Ed's first message on the machine came the next day. He found it when he came back from breakfast at his local café. The voice was Simone's, the language French.

'Ed, I don't know quite how to put this, but, well, all those things you said about how I, we, should approach Mark. Don't you think they might help you in trying to get Çāo back?'

Ed thought about it. He was confident that Çāo would come back, perhaps too confident, as he waited for reason to align with emotion and propel her in the right direction. He was not exactly love-bombing her. Perhaps he should feed her emotional needs from a distance.

He set about writing his wife a letter, telling her how much he missed her, even though he deemed it obvious. His words moved him deeply, perhaps because he had not acknowledged the depth of his pain before. He ended with phrases of condolence on the death of Mao Zedong. When he had addressed, sealed and stamped the envelope, he took out the picture postcard of London he had brought back for Mark and wrote him a few cheery lines, beginning with *My dear friend* and addressed to *Adubo*.

Ed did not blame himself for Çāo's defection. Nor did he blame anyone else. It was just an unfortunate mistake that needed to be put right. He did, however, decide to follow his own advice to Simone by getting himself in better shape for when she came back. One step in this process was to conserve both brain cells and waistline by cutting down on booze; another was to get back to rowing.

*

It was good to be out on the river, especially in the morning, before the city started to send its bustle across the water to disturb one's concentration on the sound of oars interacting with water in a rhythm conducive to peace. The estuary could be glassy calm then; you felt you had a place in another, simpler world, where nature ruled, caressing you with its velvet glove. When you rowed in company, you could feel the friendship building wordlessly. *I'll bring Mark out here when we get him back. He can pay his tithes to the Club instead of to Omomnos.*

The Club welcomed his return. The distraction of politics had damaged its income. Its ethos was apolitical: to unite in comradeship all those who could pay their fees. Ed was glad to be one of them. He enquired about Lourdes; she was still an active member. He wondered how he would feel when he saw her again.

It was her voice that made the first contact.

'Well, well, well, look what Neptune has cast away.'

Ed's first response was to its silkiness, not its irony. He looked up from his glass of the bar's finest milk, held her cool, assessing gaze and did not answer. She dropped her smile.

'I heard the world has given you a buffeting. I'm sorry.'

'Don't be. I'm on the up-and-up. I earn a legitimate salary. I'm a university teacher and a home-owner. My future is bright.'

'With a lot of help from my brother. And his friend Moisés.'

'To whom I'm grateful. Really.'

'I'll tell them. They thought you'd forgotten.'

He had not forgotten the desire her smooth, tanned skin aroused in him. It drew him like a whirlpool as he watched her lithe figure move on through the bar and out.

His answering machine held a message from Simone: *I have no news of Mark but please phone me.* He did so immediately.

'Nothing from Mark, I've been in touch with his sister, Henrietta. They were once so close that I was jealous, can you believe?'

'I wish I had a sister, or a brother. Sorry, what did she say?'

'She said that once Mark got an idea into his head, he would see it through at any cost.'

'I'm beginning to think that Mark used to be a very different person. Portugal has changed him.'

'Living abroad changes everyone, Ed. You and me, too.'

'You could be right. How are their parents reacting?'

'They don't seem to care very much. Henrietta says they gave up on Mark when he married a Frenchwoman.' She sniffled.

'Hey, don't blame yourself for the idiocy of Mark's parents. Calm and strong, remember. What else did Henrietta say?'

'She advised me to keep a record of all Mark's and my contacts with Omomnos, to write down any details of its members and supporters that I could find, in case I ever had to go to court.'

'Good. I second that. Look, Simone, do the parents and the sister have the Pangaia address?'

'Yes, I gave it to them, so they could write to him.'

'That's great, but please beg them not to write anything hostile.'

'I have done that already. I think they understand.'

'Fabulous. How are *you*, Simone? Are you eating properly?'

'Yes, I am. Since you told me it was so important for Mark, I make a lovely French meal before I cry myself to sleep.'

'Simone, we're going to have Mark drying those tears of yours sooner than you think. Remember that.'

Ed himself was content to sleep alone, to think of Ção before he fell asleep, and then to dream of Carolina, or Frances, or Lourdes. It was mostly Lourdes now. He was happy when he glimpsed her at the rowing club, discomfited if she was in male company and surprised that she did not seek him out.

When he finally caught her alone, Ed invited her to row with him that evening, and, as he hoped, their joint venture onto the water brought them back into harmony. After they had stored the equipment, it seemed natural for them to drive together in Lourdes' Volvo along the coast road to Cascais for supper. They ate barbecued chicken in a small restaurant in an alley that wound up a hill behind the fire station. The aroma of charcoal and grilling meat overpowered that of the sea and staked a permanent claim on Ed's memory, together with the teasing smile that played on Lourdes' lips and flickered in her eyes. He was caught off-balance when she began to talk about Pangaia.

'I hear you've been mouthing off about a movement called Pangaia. You shouldn't do that, Ed.'

'What are you on about? Who told you that?'

'News gets around, Ed. The powerful can have secrets, but the plebs can't.'

'You mean you know that Mark Rotherfield has gone to live with them?' Lourdes nodded.

'And you know I'm helping Mark's wife to get him back?' Lourdes nodded again.

'And why on earth should I not do that?'

'Because you're putting both of you in danger. And you're missing the point.'

'Which is?'

'They don't want Mark. They want his money and his property. If you're a still businessman, cut a deal, before it's too late.'

'Tell me, Maria de Lourdes, why I should be afraid of a sex-obsessed guru and his demented followers.'

'It's not them you need to worry about, Ed, it's the people who look after them and use them.'

'I don't go for conspiracy theories.'

'Me neither.' She lowered her voice. 'But ask yourself this. Pangaia has been operating for over five years, yet it has never been investigated.

Why? People have left spouses and families and friends to join it, but not a single story about it has appeared in the news. Why?'

'I'd very much like to know.'

'They have a place in the countryside where nobody can stick their noses. Hm, useful. They have a willing labour force that does a lot of digging. Why? To plant things, for sure, but maybe also to bury things. What? Not bodies, that's for certain, and not drugs, either, or Paulo would know about it.'

'This is getting a bit far-fetched. Don't tell me the government is behind it.'

'Our governments come and go, but our allies stay the same. They support us, sometimes against our governments, and from time to time they ask favours in return.'

'Oh, I see. You mean something like they're burying weapons for a resistance movement to use when Ção and the Maoists grab power and invite the People's Liberation Army to hop over from China. No, that's just absurd! NATO has got an underground facility down the road here at Oeiras, and makes no secret of it. They don't need help from a Dad's Army of hippies!'

'Ed, all I'm saying is be careful. Don't risk your life, not even for a friend.' She finished her water. 'And if you're determined to die, make love to me first.'

Ed would happily have complied in the restaurant, then and there. He suggested going to the house he rented to Len and Seamus, where he still kept a room, but Lourdes had already booked a room in a seafront hotel. They ran the short distance there, laughing as they arrived. The moon was new, the sky unclouded, the stars reflected in the water of the bay onto which their balcony looked. They left the french windows open so that they could hear and smell the sea as they made love on the floor, then in the bed. After that, they shut the window on the outside world and made love under the shower, and then again in the bed. Lourdes was an athletic lover, as Ed had expected, but she surprised him by being demanding and joyous as well.

Thoroughly sated, he slept well, but woke at eight a.m. both scratched and sore. Lourdes had gone, leaving no note. Ed ate breakfast in the hotel, then walked the short distance to the railway station and caught the first train back to Lisbon. His wounds felt like marks of distinction.

Ed had an appointment with Simone the following Saturday, so they could bring each other up to date on new developments. On the way to the café, Ed tried to discern whether anyone was following him. He thought about a dozen people might be, and gave up the effort.

*I'm not giving in to paranoia. I'll stick with logic.*

Simone did not look good. Her face bore heavy makeup that aged her, and her slim frame was starting to bulge in what Ed considered the wrong places. She could not raise a smile when she greeted him. They spoke in French and kept their voices low.

'Ed, I have been getting reports about Pangaia that are, frankly, worrying. They say that it has politicians as secret members or supporters.'

'Well, any cult is likely to have a few. They'd hardly go public about it, would they?'

'No, but Pangaia has many, and they cover the political spectrum.'

'What, including the Communist Party?'

'Yes.'

'Well, that's good, because it means that what I've heard recently is a load of nonsense.' He recounted what Lourdes had told him. 'Communists are not going to join an organisation that stores weapons to use against a Communist army, are they?'

'Ed, I'm scared. Pangaia getting its hands on the levers of power is worse than its playing silly cold war games in the night. Especially now, now that I need Mark more than ever.' She placed her hands on her belly. Ed realised what she was going to tell him.

'I have some wonderful news, Ed.' Her eyes began to liquefy. Ed hoped she could hold the tears back. She took a deep breath. 'I'm pregnant.'

*Oh no, not another one to save!*

'That *is* good news, Simone. Mark will come back to look after his baby. I know it. Congratulations!'

'Oh, Ed, I am so frightened! What can we do in the face of Pangaia?'

'We don't have to fight Pangaia. We only have to get Mark back. Lighten their load for them. Let's not invent enemies.'

*

Ed's own thoughts were much with Lourdes. Her athletic sexuality would help him prepare for Çāo's return, and her animal magnetism made her enticing company. Yet she, too, proved elusive. Ed began to spend far more time than he needed to at the rowing club. Eventually, he met her as she arrived there for a morning session.

'Oh, hello, Ed. Some time no see.'

'I've been trying to get in touch with you. Where have you been?'

'Oh, here and there. You know me, I'm not such a creature of habit, really.'

'I'd like to see more of you.'

'You would? You've already seen all of me. There isn't any more.'

'I loved what I saw.'

'Good. We took each other out for some exercise. That's it. Thank you and goodbye.'

Ed was astounded.

'That's it?'

'I satisfied my curiosity, and I got the impression that I satisfied you.'

'Then let's keep on satisfying each other.' *What's the problem?*

'No, Ed. If you really want to know, I thought you'd be a better lay. You know, frankly, you're like a poorly designed car: all thrust, and low manoeuvrability. I'll be surprised if nobody's told you that before.'

Nobody had. Ed struggled for a comeback and could not find one. Anger and humiliation paralysed him as his unbelieving eyes followed Lourdes' smooth passage towards the stored boats.

When Ed arrived home, still miffed, he grabbed the contents of his mailbox and stomped up the stairs. Inside the flat, something in the mail clutched in his fist cut into his hand and caught his attention. He pulled out a crushed postcard.

*Mao is dead and so is Maoism. Woman alone is the word, the truth and the life. Your ex-wife, Çāo xxxx*

He smoothed the card, drew it to his lips and kissed his wife's name. Blood from his hand distorted the view of Conimbriga on the other side. He felt a surge of joy.

*Contact!*

# 19 TWO IS COMPANY

Ed was elated. He dumped the rest of the mail on the hall table and went to the bathroom to clean his cut hand. The eyes that looked back at him from the mirror glistened from more than the sting of the disinfectant. However long the journey, his wife had taken the first step back to him.

Only much later did Ed remember to check the rest of his mail. It comprised a couple of bills, a reassuring bank statement and a letter with a Brazilian stamp. The letter was from Clarice, the blonde bombshell he had encountered at Interlingua International. She told Ed that she had made good her plan to set up her own language school in Brazil. In two weeks' time, she would be in Lisbon to recruit teachers. Could Ed put her up for a week, and would he, in any case, like to discuss a possible partnership?

*Why not?* Ed was always willing to talk business, and if Ção came home earlier than seemed likely, he could simply hustle Clarice out of his flat and into a hotel, which she could clearly afford now. He immediately wrote back to Clarice with an enthusiastic double affirmative. He also asked her to bring over some feminist literature from Brazil, to help him learn to talk to his wife on her own terms.

Before that could happen, Ed went to meetings at the University to prepare for the new academic year. Carolina was still away, in Iran, but the rest of his English-teaching colleagues were there, together with a couple of new ones, hired to meet the heightened demand for English now that Portugal was no longer the international pariah it had been under the fascist régime. After the meeting, the teachers adjourned to the bar, where Ed told them what had become of Mark, and asked for ideas on how to bring Pangaia and its dangers to the attention of his students. Ashley Beecroft had the most forceful suggestions.

'Make it a project. You can do anything that way. Last year I had a class refit a boat. In the summer, a group of us sailed it down to the Algarve and back. Then we sold it and split the profit.'

'Nice, but I'm supposed to be teaching English.'

'That's the beauty of it. As long as they do everything in English, it's a perfectly legitimate way to learn the language. Better than most, I'd say, given how it builds their motivation.'

'So something like a project to examine cults in Britain and Portugal, and compare them?'

'Yeah, with plenty of role-play on how to resist the bloody things.'

'You never know,' Xavier put in, 'your students might come up with ways to get your friend out.'

'It's certainly worth a try.'

Ed decided to devote one class a week with one of his three groups to his awareness-raising project. When he put it to the students, his suggestion was not very well received, but his enthusiasm eventually won them over, especially after he had made clear his personal motive for focusing on cults. He kept in touch with Ashley for advice, and sat in on classes of his to see how Ashley handled project work. Ed was interested by his colleague's relaxed attitude to teaching, and relieved to see how well the students responded to it. Ashley was eternally patient, always supportive and encouraging, and this seemed to release his students from their linguistic inhibitions. Ed saw Ashley focusing on interaction, whereas he himself tended to focus on product. Maybe they could learn from each other.

The University's language teachers were not a gossipy crowd. They had a strong sense of solidarity with each other and with the people they taught, and tended to spend their time together talking about the shifting sands of higher education and their own precarious place therein. Nevertheless, Ed's lightning marriage and his wife's desertion were known about. So when Ed asked Ashley for advice on getting Ção back, he did not feel the need to explain the situation in detail beforehand. The older man gave Ed a knowing look and laughed.

'Are you sure you really want her back?'

'Of course I do. She's my wife. I love her!'

'It's a wonderful thing, love. Does she love you?'

'Of course she does! She's just sent me a postcard! It's a sign she wants to come back.'

'Well, if she wants to come back, she will eventually. Meanwhile –'

'Meanwhile what?'

Ashley smirked.

'Life is long and the field is wide.'

Ashley's reputation as a womaniser had not escaped Ed. But he was also known to be a devoted father, a state that Ed aspired to and the reason he thought that Ashley might have something of value to say to him.

'Some nice young women in my class, don't you think? They liked you.'

'That's very considerate of you, Ashley, but I keep my relationships with students strictly professional.'

'Come now. A little bit of language learning in bed never hurt anyone, in my experience. How did you learn Portuguese so fast, Ed? By the way, Carolina should be back next month.'

Ed felt himself blush as Ashley's smirk widened.

When Ed next went to the airport, it was not to greet the Portuguese Scot back from Iran, but to welcome Clarice from Brazil.

Clarice had put on weight and deepened her tan. Ed, too, was darker, though thinner. The tropical sun had further bleached Clarice's hair, making her even more of a blonde bombshell in Ed's eyes and brain. They recognised each other immediately. Clarice dropped her bags, ran to Ed and clasped him in a tight embrace.

'Morfeu! I see you got up for me, in more ways than one. Boy, are you pleased to see me!'

Ed drew back and smiled.

'You said it, Clarice. I *am* pleased to see you!' He retrieved her bags and guided her through the touts towards the taxi rank. Ed asked the taxi driver to pass the nearby Old University so he could show his visitor where he worked.

'What dismal fascist architecture! I've rented an old colonial-style building for my school. Or should I say *our* school?'

'You'll have to tell me more.'

Clarice moved closer to Ed and sat on his hand.

'Still married, Morfeu?'

'Still happily married, Clarry, though my wife is taking a sabbatical at the moment, without my consent.'

'How convenient.'

'And you?'

Clarice laughed, shook her hair and looked out of the window, marvelling at Portugal's capital city.

'It's so small! Where are all the people?'

'At work, I imagine.'

'They're lucky to have jobs.'

Inside the flat, Ed placed Clarice's luggage in his bedroom, then led her to the kitchen, where he opened the fridge door and pulled out the large jug of liquor that he had prepared.

'Caipirinha!' Ed poured two generous shots. Clarice downed hers in one, choking and laughing at the same time.

'Wow! Good! Pour me another, sir!' Ed obliged.

'You know what, Ed? I haven't missed you for a minute, but it is so good to see you again!'

'I know just what you mean, Clarry.' She tasted of rum and lime and distance as they kissed. When they paused for breath, Clarice said:

'You know that stuff you asked me to get you? Feminist literature? Couldn't find any. You didn't mean girlie mags, did you?'

'No, no, serious feminist stuff.'

'Couldn't find any. Our generals don't approve, so they don't allow it, the bastards. Hey, I've just realised, I can say whatever I think while I'm in Portugal!'

'Let's drink to that!' They did.

'Anyway, I've got something else for you. You like music, don't you?'

'Sure I do. I'll show you my collection.' Ed picked up the jug and glasses, and led Clarice to the party room. While he turned on the record player, she went into the bedroom, where Ed had put her bags, and returned clutching an LP cover, which she handed to Ed.

'Happy whatever. Put it on, while I go and slip into something more suitable.' She walked back into the bedroom.

The LP cover was plain, and Ed did not recognise the name on the label. When he put it on the turntable, he was assailed by some discordant music which sounded Arabic to his ears. He lowered the volume. The bedroom door opened and Clarice swayed into view, wearing Middle-Eastern clothes that left her abdomen bare.

'What do you think? I've been getting to know the Lebanese community, and their dances.'

'I like it!'

Clarice began to gyrate her hips in time to the music, in an approximation of a belly dance.

'This is my Thursday night special!'

Ed did not catch the reference, and it was not Thursday, but the sight before him was indubitably special. He sank into an armchair to appreciate it better. Clarice beckoned to him. As he rose, she grabbed his hand and led him into the bedroom. He tore his clothes off as Clarice eased her own from her undulating body. Then they were on top of the bed, the music still wailing; then he was inside her, Clarice still twitching rhythmically, telling him to let go and come as he liked. As he did so, he understood the allure of the belly dance.

Whether it was the heat of the room, the effect of the drink, the dancing and sex, jet lag, or the mixture of them all, Clarice succumbed to sleep with Ed still inside her. After a while he pulled out, cleaned up, went for a quick shower, came back into the bed and caressed the sleeping dancer.

'*Morfeuzinha*,' he whispered. Contentment relaxed his muscles, and Ed slept, too.

Clarice dozed until midday, and, after a quick brunch, hastened out and about her business of recruiting teachers for Brazil. It was not an auspicious time, soon after the start of the academic year. Ed sent her to Keith, who was the best employer among private language schools in the city, and therefore the most likely to have a surplus of qualified teachers on his books. In the evening, he took her to a Brazilian restaurant to attenuate her culture shock and to learn her plans and his potential place in them.

Clarice told Ed she had opened her school not in Rio de Janeiro but in Salvador, further north, thus nearer the Equator and more torrid. The city was also known as Bahia, its full name being *São Salvador da Bahia de Todos os Santos* in reflection of the bay's being 'discovered' on All Saints' Day. Ed knew it as the setting for *Gabriela, Clove and Cinnamon*, a novel by the Brazilian writer Jorge Amado which was currently captivating Portuguese audiences in a televised soap opera version, the first the country had experienced. The city's image as a centre of Afro-Brazilian culture and laid-back living amid Portuguese colonial architecture were good selling points for foreign teachers, while the fact that it was a thriving metropolis meant that it had plenty of potential language students for them to teach. Clarice's drive and energy had succeeded in getting the new school launched, but she wanted someone with business acumen to consolidate and develop it.

'Wouldn't a Brazilian partner be better?'

'I already have one. He's a sleeping partner. You know, the kind of person who's much better at sleeping than at any other kind of business.'

'I'd want a say on the teaching side of things. Since I've being doing it, I've got really interested in teaching, for its own sake.'

'Ah, now, you see, that's my province. But it would be a partnership, so …'

'Do you think my wife would like the place?'

'No! I mean, you never know.'

Later, when they lay in bed and Clarice was again feeling the effects of her horizontal dancing combined with jet lag, Ed imagined himself living without Çáo in Brazil, making hay with the easy-going Clarice while the sun always shone, transforming her language school into one of the country's finest as they waited for the generals' régime to crumble like its Portuguese equivalent and offer people the same hope of doing everything anew and getting it right. But without Çáo, all those possible joys would have a bitter edge. Maybe, when the generals fell, he could entice her over to team up with her Brazilian Maoist comrades to order the new state, or to galvanise a nascent feminist movement. It was an enticing option.

Ed stayed at home the next day, planning his lessons in his usual meticulous fashion, despite imagining Ashley standing at his shoulder, chuckling and telling him to relax. He phoned Simone, but she had no news of Mark and sounded close to breaking point.

'I'm going to do something, I tell you, Ed. They can't just make my husband disappear. This isn't Brazil!'

'I know how you feel, Simone. But we've got to stay calm. Mark will come back when he's ready, and that will be sooner than you imagine, I'm sure of it.'

*Am I?* Ed asked himself. *Yes, I have to be.*

As soon as Ed put the phone down, it rang again. He expected Simone again, but he heard a different woman's voice.

'Ed? I've come to collect that dinner you offered me. Ed? This is Lisa. Davies? Interlingua International. Wimbledon? I take it your offer still stands.'

'Lisa! Of course! What a pleasure! I was expecting you ages ago. We've got a lot to talk about. Do you know I've become a full-time language teacher?'

Ed was indeed looking forward to seeing Lisa. Her experience and her no-nonsense approach might generate some ideas on getting Çáo back, or even on getting Mark back to Simone. Ed believed that time itself was enough to achieve that, but time seemed to be calling for a helping hand. He had given Clarice her own set of keys. Ed knew she did not expect him to wait for her and take her out: she just wanted him there later, for sex and sleep.

Ed prepared the rest of his lessons for the week, then set out into the warm, humid autumn evening. The rain held off as he ambled down the Avenida da Liberdade, assailed by the din of car engines and horns and by the reek of their exhaust fumes. Interlingua International had its Lisbon headquarters there, just down the road from a smaller, rival establishment called the Oxford Institute. Ed waited in the large entrance hall until the unmistakable, slim figure of Lisa Davies came down the stairs and greeted him. She was as intense as before, but her air was happier, more relaxed, more prosperous.

The rain still held off, so Ed walked Lisa up into the Bairro Alto, an area of bars, restaurants and discos both posh and proletarian, to a small eatery that served quality food with no pretensions, which he thought suited Lisa's character. He was disconcerted to see a group of English teachers from the Sussex School already ensconced there, but they returned his cheery wave and then ignored him.

Lisa expertly filleted large fresh sardines while Ed demolished charcoal-grilled chicken. As Ed poured the full-bodied local red wine, Lisa asked after his business.

'Well, the Revolution made supermarkets unwilling to invest here, and small grocers never had much to invest anyway. But I got enough of them interested to set the ball rolling. Then my bosses in England got cold feet. They offered me a job back home but I was in love with Portugal and in Portugal, so I left them and stayed here.'

'How on earth did you make ends meet?'

'It was touch and go for a time. Thanks to your course, I realised I could do this teaching thing. I managed to get a language instructor's job at the Old University and found I enjoyed it. I indulged in a few commercial things until they started paying me, and, now that they have, everything's hunky-dory. How about you? You look, what —

successful?'

'Well, yes, sort of. I've risen through the ranks of Interlingua International.'

'Blimey, you were already in charge of that teacher-training course.'

'You're right. And now I'm Deputy Director of Studies of the whole shebang. You know the best thing about all this? As the salary went up, the work got more interesting.' Lisa smiled.

*Lovely-lips Lisa.* Ed watched them close over a piece of sardine.

They ended the meal with small cups of espresso coffee. Lisa asked for a drop of milk in hers. Ed told her, for future reference, to ask for a 'garoto', a little boy, when she wanted her coffee like that.

'Of course, if you want a boy, I'm your man.'

Lisa looked at him appraisingly.

'Aren't you married these days? You made such a point of it in Wimbledon.'

*That's what Clarice said. Ah, yes, Clarice. Lisa plus Clarice. Now there's an idea.*

'Hello, dreamer!'

'What? Oh, I am, yes. It's just that my wife's on sabbatical, from me. How about you?'

'Me? I'm not married, except to my work, to which I'm always on call.'

'In that case, Lisa, let's go to my place and relax together while we can.'

'That sounds promising.'

Ed gestured for the bill.

Outside the flat door, Ed pressed the bell. Lisa looked at him askance.

'Just in case my wife's come back.'

Lisa's look turned dark.

'Unlikely.' Ed smiled. The door opened. Clarice, wearing a negligee, stood on the threshold. Lisa's eyes radiated fury.

'Clarice, Lisa. I'm sure you two remember each other, don't you? From Wimbledon.' Ed ushered Lisa in. She shouldered Clarice out of the way as she entered the flat.

'Of course I know Clarry the Cow. This is the God-damned bitch who's trying to steal my students!'

Clarice looked crestfallen. Then, seeing the attention with which Ed helped Lisa off with her coat, and the way he looked at her as he did so, fury flowed onto her face, too.

'You little bastard, Ed!'

'Hey, calm down, both of you. I just thought we could all get along, have a bit of fun together.'

Lisa looked at him in disbelief. Clarice glared at them both, then the anger left her face and she began to laugh.

'OK, Ed, I'll show you something. Take Miss High-and-Mighty here into the lounge and put on that music I gave you. I'll bet *she* didn't bring you a gift, unless you count – Hmm, just do what I said, OK?'

Clarice disappeared into the bedroom. Ed thought he knew what she was up to. He gave Lisa what he intended to be a soulful look and guided her into the party room, where he sat her in an armchair, put on the Arabic music and offered Lisa a caipirinha. When he returned from the kitchen with the jug and glasses, Lisa had moved onto a bean bag. Ed sat in the armchair, facing her. Lisa's eyes were as icy as the caipirinha. Nevertheless, she clinked glasses with Ed and her thin, expressive lips enunciated a cut-glass 'Cheers' at the moment when the bedroom door opened and Clarice swayed into the room clad in her Brazilian-Lebanese dancing outfit. Ed moved his gaze from Lisa to Clarice as she sashayed towards him. He looked at her body as she picked up the glass he had filled for her. She downed its contents in one swallow, then turned her back on Ed and moved in time to the music over to Lisa. Lisa looked stricken as Clarice got too close for comfort. She pushed herself deeper into the bean bag. Clarice straddled her, rotating her hips and her breasts so that the tassels of her tunic brushed Lisa's face. Lisa began to laugh. Clarice continued, increasing the pace. Her momentum popped open two buttons on her blouse, and one breast slid free of it; this breast she wiggled in front of Lisa's face, bringing it ever closer. Lisa sighed. Her hand shot out, clasped Clarice's lower back and pulled her even closer as her lips came together over Clarice's exposed nipple. Clarice stopped dancing long enough to shed her blouse completely. Lisa turned her attention to Clarice's other nipple, then used both hands to stop her dancing and pull her down, face forward, onto her lap.

Ed jumped out of the armchair. In time to the music, he unzipped his jeans, pulled out his erect penis and danced towards the two women. This was something he'd dreamed of. He caught Lisa's eye. It was glazed. It did not look pleased to find him in its sights. For a moment, Lisa left Clarice's breasts.

'Ed, there's no room for you here. Get out.'

'Oh, come on! The three of us! Look at this!'

Clarice was undoing Lisa's blouse. She turned her head and gave Ed a withering look.

'Sod off, Ed!'

'No, seriously!'

'I am serious, Ed, and I said sod off!'

'You don't mean that. Lisa!'

'You heard what the lady said, Ed.'

'Maybe I'll just stand here and –'

'You've got a spare room, haven't you? Go and use it!'

'But –'

'Sod off, Ed!' Lisa and Clarice chanted in unison and went on disrobing each other. Ed watched as he backed out of the room, then came back in. He held up his hands to forestall further insults, grabbed the jug of caipirinha, turned on his heel and attempted a dignified exit, preceded by his rigid penis. Giggles followed him. Other sounds interspersed the music, which he could hear from the spare room. As he drank himself to sleep, for the first time he felt humiliated by the ostensible cause of Ção's desertion being a woman.

A cold draught woke Ed the next morning. He made a mental note to fix the spare room window. He felt fine, but had a nagging suspicion that something was wrong. Then he remembered. He looked at the caipirinha jug, but it was empty. The flat was silent. He got up and padded towards the main bedroom. He stopped outside it and listened. No sound. Ed held his breath and opened the door. The bedroom was empty, the bed made. He went back to the spare room, via the empty party room, collected the caipirinha jug from the spare room and took it to the kitchen. Two notes waited for him on the table.

Lisa had written: *Thanks, Ed, I always fancied her, never thought. XXXL.*

Clarice's note read: *Gone to a nice hotel See you in Bahia Clarice (not Clarry).*

Ed crumpled both, binned them and headed for the bathroom. When he came out, refreshed from a hot shower, he made some breakfast, took up his pen and set about love-bombing his wife.

So intent was Ed upon this task that he ignored the phone when it rang. It insisted, so he settled it off the hook. When he finished his letter, he pushed it into an envelope which he addressed to Ção at João's house in Conimbriga. As he sealed it, he noticed the phone and put the receiver back in its cradle. It rang. Ed picked it up, hoping to hear a man's voice. It was Simone.

'Ed, I've spoken to Mark. He called me.'

'Great!'

'It's not great. He was incoherent! He went rambling on and on about 'revolution number one' and singing some children's song.'

'Was that all?'

'Yes. He cut off abruptly, or was cut off, I don't know. Then, today, a letter arrived. It's just a slip of paper, with these words: *Free, you're mine. Instead?* It's Mark's handwriting, so I know it's from him. What does it mean, Ed?'

## 20 DESPERATE MEASURES

Winter is the wet season in Lisbon. When the rain makes good on its ever-present threat, it lashes the cobblestones with such force that you can see it bounce back off them. There is no gentle drizzle, though an economic migrant from Stevenage might be told often that he must be enjoying this manifestation of the weather of his homeland.

Lisbon taught Ed the wisdom of carrying and using an umbrella in winter. As he hastened down the Avenida under one to meet Simone, the city did look less foreign to his eyes after rain had washed the buildings, settled the dust and persuaded the pedestrians to pick up their pace. It was familiar territory to him now. The line between home and abroad was shifting politically, too, as Europe exerted its centripetal force to draw in its Western outposts. Ed's homeland had joined the European Economic Community less than three years previously, and now Portugal had applied to do so, too. Ed saw in this yet a further step back from revolution, a step that opened up future business opportunities.

Simone was waiting for him in the café.

'Don't apologise, Ed, you're not late. I try to arrive early for appointments now, so that the little one has time to settle in before we start.'

Although her pregnancy did not show, her eyes had a radiance that contrasted with her care-worn face. Ed saw that Simone's mid-morning snack consisted of a milky coffee and a custard tart. Since she could clearly cope with the sight and smell of those items, Ed ordered the same for himself.

'Do you remember a British pop group called The Beatles?'

'Yes, they were quite popular in France as well. I heard they gave up.'

'Yes, sort of. They disbanded a few years ago. That wasn't a children's song Mark sang to you. It was one of theirs.'

'Oh, I see. Does it have a message? Is that why he was singing it?'

'I think so. It says that the only important revolution – Revolution Number One – takes place in people's heads, not in the streets. I think they wrote it after visiting some guru or cult in India. Anyway, cult leaders love it, as you can imagine.'

'So you think Mark has swallowed that message wholesale?'

'I think he tried to.'

'Then what about the letter?' Simone drew a sheet of paper from an inside coat pocket and laid it flat on the table in front of Ed. He looked at the neat words placed squarely in the middle: *Free, you're mine. Instead?*

'Ah! I get it. Simone, this is good news! Mark took the words of that song and changed 'your mind' to 'you're mine', and he's put in punctuation. Punctuation means something to Mark. He's thinking of you, he's thinking of alternatives and he's thinking of freedom. I could be wrong, but I believe the penny has dropped and Mark realises he is in deep shit and he wants out. Out of Pangaia.'

'Yes? Do you think so? Oh, Ed, we really hope you're right!'

'I think now is the time to tell him you're pregnant. If he phones, you can tell him directly. If you write, you'll have to allude to it so that he'll understand but his captors won't. The last thing they want is more competition for his money.'

'Do you honestly think that will make him run away from them, and come running home to me and the baby?'

'If he can, he will. I'm certain of it!'

\*

With Mark's return home seeming imminent and Ção's inevitable, Ed himself flew back to England for Christmas with a light heart. He forgot to take gloves, and the cold shook his hands with unwelcome intensity. Fortunately, the Vicarage was warm, both physically and emotionally. The less English he became, the more Ed appreciated his parents. They supported him to the hilt in his campaigns to get Ção and Mark back to their rightful spouses. Nonetheless, his mother let slip a comment that a woman who treated her son the way Ção had might best be left to her own devices; and Ed's father failed to contradict her.

His friends were less concerned about him than about the sky-rocketing price of beer, along with everything else, and the likely effects of the cuts imposed on the country by the International Monetary Fund in return for a humiliating bailout. Ed told them that Portugal would not follow in England's footsteps; it would make its own way, and get things right. For a nation that had shed fascism without shedding blood, economic development would be child's play.

Ed knew he was just marking time in Stevenage, both appalled and reassured by the unchanging nature of the grey town. He paid some attention to a new kind of music in the air, a discordant note among the jingles, though he did not find 'punk rock' much to his taste – its singers sounded too much like himself croaking in the shower, only much more angry. He did not think it would last. He was, however, impressed by the business acumen of its leading lights, whose record label sacked them for swearing on television but had to fulfil their expensive contract. What he appreciated most about the country, apart from its bookshops, was being able to use his own language at every turn. It was a restful place, despite a pervasive fear, most noticeable in London, of further bomb outrages as part of the Irish 'troubles'. Ed was happy when the time came to return to Lisbon, to get his classes going and his life moving again.

He was greeted by the news from Simone that she had finally gone to the police, reported Mark missing and told them where she believed he was. The word 'Pangaia' had produced a deeper chill in the cold air of the police station. The officers she spoke to pointed out that if she knew where her husband was, then he could not be missing. They became more sympathetic when she mentioned her pregnancy, but they promised no action. Mark had phoned Simone on Christmas Day and again on New Year's Day, both times stressing how happy he was at Pangaia. However, his voice had sounded extremely strained, as though he were under duress.

'I'm sure he was just reciting a script. I could almost see the other disciples at his shoulder, making certain he stuck to it. That's why I didn't mention the baby. Even so, it's obvious to me that he doesn't want to be there.'

'Good. But we can't just walk in and grab him out of their hands, Simone. That would put us on the wrong side of the law.'

'The law doesn't appear to be on our side anyway. Ed, I've got to do something!'

'Yes, you're right, you must. If Mark won't come to you, you'll have to go to him. How about this? You go up to the village, stay outside the compound and track his movements. Show him that you are there, and that you are not alone.' Ed nodded towards Simone's belly. 'I'm sure he'll come to you, when he realises.'

'And if he doesn't?'

'He will.'

Alone in bed that night, doubt assailed Ed. Would Mark really just walk away from Pangaia of his own free will? Would Çāo understand soon that she wanted and needed to come home? And if they didn't? He fell asleep and dreamed of a tidal wave rolling in from the Atlantic and sweeping over both Pangaia and Conimbriga, drowning everything and everyone.

Ed got his classes re-started and paid special attention to the one he had doing project work on Pangaia. He put out feelers for students willing to undertake some more practical work on the subject, and was pleased to find several takers. Ed pooled them with those among Simone's other friends who had volunteered, and organised a rota for people to accompany Simone up to Vila Abade. There she would wait near Pangaia's headquarters where Mark could see her if he came out, while the others would conceal themselves in positions from which they could track every movement in and out of the compound. When Mark came out to Simone, they would all make a quick getaway in the car, so they had to leave a spare place in it when they drove up there.

They could not mount a permanent watch because they all had commitments in the city. The first time a group went, they drew a blank: nobody entered or left the compound during the hours they were there. The second time, a detail of four people left the compound and picked up supplies at a grocer's and a hardware store before returning. The third time, two cars went in but did not come out while they were watching; another four-person shopping trip took place on foot.

The fourth time, Mark came out, flanked by two men younger and more robust than him; all three were singing the Beatles' 'Revolution Number One'. Mark saw Simone, stopped singing and made a move to join her. His associates restrained him and pulled him back through the compound gate. Simone ran after Mark, but they had slammed the gate shut. Simone banged on the gate and wept, but there was silence behind it. One by one, the friends who had accompanied her came to comfort her. They eventually persuaded Simone to let them drive her back to Lisbon. As they led her away from the compound's entrance, the gate opened behind them and a group of a dozen Pangaia disciples started to hurl insults, threats and finally stones at them, but did not pursue them as they ran out of sight and then to the car. None of them was hurt, but all were shaken. Simone sobbed throughout the journey home.

Ed was outraged when he heard the news.

'Damn! That's our cover blown. Now the bastards know that Simone is not alone when she goes up there. And that she knows Mark wants to leave. What's more, Mark probably hasn't realised that Simone is pregnant. I mean, it isn't immediately apparent.'

The consensus among the group of friends was that it was time for stronger action. Ed was adamant that they avoid violence.

'First, it puts us in the wrong, as far as the law is concerned, and it will be concerned. Second, we can't put Simone in harm's way. Third, they outnumber us. Fourth, they may be armed with more than stones, and fanatics are often ready to kill or maim. Do you want me to go on?'

'Why don't we just go to the police?'

'Simone has been to the police, and they aren't interested.'

'The press?' Gabriela, one of Ed's students, wanted to become a journalist herself.

'That would put the spotlight on Simone, which she doesn't want. And they wouldn't necessarily take her side. Let's keep it as a last resort.'

'I'm still not sure why they won't let him go. Their behaviour doesn't make them look good at all.'

'We've seen in our studies that these cults never like to lose followers.'

'The way Mark reacted to Simone shows he hasn't been completely indoctrinated yet.'

Ed nodded. 'Right. And he probably knows too many of their secrets already.'

Simone spoke through clenched teeth. 'They haven't got his money yet.'

'That could be the lure to bring them out.'

'It's not them we want to come out, it's Mark.'

'Let's sleep on that and come up with some ideas. Same time tomorrow?'

Heads nodded. The conspirators filed out of Ed's flat. He opened the windows and sat watching the stars compete with the city lights in an uneven struggle.

*In the end it comes down to money, and I'm the person who's supposed to know about that.*

Ed took a dark Sagres beer from the fridge for inspiration. He had acclimatised so thoroughly that he now drank his beer cold, even in winter: the chill at the back of his throat added to the impact of that first swig. With the night's third bottle, inspiration started to arrive. By the time the fifth empty bottle clinked into the waste bin, he had a plan.

In the cold light of day, Ed still thought his plan was a good one. He summoned the group to a meeting that evening and laid it before them. They thought it risky, but feasible. They would do it.

The next morning, Simone went to the bank and wired a significant sum of money from a joint account to the bank's branch in Vila Abade, for Mark to pick up in person. One of the group, Luís, then phoned Pangaia, declared himself to be a senior clerk from the bank, and asked to speak to Mark. They told him Mark was unavailable but he could leave a message. Luís explained the transfer and said that Mark could collect his money the following day.

Early the next morning, Ed, Simone and Gabriela drove up to Vila Abade in a hired car. They parked near the police station in the small town and walked towards the bank, hurrying to keep out the winter chill as well as to get in position before the bank opened. They took up their places, in sight of each other, but with only one of them visible to the guard outside the bank, should he care to look in that direction.

They were counting on Jorge being keen to get his hands on Mark's money as fast as possible, and they were not disappointed. Minutes after the bank opened, Ed saw Mark approach it, accompanied by three heavies. Ed pulled his borrowed hat down and hurried towards the bank, taking care to disguise his limp. He was the first customer to enter the bank, and he engaged the sole clerk already on duty in a discussion of how he might open an account there, spinning out the misunder-standings by making his Portuguese more rudimentary than it had been for years. The Pangaia group came in after him and had to wait. If Mark recognised Ed, he did not show it.

A blast of cold air came in as the door opened. Gabriela strode in, looking flustered and anxious. She asked who was last in the queue and started complaining loudly about bank staff always being late for work. The guard raised his eyebrows and closed the door on them. Mark's escorts glared daggers at the foreigner separating them from Mark's money. When Ed could spin out his request no further, and gave it up with many thanks to the bored clerk, the Pangaia group moved forward to take his place, but Gabriela brushed past them to the counter.

'Excuse me, I'm sorry, I just can't wait! Show a little gallantry, gentlemen!'

'Hey! Who do you think you are!'

'Get out of the way, bitch!'

'We're next! Not you, you stupid cow!'

They did not notice Simone enter. Mark did. He rushed to embrace her. As he did so, Ed started to yell.

'Help! It's a robbery! Help!!'

Gabriela began to scream. The clerk pressed the alarm button. The guard ran in, gun in hand, and saw the heaviest of Pangaia's disciples with his thick arms around Mark's neck. The guard felled him with a blow from the barrel of the gun, then pointed it at the other two heavies who scrambled to tend to their fallen companion.

'Stop where you are! You're all under arrest!'

Police reinforcements arrived, and accompanied them, in two groups, to the station. Ed explained what he had ostensibly been doing, and apologised for having jumped to the conclusion that a robbery was taking place when the group of robust young men had started shouting in a language he did not understand well. The bank clerk backed up his story. Gabriela apologised for her behaviour, claiming she was on the verge of a nervous breakdown and had badly needed to pay a utility bill before driving to see her doctor in Lisbon.

'You do understand that we women have special problems, don't you?'

The police sergeant nodded.

Simone said that she had been told that her husband, who had deserted her, was visiting the village that day. She had seen him go into the bank and, after calming herself and summoning her courage, had followed him in to speak to him; then all hell had broken loose.

The man who had been floored could offer no reason why he had been throttling Mark. His fellow disciples claimed they were all protecting Mark from his crazy wife. Mark said his wife was not crazy and he wanted to go home with her.

Barely two hours later, the sergeant completed the paper work and released Mark, Simone, Gabriela, Ed and two of the Pangaia disciples. The third one he formally arrested and sent to the hospital with an escort of his own, a police escort.

Within sight of the police station, the detained man's two companions did not dare to interfere as Mark, Simone, Gabriela and Ed got into the hired car and slowly drove north out of town before doubling back and racing down side roads that led south to Lisbon.

*

That evening they celebrated in style. With Mark and Simone's eager consent, Ed and the rescue group spread the word among all the couple's friends, colleagues and students who were in the know, as well as Ed's own Pangaia project students and colleagues. Together, they gave the Trindade beerhouse one of its jolliest evenings. Mark was confused but radiant, and quite clear on one score.

'Omomnos is right that revolution number one is in our heads. But that's not a reason to give him all our money. And Pangaia should preach the truths it teaches, not sell them.'

Faced with such an audience, celebrants hanging on his every word, Mark could not hold back from preaching some of those truths himself. *Psycho-babble blended with eco-babble*, thought Ed, before pressing Mark further on why he had changed his mind about Vila Abade.

'I realised that Pangaia wanted my money more than they wanted my mind. When I saw Simone standing there, alone, outside the compound, I knew I had to get away, to get back to my lovely wife. And when I saw Ed in the bank this morning, I knew that someone else had come to help me, too, at last.'

*At last?*

Simone explained to Mark how much they had done to try to get through to him. Clearly, Pangaia had managed to keep Mark more deeply in the dark than even Ed had suspected. Now that darkness lifted.

'This is the happiest day of my life.' Mark's face showed it.

Later, when they were home and alone, Simone made it even happier

229

with another piece of news that Pangaia had kept from Mark.

Ed's own sense of triumph that evening was jarred by the news that Gabriela brought when she arrived, late. She had tried to get the story of Mark's escape into the next day's papers, but even the lure of juicy headlines like 'TV Quiz Hero Breaks Free of Cult Chains' had failed to tempt a single one of them to take it up. Not even the State television company, which ran the quiz show, wanted the story.

Ed was also sorry that Carolina was not among the colleagues from the University who came to the beerhouse. When he got home in the early hours of the morning, he put on Woody Guthrie's *Talking Empty Bed Blues* and felt the words cut into him. Fortunately, he had drunk enough beer to send him to sleep before the words could finish their job.

## 21 INTERRUPTED DREAMS

Ed never fully decided what transformed Mark: whether it was the new outlook that the Revolution had brought to the country, the change that Mark had wrought inside his brain with his own Revolution Number One, or his experience of being imprisoned by Pangaia and sprung by his wife and friends. Mark was certainly a new man. No longer did he look down on people who did not come from a moneyed background like his own. He renounced the art of the back-handed compliment. Instead, his pleasure with life infused his relationships, which he was quick to show that he valued.

On a practical level, Mark went back to doing a few hours a week at the English Council, where he discovered that it could be interesting to listen to his students as well as talk to them. They started to make real progress, and Mark began to get respect as a teacher, not just as a former TV celebrity. Simone continued to teach French at the Sussex School, but, with Keith's ready consent, reduced her hours and brought her timetable more into line with Mark's. They did not need the money it brought, but Mark was coming to share Simone's view of work as a value, and to enjoy the social aspect of teaching. They often invited the rescue group to their place after work or at weekends, and invited Ed more than most. Their flat began to seem like his second home in the city.

Ed noticed that they never invited him alone. There would always be at least one personable young woman, apparently unattached and eager to make him smile. His friends' match-making efforts, however, failed to overcome the barrier of Ed's preoccupation with Ção. Indeed, their favourite topic of conversation – plans for the coming baby – served to remind Ed that he and his wife had plans of their own, plans that he needed to rekindle her awareness of.

Ção did not contact him. Either Ed's love-bombs were not reaching their target or else they carried the wrong payload. Ed was disturbed by the contrast between his success in getting Mark back to Simone and his failure to bring his own wife home. One night, after seven bottles of Sagres had clinked on top of each other in his waste-paper basket, Ed decided the reason was that he was trying to get Ção back by himself, whereas the rescue of Mark had been a team effort that had benefited from brainstorming.

Ed chose to approach Mark and Simone for help first. He insisted on meeting them alone, without any candidates to ease his Ção-deprivation blues. Mark was still convinced of the priority of Revolution Number One.

'You've got to sort yourself out before you can sort out Ção, or anyone else.'

Simone was more pragmatic.

'Try and put yourself in her shoes. How does she see the situation? Let her know that you can see and understand her point of view as well as your own. In the end, you may have to let her go so that she can choose freely to come back to you.'

'I can see the logic, Simone, but you never thought for an instant of letting Mark go, did you?'

'Not for one second! But, you know, thinking is one thing and doing is another. And Mark came back when he decided to. If I'd had my way, he would never have set foot inside Vila Abade in the first place.'

Ed was not convinced, but he did not intend to allow his pride to prevent him from getting his wife back. He went home and let hot coffee – *a thimbleful of black slime*, as Carolina called it – inspire him, or at least keep him thinking, throughout the night. By the time dawn reddened the awakening city's cloud cover, Ed had identified the main stumbling block: João; more precisely, his own attitude towards João.

He could not see anything wrong with that attitude, for it seemed logical to hate a favoured rival, but he understood why Çāo might think differently and despise him for it.

Ed located his writing pad and wrote the hardest word: sorry. He apologised for not being the husband Çāo had expected, for failing to respect her parents, for not being a Maoist, for being a male chauvinist pig, for not listening to her, for being hostile to the woman she loved. He could have continued, but he reasoned that overkill was the enemy of sincerity. To begin with, he did not mean much of what he wrote, but the more he tried to think about his behaviour from Çāo's point of view, the more his heart crept into his apologies. He tore the letter up and started again, willing himself to feel what he wrote. He ended by writing that he understood why Çāo did not want to see him, but that he thought it was time for all of them to meet and talk things over calmly.

He expected a reply. When it did not come, Ed sought further advice from Simone.

'I think you should give her an extra reason to meet you, one that will benefit just her. For instance, have you got still something of hers that she might like to have back?'

'I haven't come across anything. She cleared all of her stuff out of the flat. But I haven't been looking for it. I will now.'

Ed looked, but Çāo's self-removal had been unusually painstaking. He found nothing of hers. He went to Cascais to collect his rent from Seamus, and searched his own room there, but found no trace of Çāo.

As he handed over the rent, Seamus proposed a deal.

'If you want to sell this place, Ed, I can give you a decent price.'

'That's interesting, but I don't at the moment. Let's talk about that some other time. Look, Seamus, have you come across anything in the house that belongs to my wife?'

'No, mate, I don't think so. Unless that old headband is hers.'

'Headband? Let's take a look.'

Seamus led Ed to the kitchen, where he opened a store cupboard.

On top of a pile of dusty newspapers lay a black velvet headband. Ed recognised it at once.

'Is there a – ?'

He picked it up tenderly. Underneath was a choker in the same material. Ção had loved them. Ed remembered her once wearing them and nothing else. The dust in the store cupboard affected his eyes.

'These are hers, Seamus. These are perfect.'

'Take 'em.'

Ed wrote to Ção that he had found her black velvet headband and choker and thought she should have them. He asked if he might bring them to her. As soon as she got the letter, Ção phoned. She said Ed would be welcome at the farmhouse the following Saturday. Her voice was warm.

Ed hired a car for the drive up to Conimbriga. The air was cold and damp but the rain held off. The farmhouse looked run-down and even less welcoming than the dogs. João came out and shut them up. Ção followed her out and greeted Ed with a peck on the cheek. The touch of her lips was a joy, a harbinger of pleasure to come, even though it evoked a pang at the temporary loss.

They went inside. The two women were dressed identically, as though for farm work. There was no sign of a daughter. Ed tried to see João through Ção's eyes, but gave up. Nevertheless, she was the one he concentrated on, once he had given Ção her headband and choker, together with a cassette by The Dubliners that included a traditional Irish folk song called *Black Velvet Band*. Ed had presents for João, too: an orchid and a set of paintbrushes.

'Last time I was here, I saw you'd started painting the window frames. I noticed your brushes were not the best. Thought you might like these.'

'That's very thoughtful of you. I like orchids, too.'

'If you still need to finish that job, I can give you a hand right now.'

'Sure. Why not? We can have a chat while we're at it. If we're lucky, Ção will make us some lunch, won't you, sweetheart?'

Ção agreed, though no pleasure shone in her eyes.

Ed and João worked steadily as the sun warmed up the day. They spoke little. When they did, neither interrupted the other, like two people engaged in a tussle to show who was the better listener. Ed tried but failed to find João attractive, even though he imagined how she might, if she ever wanted to, exacerbate rather than mask the feminine nature of her features. He could not work out how Ção might find her appealing. Even as a man, all his male friends were, in his opinion, better looking than João, and so was he. Nor did he find her especially interesting to talk to. He realised she was kindly leaving aside her feminist diatribes, for his sake, but the opinions she did give voice to were as banal as any he heard in bars or on buses. He turned when he heard Ção's voice call them in to lunch. When he saw the beatific way his wife gazed at João, it hit him that the love between Ção and João might be myopic but it was not necessarily shallow.

Over lunch, Ed told them about rescuing Mark from the clutches of Omomnos. He hoped Ção would see it as a parable that could apply to her own behaviour. To keep things smooth, he did not emphasise the point. João surprised him by wanting to know the details of the sect. She was as scathing about the cult as he was.

'Money for nothing, and virgins to screw. That's all Omomnos or any of them want. You notice one thing about cult leaders? They're all men. When a woman starts a religion, then it'll be time to listen. They should cut that Jorge's balls off and use them to choke him. Though that won't happen in this country. Your friend was right, Ed, when she warned you to be very careful. You've upset some powerful people. You'd best watch your back. Whatever you might think, I don't want my darling Ção to become a widow.'

Something nagged at the back of Ed's mind, alongside the thought that he might also profit from trying to see his wife as João saw her. After lunch, he helped João wash up, then announced that he had to get back to Lisbon. João smiled; Ção looked disappointed. They both came out of the house to see him off. Ção kissed him with affection, João formally. As he got into the car, Ção dived back into the house, then re-emerged wearing the velvet headband and choker, laughing and waving gaily as he drove away down the track. *Contact*, he thought. *Even with João Ladrão, The Big Thief.*

On the outskirts of Lisbon, he had to brake sharply when the driver in front of him made a last-minute decision to obey a changing traffic light. The thought at the back of his mind jolted into the front.

*I didn't mention Lourdes' advice. I'd never say the bitch's name in front of Ção, or João.*

Ção phoned that evening. She thanked Ed for the gifts, for being friendly to João and helping them with the painting. 'João says you're welcome any time you want to give us a hand. With due notice.'

Ed identified the warm note in her voice as uxorious love preparing to get its act back together.

On the Monday, at the University, he ran into Ashley. Ed told his colleague about his trip to Conimbriga.

'Good man. Strike while the iron is hot. Time to go for broke. By the way, your other iron in the fire is back in the forge.'

'What are you talking about? Your mixed metaphors are frying my brain!'

'Carolina. She's back, a while now.'

'That's good news. Wonder why I haven't seen her. She hasn't been in touch.'

'Well, I guess she's busy. And she's teaching mornings now. Get after her, you lucky boy! Spoilt for choice, eh?'

'For me there is no choice. I'm a married man, in love with my wife.'

Ed's cheeks burned as the scepticism in Ashley's eyes made him acknowledge in his own mind how much he wanted to see Carolina again.

Ed wrote once more to Ção, in the same vein as before. He apologised for any pain he may have caused. He told her how he had never stopped loving her even for one moment. He dwelt on how he really would like their marriage to work and how he dreamed of having her in his arms again, but because he respected her wishes and did not want to cause her any more pain, he was going to give her the space to work out what was right for her.

*As though I don't know!*

As icing on the cake, Ed offered the couple the use of his room in the Cascais flat if they wanted a place to stay near the city.

As he licked the envelope, Ed imagined tasting again the underside of Ção's tongue. He kissed her name above the address just before he slipped the letter into the post box.

Ed was marking students' essays when Ção phoned. Her voice was warm but sad.

'Ed, for once I don't know quite what to say.'

'Say you're coming home.'

'Ed, I can't, I simply can't.'

'Why not?'

'I got your letter, of course. You're so sweet. It's just – I've had all the time and space I need. I've made up my mind. I'm with João now. She is my future and that is my decision.'

'Ção, my darling, you don't know, you can't know! Can João give you children?'

'She already has. Goodbye, Ed.'

The line went dead. Ed gently put the phone down, closed the shutters with difficulty against the strong afternoon sunlight and put half his mind back to his marking, while the other half searched for the next strategy to try.

Ed still had no satisfactory answer, though he gave it all his thought that evening, when he came out of the room that his Business English class had now been officially allocated at the University. The cool, clean air that washed over him as he passed through the entrance doorway brought no clear counsel. The moisture on the grass outside told him it had been raining, so he took care not to slip on the steps leading down to it, hunching into his leather jacket as he descended. He moved to avoid a female figure standing at the bottom of the steps, then realised she was talking to him.

'Are you going to offer a welcome drink to a lass just back from Persia, then?'

'Carolina?'

'Because if you are, I have a personal taxi waiting to take you to a den of iniquity of your choice.'

Ed pulled Carolina towards him and held her slight body hard against his. Her hair was damp. In the car, they kissed, and the warmth that rose from Carolina's body made Ed realise that winter was passing.

They caught up with each other's news in a bar in the Bairro Alto called *Poppy's*. It was kitsch but comfortable and quiet. The trip to Iran had given Carolina and her husband hope that the Shah's régime was on its last legs, as Caetano's had been in Portugal when Ed first arrived. Like in Portugal, the régime's demise would be followed by an era of human rights, democracy and religious freedom; their Baha'i faith would flourish as never before. The question was whether or not to go back before that happened, or to wait until it really had come to pass but miss the fun of the revolution itself.

'At the moment, it's truly not a great place for a Portuguese Scot with a gabby mouth, but Firouz wants to be part of the change. And in our religion, we don't do divorce.'

'You know, if you do go, I'll really miss you.' Ed surprised himself by the intensity with which he uttered the words.

'You will, will you? Well, then, take me to your dark little flat and show me how much, since I'm still here.'

Inside the flat, Ed threw open the windows of the bedroom to let in as much moonlight as he could. Carolina closed them again.

'I like the dark. I love the feel of you, you know, and I'll feel you more strongly if I don't see you as well. And if you don't see me, you can imagine I'm your little Sow.'

'Ção.'

'Ção, Sow, Cow, the little monster who's still leading you a merry dance.'

'Forget her. I love to see your face and your beautiful body, but even in the dark my mind will see them. Yours, and nobody else's.'

'My, you've been practising your chat-up lines.'

'No, I'm out of practice, actually.'

Carolina unbuttoned her blouse and let it slip to the floor. Ed stared at her small taut breasts. The palms of his hands tingled. Carolina stared back at him.

'Let me help you get those trousers off before you burst them.'

She did. She even forgot to turn the light out before she had sucked Ed dry and then had him bring her to a slow orgasm that seemed to send her on a journey inside herself from which Ed wondered if she would return. She did, and lay there under him, kissing him gently until Ed fell asleep and she drifted after him.

Ed had a nightmare: he was enclosed in a black van taking him from a prison in Teheran to the execution ground. Although naked, he was neither handcuffed nor tied. The siren screeched. Then he was awake, Carolina's soft red hair in his mouth, in his own bedroom, with the telephone ringing in the room next door.

Ed kissed Carolina on her throat, eased himself off her, got to his feet and went next door to see who was calling in the middle of the night.

It was Simone. She sounded very far away.

'Ed? Can you come over here please. It's Mark. He's–, he's dead. Suicide.'

# 22 SUICIDE?

Carolina drove him there. On the way, Ed tried to think, but Carolina drove erratically, which distracted him. Simone was waiting at the entrance to their block of flats, huddling against far more than the pre-dawn chill. Ed felt her shivering as she embraced him and then transmitted her tremors to Carolina before pulling away and saying to them both, in a distant voice:

'Come up and see.'

They took the lift in silence. Simone unlocked the flat door and led them in. They stood in the hall looking into the open living room. Mark's body, clothed in smartly casual attire, lay in a foetal position, but face-down. A noose girded his neck. The noose had been attached to an improvised beam that had been set up between two tall cupboards. The beam had come crashing down. An overturned stool lay between the cupboards.

'Don't touch the body, please. It *is* Mark.'

The impersonal pronoun describing his friend pierced Ed's armour.

'Poor old Mark.' He let out a sob, then pulled himself together.

'Let's be practical. Simone, you have to call the police. Carolina, we should leave, before we contaminate any evidence.'

Carolina was staring at the noose.

'Something is wrong here.'

'Everything is wrong here.' Simone's voice was low but steady.

'When did you find the body?'

'Shortly before I phoned you, Ed. Some students asked me out yesterday evening. A twenty-first birthday celebration. We were all girls.

I phoned Mark after class, from the School. He said go. He seemed normal, happy. He didn't say anything that sounded like a goodbye. This is wrong.'

Ed and Carolina waited while Simone summoned the police. Then all three of them went back down to the street. Simone waited for the police where she had waited for her friends. Carolina hugged her.

'When you're through with the police, you'd best come and stay with me. You may not want to be here.'

'Thanks. I will come.'

She was no longer shivering but stiff in Ed's embrace when he hugged her in his turn.

'Whatever I can do, Simone, I will. Just tell me what.'

'OK.' Simone turned and went back into her dark, silent block of flats.

They walked quickly to Carolina's car. Ed held the door open for her.

'I'll walk home, myself. I need to think.'

'You think too much, lover boy. You were better when you were an all-action business man.'

'Drive carefully, Carolina.'

Ed walked across the city as dawn turned the sky the colour of fresh blood. He thought about what he had seen. By the time he reached Largo do Andaluz, he had come to the conclusion that Mark had been murdered, and that both Simone and Carolina had worked that out before him. They had understood instinctively that the suicide scene was a set-up. Ed had realised what was wrong: even if his body weight had not brought the improvised beam crashing down while he was still alive, the length of the noose meant that a tall man like Mark would not have hung suspended but would have stood with his feet on the ground. Not to mention the absence of any apparent motive, warning or explanatory note.

Ed checked his door and his flat carefully. There was no sign of any actual or attempted intrusion. Nevertheless, he closed and fastened every open window and shutter before making himself a breakfast of scrambled eggs, toast with marmalade and half a bottle of whisky. After that, he slept until the afternoon. When he woke up, Ed wished he had not, but he got up, showered, took some aspirin and phoned first Simone then Carolina. Neither answered. He turned on the radio for the news. No mention of Mark's death yet. Since he did not have classes to give, he spent the rest of the day planning how to expand his cult-awareness efforts at the University, in Mark's memory and to help prevent further tragedies, if he could. In the evening, the television also failed to report the demise of its former star, Mark Rotherfield.

The next day, Ed packed a couple of bags and took them to his flat in Cascais. Seamus seemed pleased of the company.

'Stay as long as you want, mate. It's your house, like.'

Carolina phoned him the next day. By then, Ed felt even more certain that Mark had been murdered.

'I got the message you left. Simone's with me. The police told her it was a routine case of suicide. Kept asking her about any arguments they'd had, as though she'd driven him to it. It's crazy, Ed. Mark had just regained his life. He wasn't going to throw it away again!'

'You don't buy the idea of suicide, either, do you?'

'No, of course not. No motive.'

'But the scene in the room?'

'What do you think, Ed?'

'Well, the foetal position is a defensive position. It's a position you take up. You don't fall into it.'

'And that improvised beam couldn't hold a body's weight.'

'If it ever had to. That noose looked a bit short to hang a tall man like Mark from the height of a kitchen cupboard.'

'So you agree. Here, Simone wants to speak to you.'

Simone's voice had changed. It had become strong and determined.

'I tell you, Ed, I'm going to nail those bastards. You know they killed Mark.'

'Yes.'

243

'They killed my husband and I'm not going to let them get away with it! They got Mark, but they didn't manage to steal most of his money, and I'm going to use it to get them. I'm glad they'll rot in Hell, but I want to see them burn on Earth first, and I've got the money to make that happen. They think they're untouchable. Well, they are going to find out different! First, they took my husband from me. Then they tried to take his money. Then, when he finally saw the light and came back to me, they took his life. I'm not going to rest until I make them pay! What else is there for me to live for?'

*Your child, Mark's child*, thought Ed, but he kept his counsel and again offered Simone whatever help she might feel she needed.

To clear his head, Ed went for a long walk along the cliffs that led north out of the town. The breeze off the sea was cool. Ed filled his lungs and limped on, thinking of cults and killers and Ção and Carolina. On his return to the quiet street in which he was now staying, Ed saw a Ferrari parked outside his house. Paulo stood leaning against the passenger door.

'Hello, Mr. Scripps. Long time, no see.'

Ed shook his hand.

'Good to see you, Paulo. How did you know I was here?'

'Well, you weren't at Largo do Andaluz, so I came over here on the off chance. Seamus told me you were staying here now. He's out, by the way. Went off to see Antônia or whatever her name is.'

'Something like that. Come in.'

Paulo reached in through the car's open window and pulled out a bottle of French cognac.

'Brought you something.'

Ed made coffee to go with the cognac, and started to take the cups from the kitchen out onto the back patio. Paulo stopped him.

'No. This is business. Best stay inside and be sure it stays just between ourselves.

'OK. I'm comfortable here. What's new?'

'Always something new out of Africa, as old Aristotle said.

Things change.'

'Usually for the better, in Portugal.'

'Not always. I'm sorry about your friend Mark.'

'Thanks. I'm devastated, if you want to know, just devastated. Still can't believe he's dead. Mark Rotherfield.' Ed shook his head. 'Did you read about it?'

'It isn't in the papers. I heard about it on the grapevine.'

'Long tentacles your grapevine's got. Did it tell you who was responsible?'

'Mark himself, one way or another. Work it out.'

'I have, and it all comes back to Jorge. Omomnos.'

'Leave it alone, Ed, if you know what's good for you. It's bigger than you. Much bigger.'

Paulo looked uneasy, for once.

'There is something else. Ed, you're going to have to start thinking about money again.'

'That's all right. I used to do a lot of that.'

'So you won't mind too much. Though I mind, because this is not my style. Unfortunately, I've been forced out of my main line of business, and that has had a negative domino effect on my turnover. To put it bluntly, Ed, I need the money I lent you back.'

'What? Paulo, you can't mean that! You've got to be joking! I'm your long-term security, right?'

'No, you never were. I was just being friendly, trying to help you.'

'Oh, I see. For your sister's sake?'

Ed still harboured good memories of Lourdes' body, except for her tongue.

'No, for mine. I've done rather a lot for you, Ed, if you think about it, and you haven't given a lot back.'

'If you need money in a hurry, why don't you sell your flash motor?'

'Yes, I could sell the Ferrari and a few properties. If you were to give me some incentive.'

Paulo's confidence was back. He smiled suavely.

'Moisés also did you a big favour, got you that degree from Lourenço Marques University. At my request. You're a good-looking lad, Ed.'

Ed emptied his cognac into the coffee cup and swallowed it. The coffee gave him a burst of energy and he savoured the way the liquor smoothened its tang in his mouth.

He met Paulo's gaze.

'I like it when things are clear. I'll get you your money.'

As he listened to the sports car roar off down the habitually quiet street, Ed felt energised not only by the coffee but also by having himself to save once again.

He thought of asking Simone to lend him enough money to pay off Paulo. He knew she would let him have it at the drop of a hat, if she had it, but it was distasteful to Ed to ask under her present circumstances. Lourdes had been his only other rich friend. He had never asked his parents for money; he doubted their savings could match his present needs.

Ed was still ruminating when darkness settled over the seaside town and the patio where Ed sat. His position was not so bad. At worst, he could approach a loan shark, buy himself some time. Or save all that trouble and give himself to Paulo. A bit of homosexual experience would not kill him; it might even teach him something he could use in his regular love life. But Paulo was the type of person who liked to show off, and Ed baulked at the idea of being paraded as Paulo's latest conquest.

A shadow briefly fell from the living room window. Ed thought he heard footsteps inside. No light went on. He catapulted himself from his chair on the patio to the kitchen door and crouched there outside it, hidden, he hoped. Silence. Darkness. He eased the door open. He was glad the hinges did not creak. Ed rose and entered the kitchen. He picked a meat knife from the cutlery rack beside the sink and crept to the door to the corridor. It was ajar. A shadow flickered towards him.

The chorus of *Seven Drunken Nights* started and ended in quick succession. Seamus stood before him.

'Bloody hell fire, man! Look at you!'

Ed relaxed his grip on the knife.

'Bloody hell fire! Can a man not come quietly into his own house without being threatened?'

'Sorry, Seamus. I'm sorry. I'm not threatening you. Here, let's sit down and have a bevvy.'

They did. Ed apologised again, and tried to explain.

'I'm a bit over-wrought these days. And it is my house, if you remember. Although –'

'Tell me you want to sell. I thought you'd come round to it.'

'Can you pay cash?'

'Only if I have to.'

'You do. Can you pay soon?'

'If the price is right.'

'Are you sober enough to talk business?'

'As much as you are.'

'Good man. Let's have some light in here, and hammer out a fair price.'

Less than an hour later, they were toasting their deal with *vinho verde*. Then they strolled down to the bay to eye the talent taking the evening promenade. Ed felt like a bachelor again, in charge of the life ahead of him.

*

Mark Rotherfield's burial took place at the Protestant cemetery on one of Lisbon's many hills, not far from the English Council. They laid him to rest within shouting distance of Henry Fielding. The novelist had come to the city to improve his health, and been disappointed.

Ed wanted to talk to Simone, and to Carolina, but Carolina was physically supporting Simone, who was weak and wan and weepy, amid a group of women that included Mark's mother and sister, who had flown in together from England. Ed had not weathered the days since Mark's death well. Every night now he lay awake for hours thinking of

Mark's cruel end. Perhaps because of the insomnia, he felt as though a hammer was regularly crashing into his brain; the pain of it disrupted his powers of reasoning.

As the clergyman from the Protestant church attached to the cemetery, whose presence Mark's family had insisted upon, drew the ceremony to an end, and Mark's coffin was covered with the dark earth of his adopted home, the hammer in Ed's mind finally left his brain in peace.

Ed was last in the line to pay respects to the widow, and Simone asked him to accompany her over to the adjoining park, where Carolina and some members of the erstwhile rescue group had set up a refreshment table below trees that sheltered it from the heat of the afternoon sun. Simone seemed to gain strength with every step.

'Ed, I'm going to get those bastards.'

'Simone, whatever you do, don't put your baby in danger. Your baby is Mark's last gift to you.'

'Apart from all his money. And I can't help thinking that my baby and I are already in danger. A little more will not make any difference.'

Ed left Simone to the attentions of other sympathisers, who had turned out for her in force, whereas few of Mark's one-time hangers-on had come. Trying to get close enough to speak to Carolina, who was elusive, Ed found himself on the edge of a group that Simone was addressing in determined tones.

'Let me try and be rational, if I can. Murder by suicide – we know how it's done. First you dig up all the dirt you can on your victim and get it published. This establishes apparent motives for suicide. What you can't find, you invent, of course. Then you kill him. Or her, and make it look like suicide. Hanging or falling off a bridge are old stalwarts. You have to make it look plausible, so the coroner and the public will swallow it, but you leave some detail that tells those you want to warn off what really happened. If you've got any kind of organisation behind you, that makes it easier. Yeah, like a cult. Which will also have plenty of money to buy those who are reluctant to swallow it. Of course, you threaten them, as well. Carrot and stick, right? Oh, yes, and if you hang him, get the press to suggest 'auto-eroticism'. No-one loves a wanker, do they?'

Gabriela from the erstwhile rescue group was brave enough to contradict her.

'But that didn't happen with Mark, did it? Nobody found or spread any dirt about him.'

Simone's answer was rapid.

'No, because they wanted to keep everything out of the public eye. The strange thing is that they have succeeded, so far. That will change. You know, none of this is new, except to me. Now I've got money, and I'm going to reveal this murder for what it was.'

Ed realised it was not the time to be seeking the company of Carolina. It was not the time to be pursuing anybody. The tide of history that had appeared inexorable in the country and in his own life had slowed and spread, if not turned. He could no longer predict either. Even in the new Portugal, a man's murder could go unnoticed, or be wilfully ignored, and his own wife could be reticent to return to his love. Well, he would not abandon either Mark's memory and Simone's thirst for justice, or Ção's future. What he would do was resume a can-do attitude towards the direction of his own life.

Before he left the gathering, Ed went to take leave of Simone. She took him to one side and told him she would be returning to France, temporarily. Keith had offered to hold her job open for her until the October start of the academic year. She was in a loquacious mood, afire with righteous indignation.

'You know what's underneath all this, Ed? Religion. Or rather the idea that anything that is done in the name of religion is good, that religions operate in a special sphere above the law, where reason must be kept at bay.'

Ed recalled his own family background.

'My father doesn't think that, even though he's a Church of England vicar, same as the chap who's just laid Mark to rest.'

'Are you sure, Ed? When it comes down to it? Well, I can't change that: it'll take centuries of education, and even then, who knows? But in a country like this, I can try to make them stop applying that untouchability to just any religion. I can portray the cult that stole Mark from me and then killed him as a cult that threatens their religion.'

'Christianity?'

'Catholicism, Ed. Ninety-five per cent self-declared Catholics in this country, did you know that? I can be one, too. A devout widow. France is a mostly Catholic country, after all. Like in France, the people here won't want false prophets and 'pagan' cults luring their sons and daughters away from the true Church.'

Simone saw a sceptical look cross her friend's face.

'You want to know how one woman is going to do that. Not one woman, Ed, but one woman's money, money to pay for everything that can be done and for what cannot officially, legally be done. To get the Church, the media, the law, all on my side.'

'That might not be enough, Simone.'

'You're right, but even so. Have you got any friends in Sicily, Ed? I'll stop at nothing, to make those bastards pay! You think Pangaia will still be in Portugal in ten years' time? Believe me, Ed, it won't!'

Before Ed finally got away, he was accosted by a lanky woman he deemed a little older than himself. She had Mark's features and accent, though her face was tighter.

'I say, excuse me, you must be that fellow Mark was always going on about.'

'Was he? I dare say. Ed Scripps.'

'Yes, you did well, in his eyes. You went from *Mr Scripps the Trader* to *My Best Friend*, in a few months.'

Ed smiled.

'I tried to help him. A lot of us did.'

'Mark appreciated that.'

Ed's face clouded. Guilt knotted his stomach.

'He might still be alive if we'd left him in peace.'

'That's what Mummy and Daddy say, but it isn't true. If you'd left him to rot, he'd be dead inside. When he really died, physically, he knew he had friends and a wife who loved him. His family – us back in England, I mean – did not one single bloody thing for him. So, thank you, *Mr Scripps the Trader*, my brother's best friend.'

As Ed limped out of the park, the sun beat down on his unprotected head and neck. He hailed a taxi, thankful that he could still afford it.

## 23  Final Warning

Portugal celebrated the anniversary of the Revolution, 25 April, less fervently in 1977 than on earlier occasions. People's attention now focused more on down-to-earth matters like inflation, which had reached forty per cent. In contrast, the Portuguese political tsunami was still making waves on the other side of the Atlantic, in its former colony of Brazil, where Clarice had made her home. There, to stifle the demand for freedom, the fascist generals who held power had tentatively allowed a little strictly supervised democracy. Given the chance, Brazilians had voted for more democracy and less dictatorship, and now the military régime was making a last, desperate attempt to slam shut the floodgates it had opened. That, too, was not a major topic of conversation in Lisbon. Ed was glad Clarice had failed to lure him to Brazil, where repression was again the order of the day.

Mark's death still kept Ed awake at night, but not every night, and no longer all night. Ed now immersed himself in day-to-day concerns: conveyancing and classes among them. He continued to await his wife's return, but began to accept that it might not happen soon. He had made up his mind not to let the anticipation paralyse him.

Ed would have loved to hold a farewell party for Simone before she left for France, but Simone told him she did not want one.

'There's no cause for farewells. I'll be back so often you won't realise I've been away. Anyway, emotional goodbyes wouldn't do the baby any good, not to mention the alcohol I'd be more than tempted to accompany them with.'

Once her house guest had departed, Carolina came back forcefully into Ed's life. She found him at the University, tricked him into laughing his way out of the deepest levels of his depression and brought him home to her flat. Ed was surprised how big it was.

'Well, I need it and we can afford it. The benefits of marrying into a rich family, never despise them.'

She was categorical about where Ed and she could or could not make love.

'There's the room I'm keeping for Simone, there's the room with the marital bed, there's the future nursery, there's the room for visiting relatives. They're all sacrosanct. You can screw me in either of the other two bedrooms, the living room, my study, kitchen, bathroom, wherever else takes your fancy. Or mine.'

Carolina took Ed's fancy in any and all of them. She gave herself generously, and Ed was attentive to her needs. His one night there turned into a full week. Carolina's bubbly personality and acerbic wit brought Ed ever closer to his old self. As he relaxed, his proactive nature reasserted itself. Carolina energised him, and the more energy he bestowed on her, the better she liked it. It was a virtuous circle.

Carolina surprised Ed one night by guiding him into the marital bedroom.

'What's going on?'

'A wee bit of role-play, so you'll maybe understand me better, if you want to.'

'I do.'

'My husband packs a good right hook.'

'What?! Are you serious?'

Carolina nodded.

'The bastard!! Look, I am not going to hit you, now or ever, not even in jest.'

'No, it's the other way around. If I even defend myself, he gets more violent. You wouldn't believe what a make-up artiste I've become, disguising all the bruises. And next time you're on top of me, which I trust will be very soon, remember there's a couple of cracked ribs beneath you. No, *I* want to hit *you*, the way I can never hit *him*. You're a big strong lad, you can take it, right?'

'Try me.'

The rush of blows Carolina instantly unleashed upon him caught Ed by surprise and sent him sprawling.

'You all right?'

'Sure.'

'Get up.'

This time Ed was prepared. He moved out of range of some of Carolina's punches and slaps, parried others, and let a few catch him, while Carolina let out a stream of invective in three languages. When he sensed her tiring, Ed drew Carolina into an embrace and held her as her words turned into sobs. Then he took her to the bed, undressed her, shed his own clothes and made love to her as gently as he knew how.

Carolina was up early the next morning to get away to her morning class at the University. Ed came blearily into the kitchen and found her there preparing toast and coffee for them both.

'Ready for round two, are you?'

'Not just yet, Carolina.'

'You've no idea how much I needed that. You're a good man, Ed.'

'Sure. Have you put sugar in for me?'

'Just the one. You know, *you* could be just the one it'd be worth a Baha'i girl going through the shame of a divorce for. It'd mean waiting a year, though. Ah, I can see from your face you'd not be happy waiting that long. Anyway, don't push your luck, sunshine. Here's your breakfast. I've got to go. Let yourself out when you're ready.'

Ed let the coffee go cold. Did she really mean it? Ed had assumed he was just a plaything to Carolina. She fascinated Ed, and in bed their harmony was unmatched in his experience. But … he loved his wife, and his heart could have only one mistress.

Ed made himself some fresh toast and some tea, showered, dressed and gathered his stuff. He found a sheet of paper, scrawled a note and left it on the kitchen table.

*See you soon. Ed xxx.*
*You lying bastard,* he told himself with a wry grin.

*

Ed moved back to Cascais, where he sorted out the details and paperwork of selling the flat to Seamus. Seamus had split up with Antônia, and was eager to find a replacement. Or at least to vet likely candidates. He and Ed found plenty of those in the town's discos, and even strolling its waterfront. As their tally of one-night stands mounted, Ed pushed back the day he hoped Ção would return. To Seamus, he paraphrased his father's favourite saint, Augustine: *Lord, make my wife virtuous, but not yet.*

At the university, Ed's efforts to raise his students' awareness of cults continued, with greater fervour. He no longer limited those efforts to a single group of students. The students were always interested, but a few simply did not believe him about Pangaia, Omomnos and Mark. Several, though, had tales of their own to tell.

As soon as Ed received the flat-sale money from Seamus, he contacted Paulo to tell him it was ready for him. Paulo seemed barely interested.

'I'll send my sister to collect it.'

Lourdes duly arrived, driving a new Volvo.

'Want to drive?'

Ed did. He drove the smooth Swedish vehicle along the coast north towards Azenhas do Mar, but thought better of visiting Mark's cherished village and stopped at a resort called Praia das Maçãs – *Apple Beach* – where they sat in a bar overlooking the fine sand as the evening sun fought an Atlantic mist. Lourdes was tanned, fit and relaxed. Ed told her how good she looked.

'Well, things are working out for us, all of us, except sometimes for that no-good brother of mine.'

'Working out? What do you mean?'

'We're getting everything we wanted from the Revolution. People in this country have never had so much personal freedom. We've brought our boys home from Africa, and left the locals to kill each other. We never educated them to the level where they could run a modern state, so in, say, ten years, they'll be begging us to come back and run things for them. Meanwhile, a young man with entrepreneurial talent could clean up there.' She looked at him pointedly and took a sip of her chilled white wine.

'I'm not going anywhere. I'm happy here. I'm staying for the long term.'

'You know, maybe you should reconsider that.'

'How else are things working out for you?'

'Well, the amount of absolute poverty in this country is falling. That means that the next generation will be better fed, better housed, taller, healthier and no doubt more self-obsessed than us. They won't want to risk all that by snatching the wealth from its rightful owners, such as my family.'

Ed absent-mindedly took a sip from Lourdes' glass. She called for a clean glass and poured them both more wine.

'Lourdes. Do you know who killed Mark?'

'Sure, Jorge "Omomnos". But you know that, too.'

'Yes, I think so. For his money, I presume.'

'Mostly. You don't need to know the details.'

'What I need, Lourdes, is vengeance. For Mark. I don't want Jorge to live!'

'I can understand that. Really. But why are you telling me? What do you imagine I can do?'

'I know Paulo has contacts who are good at fulfilling contracts. I know I owe Paulo, and I'm ready to give him whatever he wants in exchange for them.'

Lourdes laughed, then abruptly stopped. She shook her head.

'Ed, really. Grow up. You're out of your league. Sure, Paulo has contacts of the kind you're hinting at, but these days he doesn't have much influence over them, if any. Ed, stop playing with fire or, believe me, you'll get roasted, and I hate funerals.'

She poured the last of the wine and drank it slowly. Ed's stood untouched. Lourdes noticed, picked up his glass and drank its contents, gazing levelly into Ed's eyes.

'Don't look so sad and bewildered. Let's find a sheltered spot among the sand dunes. It's second-chance time.'

*

Gabriela often smiled at Ed in class. This time, from start to finish, her long dark hair framed a face that seemed to be making a constant unsuccessful effort to keep the world's greatest joke to itself. When Ed wrapped up and bid the students all a good evening, she bounced to her feet and came over to him, grinning without restraint.

'Hey, Ed, I've got something for you, something to make you happy.'

*I don't doubt it*, Ed thought.

'You're a football fan, I know. What's your team?'

'Stevenage Athletic.'

Gabriela's face fell.

'I mean Stevenage Borough. Athletic didn't follow my advice and went bust. New club. Chiltern Youth League, but we'll be back in the Southern League in no time.'

'Don't you follow some other team as well? Someone I might have heard of?'

'Yes, actually. Liverpool. Champions of England.'

Gabriela's face lit up again.

'You know they've got a big match this month.'

'Sure. Borussia Moenchengladbach. European Cup Final. In Rome. I hope it's on telly.'

'Forget that. Look, my paper wants a Portuguese-speaking Englishman to accompany the journalist they're sending. To give a Liverpool supporter's insight with comments that he can put into his articles. I suggested you. There's no money in it, but you get a free flight, hotel, and you see the game from the press box. What do you say?'

Ed crushed Gabriela's soft frame in a bear hug.

'I say you're an angel, Gabriela, an absolute angel! You're not kidding me, are you? This is a dream come true!'

The journalist, Manuel Rocha, was already in Rome, soaking up the atmosphere, when Ed took the plane. As they crossed the Mediterranean, Ed reflected on developments in his life. Lourdes had deemed his lovemaking in the sand dunes 'satisfactory' and hinted he might get a further chance to demonstrate improvement. He didn't appreciate women rating him, but his businessman's brain could see the usefulness of performance appraisals. His mind turned to a more sombre matter: the apparent impossibility of bringing official pressure to bear on Pangaia. Well, its friends in high places would have to sing a different tune if, or perhaps when, the killer cult decided it needed to eliminate more than one member at a time. The thought of whom its next victims might include chilled Ed until the coast of Italy appeared below him and he remembered why he was travelling.

Manuel was an amiable, portly man nearing forty who shared Ed's penchant for modest good living and was also serious about his job. So serious that as well as Ed he had brought over a Portuguese-speaking German to give the other side's view. Ed was not best pleased to renew his acquaintance with Calvin, but, away from his normal habitat, Ção's former Sussex School teacher proved affable and forthcoming, as well as knowledgeable about football and Rome.

Ed had swotted up on the history of Liverpool FC and the composition of its present team, so he was able to match Calvin in providing Manuel with comments that he could use. Naturally, he far outdid the German in exuberance as Liverpool took an early lead in the Olympic Stadium, withstood the pressure that followed Borussia's equaliser, forged ahead in the second half and sealed the victory that gave them Europe's top trophy, for the first time, with a late penalty. Together, Ed, Calvin and Manuel toured Rome's bars afterwards, interviewing festive Scousers and distraught Rhinelanders to add depth to Manuel's reports and their own hangovers the next morning. Their own party continued all the following day, and barely let up even on the flight back to Lisbon. Somewhere in that time, they each poured out their hearts to the other two and promptly forgot what they heard, though Manuel's refusal to discuss Pangaia lodged in Ed's mind, as did a comment the drunken Calvin passed down from his pulpit:

'Herr Scripps, you have made a cult of your wife.'

Ed clutched a tacky replica of the European Cup as he said goodbye to Calvin and Manuel outside Lisbon airport's arrivals hall, convinced that he had made two new friends for life, thanks to Gabriela. He took a taxi to Largo do Andaluz, to empty the mailbox and crash there for the night. He should have done that earlier, to make sure the utility bills got paid. Indeed, when he got there, the mailbox was stuffed full and the electricity failed to come on when he pressed the switch just inside the flat door. He stood still and let his eyes get accustomed to the darkness. The moment they did, he let go of the replica cup. The sound of its fall was muffled by the papers on which it landed. His flat had been trashed again. This time, the intruders had made a thorough job of it, sparing only the fittings. Doors, left open, still stood on their hinges; light bulbs still hung from ceilings. Ed located the fuse box in the hall, opened it and pressed a couple of switches. Electric light illuminated the devastation.

Every personal item that could be broken had been smashed. Every piece of paper in the flat had been ripped to pieces and tossed on the floor. Ed looked at scraps of his student records, his wedding photos, his Lourenço Marques and Open University degrees. He picked his way among the shreds and shards to the kitchen, hoping to let the taste of beer mask the bitterness in his mouth. The wreckage of plates and glasses vied with broken empty bottles to tear at his shoes and menace his ankles. Ed opened the fridge. On the shelf above the vegetable compartment, his passport sat, intact, in a quagmire of congealed blood. The blood had dripped from the severed neck of a plumed cockerel that lay on a shelf above it. Otherwise, the fridge was empty. Ed staggered across the kitchen, opened the door onto the balcony stepped outside and drew in slow breaths of the cooling night air. He sat on the bare iron floor that was also the top of the fire escape and contemplated how best to ensure that he might still have a future to think about.

\*

Well before sunrise, Ed got to his feet, went back into the kitchen, made his way to the main bedroom, threw himself onto the ripped mattress and plunged into sleep. When the morning heat in the enclosed room woke him, he got up, ascertained that the water, gas and telephone had not yet been cut off, then washed and called the police, not that he expected much help from them. When he returned to the bedroom to put his dirty clothes back on, he noticed the two unused bullets at the foot of the bed. Gingerly, he picked them up and slipped them into his pocket, where they felt cold through the lining.

The police, once they arrived, found some neighbours below to interview. One family had heard nothing, but an old lady living alone had been kept awake a week previously by what she believed to be loud music and things breaking, which she had assumed to mark just another bloody foreigners' party, though she hadn't heard the usual shouting. The police told Ed to pass by the nearest police station to file a report: the little cash in the flat had disappeared, and occasionally thieves got caught. Meanwhile, he should clear up, wearing gloves so as not to cut himself: they did not want anyone to get hurt.

Ed went out and purchased suitable gloves from a hardware store. On his way back, he bought a newspaper from a kiosk and read it in his local café, where he challenged his unsettled stomach with pastries and tea. The lead story, for once, was from abroad. In Angola, pro-Moscow stalwarts within the government had become alarmed at President Neto's tendency to speak and act without consulting the country's Soviet backers, and especially at his refusal to grant the Soviet Union permanent military bases within Angola. They had made a bloody attempt to overthrow him. Neto appealed for intervention by the Cuban troops stationed in the capital, who had helped Angola to contain South African invaders in the south and those from Zaire in the north. The Cubans hesitated, but then sent in tanks and crushed the attempted coup. Ed read every word of the reports, and the analyses. Then he went and bought more newspapers, and read all they had to say about the war-torn African country, while his subconscious mind worked on his own predicament.

The two bullets weighed heavily in his pocket.

## 24 BE CAREFUL WHAT YOU WISH FOR

Seamus was kind. He offered to rent Ed his former room in the flat in Cascais. Ed, however, believed his moving in there might infect his friend with some of the danger he himself was in, so he declined Seamus's offer, and instead checked into a small hotel located between Lisbon city centre and the University. He did not feel a similar responsibility to ensuring that the management avoid bloodstains on its carpets; his duties in that setting were entirely to himself.

Ed also felt a responsibility to his students at the University. At his next class, he wrapped up his awareness-raising project. He explained exactly what had happened, and that he interpreted the trashing of his flat as a clear warning to him to shut up and get out, or else. He wanted to stay in Portugal, but he did not intend to let his tongue get him buried there. He told them their cult awareness, like his, was now high enough to inoculate them all for the rest of their lives, but asked them to be cautious enough to ensure that those lives were suitably long. It was a message he had already internalised. The expressions Ed saw in response were a mixture of denial, understanding and fear. He had never wanted to bring fear into his classroom. Ed re-stated what he had affirmed at the beginning: that end-of-year marks would be based on the quality of English that each student had used throughout the year, not on any opinions voiced or attitudes shown. He would bring that year to an end as soon as was logistically possible: a piece of news that was always well received.

Before he got the chance to fulfil that pledge, he received a phone call at the hotel from Seamus. Ção wanted to talk to him. Finding the phone at Largo do Andaluz cut off, she had tried the Cascais flat. Seamus had taken the call. He had refused to give out Ed's present phone number but confirmed that Ed was no longer living at Largo do Andaluz, or Cascais, and offered to pass on a message.

Ed was curious as to what Ção wanted all of a sudden. He phoned the unfamiliar number that Seamus had given him, and asked her directly. She seemed taken aback by his abrupt manner.

'Well, I want to see you, don't I?'

'OK. Just tell me when and where?'

'Ed, are you all right?'

'No, I'm not. One of my best friends has been murdered, I've been threatened with death, and things generally are falling apart.'

'I'm sorry, Ed. I had no idea.'

'Don't worry. You're well out of it. Of course I'd love to see you. You know that. Just tell me when and where.'

She gave a Lisbon address and named an evening time that Ed changed to Saturday morning.

\*

Ed took a taxi to a part of Lisbon named Mouraria, which had evidently seen better days, though perhaps not since the Moors had in fact left, some seven centuries earlier. Ed's colleague Rupert Harley-Davidson liked to tell people that when the Crusaders had retaken Lisbon, they had massacred everyone sheltered within its walls, including the Christian archbishop. It had never occurred to them that a degree of religious tolerance might be operating within the Moorish city. The name Ção had given was the only one next to the intercom. Ed pressed the bell, and after a while the street door clicked open. He pushed it back and stepped inside. There was a central courtyard open to the sky. He looked up and saw his wife's beloved face looking down at him.

'Come on up, Ed. I'm on the third floor. There isn't a lift, I'm afraid.'

Ed bounded up the first flight of steps, then slowed to be sure he would not meet Ção out of breath.

She greeted him wearing a short, low-cut dark blue dress, as though she were about to leave for a party. She slipped into Ed's arms and kissed him with a restrained passion that reminded Ed of simpler, better days. The aroma of cinnamon filled his nostrils. He stood back from Ção and shook his head to clear it.

'Come inside.'

She led him through an open door, across a vestibule and into a large living room that contained a few pieces of antique furniture.

'What's going on, Ção?'

'Ed, I'm so sorry. Tell me everything that's happened.'

Ed told his wife about everything except his love life, or rather his sex life. When he finished, he was surprised to see tears on her cheeks.

'Poor Mark. Oh, Ed, I'm so sorry I've ignored you all this time. I'll never do it again, I promise.'

'And why is that?' He already had a strong inkling as to the answer. He had been waiting to hear the words for a long time.

'You're my husband, Ed. I love you, and I want to live with you again.'

Ed felt dizzy; his heartbeat accelerated. He noticed that although it was June, the room was cold. He managed to keep his voice, at least, under control.

'What about João?'

Ção drew a small silk handkerchief from her sleeve and dabbed at her cheeks. Then she looked directly at Ed.

'I loved João, I can't deny it. But our love was kind of destructive, and in the end it destroyed itself.'

'Does she feel the same way?'

'I think she still loves me. I've told her that it's over between us, but she doesn't want to understand. It's you I love, Ed, not João.'

'I know.' He had always known.

Ção stood up. She placed her legs apart, looked at Ed's dilated eyes, then brought her legs together and moved her hands to the hem of her dress.

'Let me show you how much I love you, Ed.'

'I know.'

Calvin's drunken words came back to him. For so many months he had worked towards this moment, when he would again enter the temple of the cult of Çāo and lose himself in its wonderful rituals.

'I already know. You don't need to show me anything.'

Çāo stared at him blankly.

'I don't understand. What do you mean?'

'Çāo, a lot has happened. I knew this moment would come but even so, it's caught me off balance. I need time to think things through, to see what's best for both of us – for all of us.'

'I know what's best for us, Ed, for you and me.'

'I don't, yet. It isn't obvious any more. Look, Çāo, are you staying here for a while?'

'Yes. Until you take me back, until we go home.'

'OK, I'll call you.'

'What? You can't just leave me here! You can't just walk out on me!'

Ed was already on the stairs. At the bottom, he heard Çāo's voice resonating around the courtyard.

'Ed? Ed!'

He pulled back the heavy wooden door and stepped out into the street. The light and the heat disoriented him. He got his bearings and headed down towards the central square, Rossio, where he could catch the underground. The scent of jasmine hung in the air.

The world looked different to Ed. It was again a place in which he could get what he wanted, provided he used patience and skill. For days, he was light-headed; he was happy. Nevertheless, he recognised an under-current of unease in his joy, and traced it back to the soul-searching that Calvin's words had provoked.

Ed went to look for Lourdes, but got side-tracked on the way, and instead spent the day in Sintra, wandering among its palaces and gardens, and wondering about himself and Çāo and their future. Sitting in a deserted summer house in the grounds of the Pena Palace, listening to the bees flitting from one delight to another among the semi-tropical vegetation outside the open windows, it struck him that what he desired was Çāo's wish to come back to him, more than her actual return. The knowledge burnt into his brain like the midsummer sun into his skin. He had achieved his desire. Now he could look more objectively at its possible consequences.

*

Ed was not used to thinking so much without acting. After a few days of it, his concentration lapsed and he understood it was time to move. He phoned Çāo again. It was wonderful once more to hear happiness in her voice when she realised it was Ed who was calling. She wanted to see the damage that had been done to the flat in Largo do Andaluz, and so Ed arranged to meet her there.

As he ascended the stairs to his floor, Ed hoped that Çāo would be waiting for him, seated at the top of the stairs. She was. As he turned into the final flight, the sight of her shapely legs triggered strong, erotic memories. She sat there smiling happily, but said nothing as he approached. Ed let one hand run over a tanned thigh as the other hand cupped the back of Çāo's neck and brought his wife's mouth onto his. They kissed with passion until they had to draw back for breath.

'Not here, Ed.' Çāo giggled. 'It's too public. Take me inside.'

Even though Ed had cleared up and cleaned up as best he could, the flat was desolate. Çāo was visibly shocked by the state of her former home. Her confident mood dissipated.

'This is dreadful Ed. It's like a bad dream.'

Ed remembered the nightmare of seeing their wedding photos torn to shreds on the floor in front of him.

'What are you going to do?'

'Put it on the market. Sell it as soon as I can.'

Çāo looked around carefully.

'You know, together we could do it up. Perhaps make it more comfortable than it was before.'

'It's too dangerous for me to live here now. And for you, too. I'm sorry. I only ever wanted to make life better for you.'

'Ed, if we're together, we will make life better for each other.'

The fire lit by Çáo's lips had flickered out.

'Let's sit down, Çáo. Let's talk things over.'

The only place to sit was on the floor. Çáo hitched up her skirt and sat in the lotus position. Ed knelt opposite her and looked into her eyes. The sadness he saw there mingled with the familiar cinnamon scent to kindle his lust. He came straight to the point.

'Did you ever love me, Çáo?'

'Of course, Ed! I do love you! How can you doubt it?' she shifted her thighs so that her skirt inched higher.

'I doubt it because you left me so easily.'

'Do you think it was easy? Believe me, it was the hardest thing I've ever done.'

'No, I don't believe you. I've realised how much you loved João. And you know what? I believe you still do.'

'How can you say that?' Çáo began to weep. 'I left João because I realised it's you I love. It always was.'

'Çáo, I want to be loved, for myself. We all do. In the end, I think the nature of the love carries more weight than the person it's coming from. I don't want to be a poor substitute for the person you truly love.'

'Ed, I – truly – love – you.' She placed her hands over her eyes and leaned forward until her elbows were on the floor, keeping her arms in place while tears oozed from between her fingers.

'I worshipped you, Çáo. I'm not sure any more whether that was love.'

'I worship you, Ed, my love, my husband.'

'It's love that matters to me now, not worship.'

Çáo sat up and dried her eyes with her hands.

'Are you saying you won't take me back?'

'Not until I'm sure of your love.'

'Where else can I go?'

'You love João. Go back to her.'

'I don't and I can't! Why do you pretend not to understand?'

'I know your father would be happy to have you back with him. You've got a sister. There's Estrela. Or you could think about a new life with your mother in Canada.'

Ção got to her feet. Fury blazed in her eyes.

'You're heartless, Ed Scripps. You think with your prick and feel with your balls! No wonder your life's all screwed up!'

Ed smiled.

Ção slapped him with enough force to send him sprawling on the floor. He listened to her high heels clacking their way out of the flat as he waited for his brain to clear. With his head still ringing, he turned onto his back, stretched his legs and fell asleep.

Ed's head ached when he woke. He had not been asleep long. As he left the flat, he closed the new mortise lock with great care. He took the underground to travel the few stops from the Park to Rossio Square, where he bought himself a panama hat to protect his headache from the sun and some aspirin to get rid of it altogether. He bought a bottle of mineral water from a kiosk in the Avenida da Liberdade, swigged from it to ease a couple of the aspirin down his throat, then sat on a bench by the Avenida's stretch of water and imagined himself asking the black swans which inhabited it what he should do about Ção and the future. A few passers-by stopped to watch the mad foreigner talking to animals, but this was Lisbon, where St. Anthony had preached a sermon to the fish in the River Tagus, so they soon moved on.

With the help of the aspirin, the hat and his unperturbed audience, Ed started to feel considerably better. He was astonished at himself for not having instantly welcomed his wife back into anything more than his arms and his confidence, yet the message arriving from his subconscious was a saying popular from ten years earlier: today is the first day of the rest of your life. Ção would no longer dictate his heartbeats. He need no longer hold back his emotions from the women he slept with, nor even from those with whom his relationships remained platonic. If Ção were to prove she truly loved him not João, she might yet succeed in reigniting his exclusive love for her. Nonetheless, Ed decided to offer first refusal to a woman who had already shown both passion and compassion, maturity and spontaneity, who both saw through Ed and saw things of value in Ed, a woman who, Ed was sure, would repay love with love.

He made his way through the muggy afternoon to her house. A neighbour was leaving the building when he arrived, so Ed took the opportunity to slip inside and walk up to her floor. Nobody answered when he pressed the bell, nor when he knocked on the flat door with his fist. He looked through the keyhole, but it was dark inside. Ed reflected that it was just as well: he was sweaty and had not had a shower that morning. *The rancid lover*, he imagined her calling him.

Ed took a taxi home, had a refreshingly cool shower and set about the task of preparing his end-of-year assessments without the meticulous records he had kept at Largo do Andaluz. He phoned her at regular intervals, but she did not answer.

The next morning Ed caught a bus to the university. Fortunately, she was teaching that morning and the schedule tacked to the notice board listed her classroom. Ed noted how efficient the administration had become in the last two years. The classroom was empty. Ed waited, but no-one came to fill it. Ed stopped and listened outside other classrooms, but none that were occupied emitted the sound of English being spoken. He went down to the basement café. Xavier and Ashley were standing at the bar, drinking coffee and beer, respectively. Without getting anything for himself, Ed went over to join them.

'Have you seen Carolina? She's supposed to be here today.'

Ashley shook his head and winked at him. Xavier put down his cup and spoke.

'Haven't you heard? She's gone. Back to Iran, for ever. She said she could see more chance of a better life there than here. Faith, hope and hubby. I guess somebody disappointed her here. Whoosh!' He made a gesture of an aeroplane taking off.

A stony silence fell among them. Ashley broke it.

'I'm sorry, Ed. I wasn't certain about you two, either.'

Xavier looked lost, then distraught.

'I'm sorry, Ed. I never thought –'

Ed managed to generate a hollow laugh.

'It doesn't matter. Let's, er, drink to new starts. What do you fancy?'

A while later, Rupert Harley-Davidson joined them. He was in celebratory mood because his wife had just accepted an important post at the Ministry of Education. His enthusiasm affected all of them. Rupert invited them all to lunch at a Brazilian restaurant staffed by political exiles, where Ed became his former animated self. After lunch, they proceeded to a beerhouse downtown, where the afternoon passed in a convivial blur.

Ed did not remember how he had spent the evening, nor even where he was, when his hangover woke him the next morning. Then he recognised his hotel room and remembered that he had bought a bottle of aspirin the previous morning. Ed rolled off the bed and staggered into the bathroom, where he tried to refresh his body and his memory with a shower. Once he was dressed and feeling slightly better, he located his bottle of aspirin, put on his hat and headed out to a nearby café, stopping to buy a morning newspaper on the way. In the café, Ed fortified himself with toast, tea and aspirin while he scanned the newspaper for reports on Angola. He found none. However, a small item in one of the local crime pages caught his attention. Apparently, the authorities had closed down an 'esoteric temple' north of Lisbon, and arrested some of its leaders, for tax evasion.

Ed's thoughts sprang to Simone.

*Bloody hell! She's done it! What a woman!!*

Then his thoughts turned to Mark and his elation disappeared.

*Too late for poor Mark.*

Ed paid his bill and left the café. The day was already hot. He hailed a taxi and gave the address of the British Cemetery. As he approached Mark's grave, he saw that he would not be alone in paying his respects.

The woman had her back to Ed. Her head was bowed. Thick, dark hair. Full figure. Long dress. All familiar.

Gabriela must have heard Ed's footsteps on the gravel behind her, because she turned to see who it was. Her misted eyes smiled in recognition.

'I see you read my paper.'

'I buy yours first.'

'It was only in mine. There won't be anything on TV or the radio, either.'

'Tax evasion?'

'If it was good enough for Al Capone, it's good enough for Omomnos.'

'It's hard to believe they've really shut down Pangaia.'

'We can go and see for ourselves, if you like. My car is here, and I've got the time.'

They drove to Vila Abade. Gabriela told Ed that she was grateful to him for more than teaching her English: he had given her the confidence to keep pressing for a job at a newspaper until someone gave her a chance. They, too, were satisfied with the way she had taken it.

At Vila Abade, the dismantling of the gates and perimeter wall had been thorough. The property was more extensive than it appeared from the outside, with orchards and kitchen gardens as well as houses. Wandering among its two dozen empty buildings was like walking through a ghost town. The cicadas were loud, though intermittent.

'Where have all the people gone?'

'The kids will have gone home. The drifters will have drifted on. The ringleaders are in jail, awaiting trial –'

'For the wrong crime.'

'With every chance of being convicted, Ed. And the people who were using this place and those people for deep cover have simply gone elsewhere and dug deeper.'

'And you think that's a decent outcome?'

'There will be no more murders like Mark's, so, yes, I do.'

Ed noted a beauty in Gabriela's features as she concentrated on her driving on the road back to Lisbon. He reflected that very soon she would no longer be his student. He was puzzled as to why Simone had been in contact with Gabriela but not with him. He asked, and Gabriela explained that Simone had tried to trace him but without success; apparently, Seamus was away. She dropped Ed at his hotel, and wrote down Simone's current phone number in France for him, together with her own home and office numbers. As Ed's mind wandered to a day when people might have a single number for all their phones, and the inherent business opportunities, his lips brushed Gabriela's.

'Bye, teacher,' she said, smiling. As she drove away, Ed savoured the after-taste. Then he went inside and phoned Simone. She answered. She was calm, thinking of the baby, who was due soon. Ed congratulated her on getting Pangaia shut down, and so fast. He confessed he had not expected that.

'Sometimes desperation helps, not that I would recommend it.'

'Was it Jorge who killed Mark?'

'No, it wasn't him personally. He just gave the orders, but the three people who carried them out are in jail with him, though I'm not sure how long any of them will actually stay there.'

'Simone, it strikes me that at the moment we have four sitting ducks. It might only take money to make their lack of freedom permanent.'

'No, Ed, don't even think about it!'

'Maybe only Jorge?'

'No, Ed, I don't want that. I wanted to stop violence, and I think I've done that. Pangaia is dead, and new cults will have a harder time in Portugal. That's enough for me. From now on, all that matters to me is my baby, my child of love.'

\*

Executives from the nearby banks were again contesting the best crowd-watching seats outside the Café Suiça with expensive cameras and their temporary North American owners, so Ed and Keith found themselves a café terrace up the hill in the smart Chiado shopping district for their catching-up and drinking session. An awning protected them from the implacable sun. An elderly waiter brought them chilled beer. Ed cooled his neck with the bottle before swigging from it. Keith poured his into a glass. They eyed the passers-by.

'Hard life, Keith, isn't it?' They both laughed.

'Ever think of moving on?'

'Me? No. I've got everything I've ever wanted here. Why should I move, unless there's a counter-revolution. And even then … I could probably adjust. How about you, Ed? Has Portugal already become too small for you?'

'No, I love it here. Unfortunately, it's become too small for me and certain other people. They are powerful and dangerous, so I have to get out, at least for a while.'

'I'm sorry to hear that, Ed. Really. You came here at the wrong time, yet made a go of things. Well, I'm sure you've got plans.'

'You bet! Make a virtue out of necessity. First of all, a year in England. Get myself a proper academic qualification for teaching English abroad.'

'You realise the gold standard is an MA in applied linguistics, I take it. Have you applied?'

'Yeah. A bit late, but maybe I can squeeze in through the clearing house, if not for a Master's then for some kind of Diploma or Certificate.'

'Go for the Master's, that's my advice. Make the world your oyster. Which part of the oyster do you fancy?'

'You know, Keith, the place I think has most potential is Angola. It's got oil, diamonds, potentially every mineral under the ground and every kind of food that grows above it. At the moment, it can't develop because of war and Stalinism, but that has got to change, and I'd like to be there when it does.'

'Helping and cashing in at the same time.'

'Exactly. What I'd really like to do is to teach business ethics, to help them transition to a decent form of capitalism instead of the usual kleptocracy. But I'll be happy enough to start by teaching English.'

'While looking for some individual, ethical business niches that you alone can fill?'

'Preferably. Another beer?'

Keith grinned and nodded, Ed ordered, and the drinks promptly arrived.

'You know,' said Keith as he filled his glass, 'I'm always looking for places to expand the Sussex School franchise. Keep that in mind.'

They toasted to future success.

*

Ed persuaded Deolinda d'Almeida to back his application for an unpaid sabbatical year from the University. In fact, she welcomed the idea.

'We weren't too impressed with your Mickey Mouse degrees, but we were desperate for English teachers at the time, so we took you on. We're glad we did, as things turned out, but we'll be gladder still if you come back a year from now with a real Master's in a relevant subject.' First her mouth smiled, then her eyes joined it. Briefly, Ed wished he were older.

*

After putting his flat on the market through an agent, Ed had one more duty to perform before he left Portugal. He phoned home. His parents had never visited Portugal; now he invited them over. They hesitated.

'Come on, Dad. Even vicars go on holiday. And I'm paying, not the parish. I'd love to show you this country. You'll probably love it, you might hate it, but you won't be bored.'

Ed got his mother to work on her husband's reluctance to 'sponge off his son'.

'Look, Mum, I'm going to be strapped for cash next year, so this is my last chance to feel rich and be the opposite of a bad boy at the same time.'

And so they came. The heat was a problem. The language bemused them. But they loved the food, the friendliness, the variety of landscape and townscape as Ed drove them the length and breadth of the country in a hired car. Most of all, they loved drawing closer to their son.

Ed saw his parents off at Lisbon airport, where he checked in the car. Then he went by bus and suburban train to the rowing club. He found Lourdes in the bar there, drinking coffee by herself before venturing onto the water. Ed's eye caught the engagement ring on her finger.

'Congratulations!' He realised he meant it.

'Oh, this? It keeps the vultures off better than my old wedding ring. How's yours, by the way?'

Ed told her about Ção, that he would give her a divorce if she asked for it again, but until then he didn't mind being married; he was not going to give up on her completely, though he had few illusions left. He talked about his plans for England first and Angola thereafter, but stressed there was no way he would burn his bridges with Portugal. Lourdes looked at him pointedly, and Ed's heart skipped several beats.

'When you come back, you can stay at my place, if you're at a loose end. You can show me what you've learned in England.'

'I'd love to. Provided you're not otherwise engaged. Excuse the pun.'

'I won't be.'

She slipped from the bar stool and kissed Ed lightly.

'Farewell, lover boy.'

Ed's eyes glued themselves to Lourdes' graceful figure as she propelled it out of the bar and towards the dock.

*Another great reason to come back to Portugal.*

At the hotel, an envelope had arrived for Ed. It bore a French stamp. He opened it and drew out a greetings card that announced the successful birth of Marcelle Rotherfield.

Inside, Simone had written three words in English that tugged even more strongly at Ed's heart-strings:

*Thanks, old friend.*

# ABOUT THE AUTHOR

Zin Murphy lived and worked in Oporto in 1973 and in Lisbon from 1974 to 1980. He is now a retired international civil servant who lives mostly in cyberspace.

He is co-author, with Joana Rabinovitch, of *Getting Through: Communicative English for Speakers of Portuguese.*

Also available by the same author,
writing as Bryan Murphy:


Angels Versus Virgins

Breakaway

Goodbye, Padania

Heresy

Houlihan's Wake

Linehan Saves

Linehan's Ordeal

Linehan's Trip

Madeleine's Drug

Murder By Suicide

SuperOldie

Printed in Great Britain
by Amazon